FIRST
DEGREE

Also by David Rosenfelt

Open and Shut

FIRST DEGREE

□

DAVID ROSENFELT

Published by Warner Books

An AOL Time Warner Company

Mysterious Press books are published by Warner Books, Inc., 1271 Avenue of the Americas, New York, NY 10020.

Visit our Web site at www.twbookmark.com.

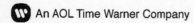 An AOL Time Warner Company

The Mysterious Press name and logo are registered trademarks of Warner Books, Inc.

Printed in the United States of America

First Printing: May 2003
10 9 8 7 6 5 4 3 2 1

Library of Congress Cataloging-in-Publication Data
Rosenfelt, David.
    First degree / David Rosenfelt.
        p. cm.
    ISBN 0-89296-754-4
    1. Attorney and client—Fiction. 2. Trials (Murder)—Fiction. 3. Police murders—Fiction. 4. New York (N.Y.)—Fiction. 5. New Jersey—Fiction. I. Title.

PS3618.O838 F57 2003
813'.6—dc21   2002024509

To Doris and Obby Rosenfelt,
Herb Jaffe, and David Laser.

If you knew them,
your lives are better for it.

Acknowledgments

I would very much like to state that I had no help whatsoever in putting this book together, but too many people know better. So in no particular order, I grudgingly thank:

All the great people at Warner, including but certainly not limited to Jamie Raab, Bob Castillo, Elizabeth Hickmann, and Kristen Weber. Very special thanks go to Sara Ann Freed, who is the only editor I ever want to have, and Susan Richman, a wonderful publicist who somehow finds the time to deal with my inane requests. Every inexperienced novelist should be lucky enough to be paired with people like this.

My outstanding agents, Robin Rue on the book side and Sandy Weinberg on the film side. Besides being a pleasure to deal with, they put up with my nonsense and still manage to do absolutely everything right.

George Kentris of Findlay, Ohio, a terrific criminal attorney and friend, who fills in my legal blanks. And believe me, I have plenty of legal blanks.

Ed and Pat Thomas of Book Carnival in Orange, California, who have been amazingly helpful and supportive, generously offering their knowledge and advice.

All of those who read the book in its early drafts. They include, and I hope I haven't forgotten anyone, Debbie Myers, Mike, Sandi, Rick, Lynn, Ross, Heidi, Adam, Eden, Todd and Bree Rosenfelt, Betsy Frank, Art Strauss, Emily Kim, Greg Creed, George Kentris, Joe Cugini, Amanda, Sharon and Mitchell Baron, Jerry Esbin, Norman Trell, Al and Nancy Sarnoff, James Patricof, Nancy Carter, Holly Sillau, and the entire terrific Heller family.

Debbie Myers, whom I could spend the next 200 pages thanking, and it wouldn't be enough. The knowledge that I am going to spend the rest of my life with her brightens every day.

I'm very grateful to all of you who e-mailed me feedback on *Open and Shut*. Please do so again through my Web site: www.davidrosenfelt.com

• • • • •

OPENING DAY.

Said separately, they're just two ordinary words.

"Opening" and "day." No big deal.

But put them together, liberally sprinkle some thirty-year-old memories, and they take on a meaning that can simultaneously bring a rush of excitement and a threat of tears. At least to me.

"Opening day." My mind's eye conjures up men in pinstripes racing onto a lush green field as the public address announcer booms, "Ladies and gentlemen, the New York Yankees!" That field is a clean spring slate; none of those players have yet made an error, or hit into a double play, or thrown a bat in disgust. Nor have they plans to.

The feeling I have on opening day is one I shared with my father and one he shared with his father before that. Today it takes on an added significance, because I'm going to continue that legacy. The experience won't be quite identical, but we in the Carpenter family are nothing if not adaptable.

I should mention the differences, subtle though they are. First of all, since I don't have any children, the offspring I am passing the sacred tradition on to is my golden retriever, Tara. Also, with the baseball season a good month away, we won't be going to Yankee Stadium, and we won't be seeing a baseball game. The particular opening that we are attending is that of Paterson, New Jersey's first-ever dog park.

I've never actually been to a dog park; I'm not even sure what one is. Tara hasn't been to one either, unless it was during the first two years of her life, before I knew her. If she has, I suspect the experience was less than thrilling, since I told her yesterday that we'd be going, and she was not awake all night in eager anticipation.

This dog park is supposed to be a pretty big deal. It was even a campaign issue in the recent election for mayor. Every candidate promised to have one, so I guess Paterson must have a lot of people like me, concerned citizens who vote the straight dog ticket.

As Tara and I drive over, I'm not getting the feeling that she's into the swing of things. She sits on the front seat, munches on a rawhide chewy, and doesn't show the least bit of interest in where we might be headed. Even when we get close, and we can hear the barking, she doesn't bother to look up and just keeps chomping away. Now I know why my father never gave me chewies on the way to Yankee games.

The park itself is nothing more than a very large dirt area, maybe the size of a football field, fenced on all sides. There must be a hundred dogs running around, getting to know each other, stopping to drink at numerous and well-positioned water fountains. Sort of a canine singles bar. There are maybe half as many humans, almost exclusively women, standing off to one side, talking and occasionally throwing a tennis ball, which sends the dogs into an absolute frenzy.

As we near the entrance gate, Tara seems to watch this scene with some measure of horror, much as I would approach a mosh pit. But she's a good sport; she checks her dignity at the door and enters with me. I walk toward the humans, and so does Tara. She'll do this for my sake, but she's not about to go fighting for a tennis ball like some animal.

The conversation, as might be expected, pretty much centers around all things canine. The dog park, the dogs, dog food, dog toys . . . it all seems fascinating, except as a male I'm not included. Tara keeps leaning against my leg, in a subtle suggestion that we bail out of here. I am preparing to do just that when a woman deigns to speak to me.

"Your dog seems a little antisocial." She's talking about Tara, and if she hadn't said it with a smile on her face, we'd be duking it out right now.

I decide to go with glib. "This isn't really her scene. She's an intellectual. Bring her to a poetry reading, and she's the life of the party."

The woman, nice-looking despite her "yuppie puppie" headband, for some reason decides this could be a conversation worth continuing. "I have a friend looking for a golden retriever puppy. What breeder did you get her from?"

I shake my head. "I didn't. She was in the animal shelter."

She is amazed by this, as I was, as would be any normal human being. "You mean somebody abandoned this dog? And she could have been . . ."

She doesn't want to say "killed" or "put to sleep," so I take her off the hook with a nod. "She was on her last day when I got her."

The horrified woman calls some of her friends over to tell them this story, and before I know it I'm holding court in the middle of maybe twenty women, all of them gushing over my sensitivity for having rescued this dog. The dog in question, Tara, stands dutifully by my side, enduring the embarrassment and apparently willing to let me take the credit, even though she was the one stuck in that shelter.

After a few minutes of embellishing the story about the animal shelter, which I am now referring to as "death row," I move smoothly into light banter. This is interrupted by a woman standing toward the back.

"Hey, aren't you that lawyer who won that big case? I saw you on television. Andy Carpenter, right?"

I nod as modestly as I can manage. She is talking about the

Willie Miller case, in which I proved Willie's innocence in a re-trial after he had spent seven years facing the death penalty. The women connect the dots and realize that I am that rare person who saves both dogs and people from death rows everywhere, and the group attitude quickly moves toward hero worship. It's daunting, but that's the price I pay for being heroic.

Suddenly, there is a sign of life and interest from Tara, as she moves quickly toward a woman approaching our group. The newcomer, to my surprise, is Laurie Collins, the chief (and only) investigator for my law practice, and the chief (and only) woman that I am in love with. She would not have been my first choice to interrupt this meeting of my all-female sensitiv-ity class, but she looks so good that I don't really mind.

As Laurie comes closer, I can see that she doesn't only look good, she looks intense. She doesn't even lean over to pet Tara, an uncharacteristic oversight which surprises me and pos-itively shocks Tara. Laurie comes right over to me, and my de-voted fans part slightly and grudgingly to let her through.

"Alex Dorsey is dead," she says.

"What?" It's a reflex question. I wasn't asking it to get more information in the moment, but that's exactly what I get.

"Somebody decapitated him, then poured gasoline on his body and set it on fire."

If you ever want to get rid of twenty adoring women, I know a line you can use. My fans leave so fast you'd think there was a "70% off" sale at Petco. Based on the gleam in Lau-rie's eye, that's exactly what she expected. Within moments it is just Laurie, Tara, and myself.

"Sorry to interrupt, Andy," she says. "At first I wasn't sure it was you. I thought it might be a rock star."

I put on my most wistful look. "For a moment there, I was."

"You up for breakfast at Charlie's? Because I'd like to talk to you about Dorsey."

"Okay," I say. "I'll meet you there."

She nods and walks to her car. I'm going to drop Tara off

at home and then go to Charlie's, which is just five minutes from my house.

On the way there, I reflect on Dorsey's death and what it might mean to me. The answer is that it means absolutely nothing at all to me, except for the impact it will have on Laurie. But that will be considerable.

Alex Dorsey was a lieutenant in the Paterson Police Department when Laurie was making detective, and she was assigned to his command at the time of her promotion. It didn't take long for her to realize that whatever he once had been, he had ceased to be a very good cop. If there was an easy way out, Dorsey would find an even easier one. He was a walking billboard for the twenty-year retirement rule, although obviously he had chosen to take his retirement while still on the job.

It took a while longer for Laurie to realize that laziness was not Alex Dorsey's biggest vice. Like most of her colleagues, she had heard the rumors that Dorsey was on the take, but she came to believe that the truth was something even worse. Dorsey was playing both sides; he was partners in business with the criminals he was supposed to be investigating. And he was such a tough, resourceful son of a bitch that he had been getting away with it for a long time.

Laurie agonized about what to do but emotionally didn't really have a choice. Her father and uncle had been cops, good cops, and she learned from a very early age that what Dorsey was doing was the worst kind of public betrayal.

Laurie developed some evidence against him, circumstantial but a compelling start, and presented it to Internal Affairs. It was not her job to prove the case, and besides, she knew that they could take it from there. Conclusive evidence would not be difficult to uncover, and it wouldn't be long before Dorsey paid for his sins.

But the first sign that Dorsey was not going down easily was the almost immediate public knowledge that Laurie was the person who had turned him in. That leak was a violation of department policy, which guarantees anonymity to those who turn over evidence implicating an officer in a crime. Laurie's action was also considered by some a violation by her of the ridiculous code of silence, which says that cops don't turn on other cops, no matter how slimy those other cops might be.

The controversy brought chaos and bitterness to the department. Dorsey had developed quite a power base over the years, and he was aware of skeletons in closets where most people didn't even know there were closets. The rank and file, and probably the department leadership, were drawn to one side or the other, and it became perceived as Alex Dorsey versus Laurie Collins. His supporters viewed her as the enemy, or worse, as a traitor.

It became apparent to Laurie that the investigation, mired in departmental and even mayoral politics, was going to be neither complete nor fruitful. So when the word finally came out that Dorsey was merely reprimanded for "improprieties," rather than dismissed and charged with felonies, Laurie's disenchantment and disgust were complete, and she left the department. She opened her own investigative agency, and I became one of her clients. Happily, I became much more later on.

A week ago, word got out that new information had surfaced and that Dorsey was facing imminent arrest. Unfortunately, that word must have also gotten to Dorsey, who proceeded to disappear. Laurie openly admitted to feeling vindicated by the turn of events, which was the last we had heard of Dorsey until today's grisly discovery.

I drop Tara off, give her a biscuit, and head over to Charlie's. It is basically a sports bar/restaurant, but it has recently added a terrific breakfast menu. One of the many things I love about Laurie is that she likes Charlie's as much as I do, which is about as much as is possible to like a restaurant. Even on Sunday mornings, when there are no games on the ten television screens, it's a great place to be.

I order some fresh fruit, hash browns, and black coffee, then sit back and prepare to listen. I know Laurie well enough to realize that in this case, when she says she needs to talk to me, that isn't exactly what she means. What she needs to do right now is talk period, and she feels a little silly if there's nobody around to hear it. So I am the designated listener.

Laurie starts a five-minute soliloquy about Dorsey, rehashing some of their history together. It's nothing I don't already know, and nothing she doesn't know I already know. She wraps it up with, "He was a bad guy. A really bad guy. You know that."

Recognizing that it is my turn to speak, I nod. "Yes, I do. He was a bad guy. Absolutely. A bad guy."

Laurie is silent for a few moments, then says softly, "The thing that bothers me, Andy, is that I'm glad he's dead. When I heard about it, I was glad."

This is a major admission from someone who, when she catches a fly, takes it outside and turns it loose. "That's normal," I say.

She shakes her head, unwilling to be let off the hook. "Not for me."

"He was a dirty cop who had it coming." I twirl my imaginary mustache and inject some humor. "Said the liberal to the conservative."

She seems completely unamused, which I have to assume reflects her emotional state rather than the quality of the joke. I try again, continuing with the same theme. "At today's performance, the role of tough law-and-order advocate will be played by Andy Carpenter, and the role of defender of the indefensible will be played by Laurie Collins."

She ignores this one as well; I should be writing them down to use on more appreciative audiences. The fact is, I can't get that exercised about Dorsey's death; the planet is a healthier place for his being gone. He represented a terribly unpleasant chapter in Laurie's life, an emotional toothache, and I'm hoping she can now put it behind her.

But she's not letting it drop, so I decide to steer the conversation toward the nuts and bolts of today's news. "Do they have any suspects?" I ask.

"Doesn't seem like it. Pete's theory is that his mob friends turned on him once he was no longer of any value to them."

"Pete" is Lieutenant Pete Stanton, my closest, and only, friend on the police force, and one of the few officers who openly supported Laurie during the tough times. I'm not surprised that he would be the one to provide her with information about Dorsey's death.

"Where was he found?" I ask.

"In a warehouse on McLean Boulevard. Kids called in an alarm when they saw smoke. Turned out it was Dorsey that was on fire."

She takes a deep breath and continues. "They think his head was sliced off, maybe with a machete. Whoever did it must have kept it as a souvenir. And the body was burned beyond recognition. They only ID'd him based on some unusual kind of ring he was wearing."

My antennae go up. "That's all?"

She nods. "But they're running a DNA test to be sure."

I'm glad to hear that. I wouldn't put it past Dorsey to murder someone else and fake the whole thing. People on both sides of the law have a tendency to stop chasing you when they think you're dead.

We talk about the Dorsey situation some more, until there's nothing left to say about it.

"Are you going into the office tomorrow?" she asks.

I nod. "Probably late morning. I'm meeting with Holbrook on the Danny Rollins case at nine-thirty."

"Wow. Practice is really taking off, huh?"

Laurie is gently mocking both the fact that I'm representing Danny Rollins, who happens to be my bookmaker, and the fact that I've got absolutely nothing else to do. I haven't taken on a significant client in the six months since the Willie Miller case. And it's not that I haven't had the opportunities. The way the trial ended, with Willie getting off and the real killers exposed,

I became a media darling and Paterson's answer to Perry Mason. I've been at the top of every felon's wish list ever since.

But I've rejected them all. Each turndown had its own rationale. Either the potential client seemed guilty and therefore unworthy, or the case wasn't challenging, or interesting, or significant. Down deep it feels like I've been inventing reasons to decline these cases, but I truly don't know why I would.

I think I have lawyer's block.

WEALTH TAKES some getting used to.

When one suddenly becomes really rich, as I have, there's just nothing natural about how it feels. It's sort of like driving an old, beat-up Dodge Dart for a bunch of years, and then somebody gives you a Ferrari. You say you won't let it change your life, but you think twice before parking it at the 7-Eleven.

My father, Nelson Carpenter, left me twenty-two million dollars. It was money he received dishonorably, taking a payment in return for covering up a crime committed by his oldest friend, who eventually became my father-in-law. My father was a respected district attorney, and to my knowledge, this was the only dishonorable act he ever committed. It set off a chain reaction that left my now-ex-father-in-law in prison and me rolling in dough.

It could have been worse, of course. My father could have done something bad and then left me poor, but instead he shocked me by leaving me all this money that I didn't know he had and that he never touched, letting it accumulate interest for thirty-five years. So for the last six months I've been trying to figure out what to do with it.

I definitely intend to be a regular contributor to charity, and I've made sporadic efforts at that. But what I really want is to find a charity, a cause, that I can attach myself to and make my own. That sounds like it would be easy, but it's been anything but.

First of all, I talked too much about it, the word got around, and charities started coming after me like I was fresh meat. Which I was. Which I am.

The low point came a couple of days ago, when the president of the Committee to Save the Otters of Guatemala Bay came to see me. She was a nice enough woman, but it was probably the tenth solicitation of its kind I endured last week, and I'm afraid I was not on my best behavior.

"Who did you beat?" I asked.

"I beg your pardon?"

"In the election, when you became president of the Committee to Save the Otters of Guatemala Bay . . . who did you run against?"

"We are not a political organization," she said defensively. "We are a cohesive, organized effort to right a terrible wrong. Guatemala Bay is being systematically contaminated, and the otters are left unprotected."

"So you ran unopposed?" I pressed.

"In a manner of speaking." Her annoyance with me was showing. "Mr. Carpenter, if we could get to the reason why I am here."

"I'm sorry, but until now, I didn't even know there was a Guatemala Bay. I thought Guantánamo was the only 'Gua' with a bay."

"If people like you don't intervene, it soon will be."

"How much of an intervention are you looking for?" I asked.

"Ten thousand dollars."

I intervened her a thousand. I'm hoping it'll be enough to get me a cute picture of the otter I've adopted, with maybe a letter or two.

Today being Sunday, that letter won't be coming, so I'll have to content myself with sitting on the couch with Tara and watching basketball. I'm feeling very comfortable at home these days. A couple of months ago, I sold my house in the allegedly fashionable suburbs and moved into the one I grew up in. It is located in the decidedly less fashionable Paterson, but it is the only house to which I will ever feel a real attachment. When my father died, I had planned to sell it but couldn't get myself to do it. Laurie suggested I move in, and since I did, I know that I've come home.

The only addition I've made to the place is a large-screen TV, which I will put to great use today. The Knicks are on at one o'clock, then the Lakers are playing Utah at four, then Nets-Sacramento at six, overlapped by Marquette-Cincinnati at seven, and finishing up with UNLV-Utah at nine. If I plan it right, I can have the pizza arrive before the Laker tip-off, just about the time I'm having my third beer.

If this were a movie, it would be called *The Perfect Day*.

My first step is to call in a bet on the Knicks, minus three against Toronto. The bookmaker, Danny Rollins, wishes me luck both on the game and especially in my meeting tomorrow with the assistant DA, who has the nerve to be accusing Danny of bookmaking. Obviously a trumped-up charge against a law-abiding citizen.

Tara gets up on the couch and assumes her favorite position, lying on her side with her head resting just above my knee. It virtually forces me to pet her every time I reach for my beer, which works for me as well as her. If there's a better dog on this planet, if there's a better living creature on this planet, then this is a great planet, and that must be one amazing living creature.

The Knicks are up by four with a minute to play when I once again feel the reverse sting of great wealth. I bet two hundred on the game, and I realize the money has absolutely no significance to me. Betting is only fun when you're worried about losing. Absent the possibility of the agony of defeat, there can't be a thrill of victory. I'd better get another beer.

It's ten o'clock when the phone wakes me up during the

UNLV game. I'm up three hundred bucks; I wish I could get excited about it.

"Hello?"

"Sorry to wake you, but you shouldn't be sleeping on the couch anyway," Laurie says. How does she know these things? Of course, she is a professional investigator; I have to remember to check the house for hidden cameras.

I stand up immediately. "I'm not on the couch."

"Yeah, right," she says in a voice that implies "You're full of shit, but who cares?" "Anyway, I just heard from Pete."

"And?"

"The preliminary report came in. The DNA matches. The body is definitely Dorsey."

"Are you okay?" I ask.

"I'm fine. I'm glad it's over," she says. "Go back to sleep."

I stifle a yawn. "I'm not really tired. I think I'll check and see if there's a basketball game on."

"You mean like the UNLV game I hear in the background?"

"Well, what do you know?"

"Good night, Andy. I love you."

"Good night, Laurie." We've been using the *l*-word for a couple of months now, but we both agree that it loses some meaning when it always draws an automatic "I love you too" in response. So we're allowing ourselves to make the decision on an individual basis, as it comes up. We're doing groundbreaking things in this relationship.

I watch the game for another three or four seconds before falling back to sleep. Somewhere around three o'clock in the morning, I get up and head for the bedroom, not waking again until seven-thirty. I take Tara for a walk, then get dressed and head for John Holbrook's office.

Holbrook has been with the DA's office for about six years, which means he's probably getting ready to head for the money on the defense side of the table. He's conscientious, hardworking, and relatively fair, a good if unexceptional attorney. Even on cases like this one, which he and I both know is of no great consequence to society, he'll be thoroughly prepared.

Danny Rollins's only role in my life is that of bookmaker, but in the numerous phone calls we have shared, I've gotten to know a little about him. He's got a wife who works as a physical therapist and two kids in high school. He skis, votes straight Republican, tries every diet fad that comes along, and can be counted on to pay off on a bet as surely as he can be counted on to collect.

What Danny does for a living is considered illegal only because of the bizarre nature of our criminal code. It's legal to gamble on a horse race at the track or an off-track betting parlor, but not with a bookmaker. You can waste the family food budget on lottery tickets, but not on the Knicks. Fortunes can be made or lost buying Yahoo! or IBM, but take the Giants and lay the points and you can find yourself in court.

I know that Danny has some connections to northern New Jersey's version of organized crime, because that is how he gets assigned the territory that he can cover. Having said that, I find him to be decent and honorable, and certainly worth getting off this ridiculous legal hook.

Holbrook is finishing a meeting in the conference room when I arrive, and his secretary has me wait in his office. He comes in a couple of minutes later and seems surprised to see me.

"Andy, what are you doing here?"

"We have a meeting on the Danny Rollins matter."

He nods. "I know, but I didn't expect you to come personally. I mean, a rich guy like you?" He looks at his watch. "And with the stock market open? I would have thought you'd send one of your people."

If you're keeping a list at home, you can write down "envious taunting" as another of the downsides of sudden wealth. "My people were busy. Besides, they don't like you. So drop the charges and let me get back to the stock market."

He laughs and opens the file. "Drop the charges? This is such a sure thing, your client wouldn't take a bet on it."

He proceeds to take me through the file, showing me the confiscated betting slips, the ledgers, and the phone records. His office has already sent all of this to me as part of discovery, and I've gone through it, but I don't tell him that.

He finishes, a satisfied smirk on his face. "What's your position on this, Counselor?"

"If you drop the charges at the end of this sentence, I believe I can convince my client not to sue for false arrest."

"Come on, Andy. I'm busy here, you know? You want to deal or not?"

I shake my head. "Not. We intend to mount a vigorous defense."

He laughs; it's quite possible he's familiar with some of my previous vigorous defenses. "Consisting of what?" he asks.

"Character witnesses."

"Excuse me?"

"Character witnesses," I repeat. "They're witnesses as to my client's character, which, by the way, is extraordinary."

"I'm sure it is. And who might these witnesses be?"

"Oh, you know, the usual well-respected, above-reproach, pillars-of-society types. Those kind of people. Would you like me to give you an example?"

He shrugs, which I take to be a yes. I open the file and take out the phone records.

I point to the first page of numbers. "Now, if I remember your stirring presentation correctly, these phone numbers allegedly represent the people who called my client to place illegal wagers. Of course, you offered no proof of this, but—"

He interrupts. "And your contention is that these fifty-seven hundred calls in one month were for what purpose exactly?"

"I can't speak for all of them, but I would suppose that they were mostly friends calling to discuss current events, exchange recipes, that kind of thing."

He's losing patience. "Come on, Andy, can we move this along?"

"Okay. Let's pick a number, any number." I point to a place on the sheet. "How about this one?"

Holbrook looks where I'm pointing. "What about it?"

"Dial it. On the speakerphone."

He starts to argue, then shrugs and goes over to the phone, no doubt figuring that it'll get me out of his office that much sooner. As he goes back to his desk, we can both hear the phone ringing through the speaker.

The female voice comes through the phone. "Carmichael residence."

A look of concern flashes across Holbrook's face as I walk toward the phone. "Is the mayor home?" I ask.

"Who may I say is calling?"

I smile benignly at Holbrook and continue. "Just tell him it's Deputy District Attorney John—"

Displaying catlike quickness that I had no idea he possessed, Holbrook leaps from his chair, moves deftly around his desk, lunges, and cuts off the call before I can finish identifying him. If he does as well on the parallel bars and horse as he's just done on the floor exercise, he's got a shot at the individual all-around.

With the phone safely hung up, he turns to me. "Are you telling me the mayor bets with this guy? Is that what this little stunt was about?"

I shrug. "Unless he's into recipes. I'll ask my client when I get him on the stand."

Holbrook is indignant. "You think this'll stop me? I didn't even vote for the son of a bitch."

"On the other hand, he did appoint your boss." I point to the list. "Care to try another call?"

"Who else is on here? The pope?"

"My client is a really friendly guy who just loves to chitchat. You know the type?"

"Yeah, I know the type exactly," he says. "Now, get the hell out of my office."

So that's what I do. I get out of his office and go to my own. On the way I call Danny and tell him that justice is about to prevail. He's really happy and asks how much he owes me. I tell him five hundred and we let it ride on the 76ers tonight. Maybe I'll win, and maybe I won't. Whatever.

My office these days is not exactly a beehive of activity. Edna, my erstwhile secretary, doesn't even look up from the *Times* crossword puzzle when I walk in. Of course, Edna wouldn't look up if Abraham Lincoln walked in. Edna is the unchallenged crossword puzzle master of the Western world, and she attributes a great deal of that amazing ability to her powers of concentration. My entrance doesn't put a dent in them.

My call list consists of three charities and a wanna-be client, whom I've already turned down, but who is persistent. It's a DUI case, which resulted in a near-fatal injury to a pedestrian. The potential client, when he came to see me, had the smell of liquor on his breath. The decision to pass on the case was not a close call.

I sit at my desk for a while, moving the papers from the right side of the desk over to the left. That makes the desk look left-heavy, so I move half the papers back to the right. The problem is, with papers now on each side, there's no place for me to put my feet up. So with my feet resting uncomfortably on the floor, I pick up the newspaper and read about the discovery of Alex Dorsey's headless body. In order to sell papers, the media usually try to make murders sound gory and disgusting. In this case, with those qualities preexisting, they are pretending to be embarrassed at having to participate in the revelations.

The meeting with Holbrook this morning, though it wasn't exactly arguing before the Supreme Court, has had an effect on me. I realize that I'm getting ready to get back in the action, that I want a case to sink my legal teeth into.

Since I don't happen to have one right now, and since Edna is paying no attention to me at all, I get up and wander down the hall to Sam Willis's office. Sam has been my accountant ever since I moved into this building.

Actually, Sam and I have exchanged professional services. Sam is nothing short of brilliant in two areas. On the one hand, he is as close as anyone I've met to being a financial genius. He knows everything there is to know about money and the rules that govern it. He also has an amazing and complementary expertise in computers, at least as it relates to financial matters. Sit him at a keyboard, and he is a true maestro.

Just a month or so after we met, Sam was accused of illegal hacking, a crime of which he was guilty. The mitigating circumstance, at least in my mind, was that he was retaliating on behalf of a client who was wronged by a large corporation. I got him off on a technicality, and we've been friends ever since.

The thing I find confusing about Sam is that, even though it must have taken a very significant amount of work and drive to learn all that he knows, he has never seen fit or been able to channel that drive into his own financial success. He should be financial guru to the corporate stars, but instead his client list reads like a who's who of schleppers. As a former low-income nobody, I had fit right in. When I came into all this money, Sam got so excited I thought he was going to have a stroke.

Sam is in his office with Barry Leiter, a twenty-three-year-old whom Sam hired out of high school. Barry has been putting himself through night school at Rutgers in Newark by working for Sam, who claims that Barry is even better than he is on a computer. Sam clearly likes the idea of having a protégé.

Sam and I have this ongoing contest that we call song-talking. The trick is to work song lyrics into a conversation. Just doing it is a plus; doing it without the other person realizing it is a total victory.

"Hey, Sam," I say, "what good is sitting alone in your room? Come hear the music play."

I expect him to ridicule my "Cabaret" opening as the feeble attempt that it is, but he doesn't seem to pay it any attention at all. The look on his face is of a man in real distress. "Hello, Andy," he says with no enthusiasm whatsoever. He then shoots a quick glance at Barry, who takes it as a sign he should leave, which he does.

"What's the matter?" I ask.

Sam sighs. "Everything."

"What does that mean?"

He takes off his glasses and rubs his eyes. "You ever meet my younger brother, Billy? When he came to visit?"

I nod. Billy lives in Pittsburgh, but he came to visit Sam last year and I met him then.

"He's been sick, you know?" I didn't know, but I nod, and Sam continues. "At first nobody noticed, not even him, but he started feeling a little weak, and it seemed like no matter how much he ate, he was losing weight."

"How much weight?" I ask.

"I thought just a few pounds, like five or ten. I've been talking to him on the phone, a few times a week, and he doesn't sound good, but he tells me he's just a little under the weather. That's how he puts it: a little under the weather." Sam shakes his head sadly. I think I see tears in his eyes. This can't be good.

He continues. "So I'm out there this weekend, for my mother's birthday, and I ask where's Billy, and Mom says, 'Up in his room. He's feeling under the weather.' All of a sudden I got a family full of meteorologists, you know? So I go up to his room . . . man, I'll never forget it as long as I live."

"What?" I prompt, although I dread hearing it.

He composes himself before continuing. "Billy . . . he . . . he's like wasting away, Andy. Right in front of me. He was this big guy, remember? Maybe a hundred and ninety pounds. You know what he weighs now? One fifteen. One fifteen! He's like skin and bones, just waiting to die."

I shake my head; there's not much to say.

"So I take one look at him, and I get mad, you know? All these months, he's been lying to me, not telling me how sick he really was. I was so pissed, I just wanted to walk out of there and never come back."

"So what did you do?"

He shrugs. "What could I do? I mean, Billy, all skin and bones like that . . . I figured, 'he ain't heavy, he's my brother.'"

Sam starts to cackle, recognizing full well that he has taken song-talking to a new level. The fact that he was willing to fake an agonizing, fatal disease for his own brother in the process does nothing to temper his glee.

I hang around for a little while, but nothing I say can take the satisfied smirk off his face, and it starts to get on my nerves. I head back to my office, preferring the company of the oblivious Edna.

Edna is not alone when I get back. Waiting with her is a tall man, maybe six foot two, with short black hair slicked back. He is wearing a leather jacket that without question cost more than it takes to adopt a family of Guatemalan otters. He is probably in his mid-forties and seems to work hard to make himself look more sophisticated than he naturally is. Fonzie joins the country club.

There's no doubt Edna thinks he's got something going for him. She has put down her crossword puzzle and has already gotten him a cup of coffee. For Edna that qualifies as undying devotion.

"Andrew, this is Geoffrey Stynes. Mr. Stynes, Andrew Carpenter." This brings to a total of one the number of occasions on which Edna has referred to me as "Andrew." Clearly, she is trying to match Stynes's sophistication.

Stynes smiles and holds out his hand. "Nice to meet you."

I take his hand and shake it. "Same here. What can I do for you?"

"You can be my lawyer," he says, the smile remaining intact.

"Come on in," I say, and move him toward my office. As he enters, I look back and see Edna giving me the thumbs-up, signifying her approval of him as a client. I close the door behind us, no doubt pissing Edna off, but that's "Andrew" for you.

Most people that come to see me take the chair across from my desk, but Stynes sits on the couch. I bring my chair over to be closer to him as we speak. He seems totally relaxed and at ease, not the demeanor that prospective clients usually display. People in need of a criminal attorney are by definition under pressure, but if Stynes is experiencing any stress at all, he is hiding it extraordinarily well.

"How did you get my name?" I ask.

"Come on, you're famous since the Miller case. Anyway, I've been watching your career for a long time," he says.

I'm puzzled and vaguely disconcerted. "Why have you been following my career?"

The confident smile returns. "For exactly the kind of situation I'm in today."

Before we discuss what situation he might be talking about, I explain some of the basics of hiring an attorney. Included in that is a standard retainer agreement, which Edna prepares and Stynes signs. Though it by no means guarantees that I will accept him as a client, the retainer establishes attorney-client privilege and allows Stynes to speak openly about his reasons for hiring me.

All of this takes about ten minutes, at the end of which Stynes is technically my client, though only for the purposes of this conversation. I will decide whether to take on his case when I hear what that case is.

"Now," I say, "tell me why you need my services."

"There's a slim but real chance I'll be charged with a crime," he says with absolutely no trace of concern.

"A specific crime?"

His smile comes back, now more condescending than before. "Yeah. Real specific."

"And what crime is that?"

"The murder of Alex Dorsey."

Since I am far from the most inscrutable person in this room, I'm sure my face reflects my surprise.

"Have the police contacted you?" I ask.

"No."

"Do you have information which leads you to believe they are going to?"

"No."

"Then why do you think you are currently a suspect?"

Another smile, smaller this time. "Right now I don't think I am. But when I killed him, I got some of his blood on my clothes. I threw them and the knife I used into some brush behind Hinchcliffe Stadium. I should have thrown them over the falls, but I was in a hurry, you understand."

Hinchcliffe Stadium is a large baseball field, a former minor league park, and it is right next to the Passaic Falls, one of the larger waterfalls in the country. Had Stynes thrown the material into the falls, that would have been the end of it.

"Dorsey wasn't killed behind Hinchcliffe Stadium," I point out.

He smiles. "Don't confuse where he was found with where he was killed. He was *found* in a warehouse on McLean Boulevard."

I've already pretty much decided I'm not going to take this case, but for some reason, maybe morbid curiosity, I keep probing. "Why don't you just go there and pick the stuff up?"

"Because if for some reason the police are watching me, they'd nail me to the wall. This way, even if they find it, there's a chance they won't tie me to it."

He's just confessed to a brutal murder with all the emotion that I show when I'm ordering a pizza. I am suddenly struck by a desire to pick up the intercom and say, "Edna, this is Andrew. Could you bring in a machete, a can of gasoline, and some matches? Mr. Thumbs-Up wants to show us how he de-capitated and charcoal-broiled a cop last week."

"Why did you kill him?" I ask.

He laughs, permanently removing any chance I would re-consider and take the case. "If you knew Dorsey, the more log-ical question would be, Why didn't somebody kill him sooner?"

"What did you do with his head?"

He smiles, seems to consider answering, then makes his decision. "That's something I don't think I'll share with you. Nor is it relevant to your taking or not taking my case."

He seems to think I might be doubting his truthfulness, so without prodding, he goes on to tell me the mixture of gaso-line and propane that he used on Dorsey's body. It is the same as Pete had mentioned to Laurie, but not reported in the news-papers.

I'd like to know more, but that desire soon gives way to an-other, even more intense one. I want to get this guy out of my office. Now.

I stand up. "Make sure you keep a copy of the retainer agreement. It is your protection against my revealing anything you've said today. I won't be representing you."

He stands. If he's disappointed, he's an outstanding actor. "You think just because I'm guilty I don't deserve a good de-fense?" he says with apparent amusement.

I shake my head. "I think everyone is entitled to the best defense possible. The guilty generally need it the most."

"Then why are you turning me down? I can afford what-ever you charge."

I decide to be straightforward. "Mr. Stynes, when I repre-sent a client, I do everything possible within the system to win. I don't want to be sorry if I succeed."

"You want me to go to jail?" he asks.

"Not as much as I want you to leave my office. I assure you, there are plenty of competent attorneys who will take your case, if it becomes a case."

"Okay," he says. "Whatever you say."

With that he walks out of my office, and I hear him saying a polite goodbye to Edna as he leaves. The meeting has left me a little shaken, which I can attribute to the casual, matter-of-fact manner in which he described committing such a horrible murder.

What I can't figure out is why I'm worried.

• • • • •

Monday NIGHT IS TIED for the best
night of my week with Wednesday and Friday. Those are the
nights that Laurie and I spend together. We don't often go out;
in fact, more often than not we stay at one of our homes and
either cook dinner or order in. We each have spare clothes in
the other's house, though since Tara is at my house, that's almost always where we sleep.

I admit there is nothing spontaneous about this arrange-
ment, but it works quite well for us. We are in a committed relationship, with all that entails, but we are not ready to live
together. This way everything is out in the open, and there are
no unmet expectations. We've chosen not to include Saturday
night on our list because for some reason we both cherish Sunday morning solitude.

Tonight we're at my house, but it's Laurie's turn to provide
dinner. While I can barely manage to order in, Laurie is an absolute master in the kitchen. Anything she finds in the refrigerator, anything at all, can become part of a terrific pasta dish.

Laurie has planted a vegetable garden in the rear corner of
my backyard, a testimony to the differences between us. She
finds it rewarding to spend her time growing things that the supermarket is already filled with. She seems to believe that if

she can't make lettuce rise from the ground, then we'll have to go lettuce-deprived. She's even growing basil, and in a pathetic attempt to curry favor with her, I've forever sworn off store-bought basil.

We're having pasta tonight, some kind of red sauce with things in it. I don't ask what those things are for fear that they'll sound so healthful I won't want to eat them. It's delicious, and with the music and candles and Laurie as company, it should be perfect. It isn't, because I'm still thinking about Geoffrey Stynes and his chilling confession this afternoon.

I move it partially out of my mind, until Laurie mentions that she stopped into the office after I had left. "Edna told me somebody tried to hire you today, but you fought him off."

I try to smile and shrug it off. "You know Edna."

She does know Edna, but somehow that isn't enough to get her to drop it. "She said you seemed upset."

I decide to try honesty. Who knows? Maybe it'll work. "I didn't like him. I didn't like the case."

"Why?"

I shake my head. "It's privileged."

She nods, fully understanding and respecting the meaning of that. It bothers me, not being able to tell her something she would so desperately want to know, but I have no ethical choice.

There are few, if any, things more vital to a defendant's protection in our justice system than the attorney-client privilege. If an accused individual were unable to be honest with his attorney out of fear that his words would be revealed, it would cripple his chances of being adequately defended. I have never breached attorney-client privilege in my life, and I never will.

Ironically, had I accepted Stynes as a client, I could have assigned Laurie to the case as my investigator and told her everything Stynes said. Once I turned him down, I clearly lost the ethical justification to assign an investigator.

Besides, there really is no absolute guarantee that Stynes

killed Dorsey. False confessions are amazingly commonplace. Of course, they're usually made to the police, not to lawyers. And the confessors are most often losers and/or lunatics. On the surface at least, Stynes doesn't fit the bill. Even more significant, the fact that he knew the composition of the flammable solution pretty much says it all.

The guy did it.

Laurie drops the issue, though she can tell that something is bothering me. Wild and crazy couple that we are, we decide to do what we often do after dinner: play Scrabble.

Playing Scrabble against Laurie is very difficult for me. We take our glasses of wine and sit on the floor, and I almost instantly find that I can't take my eyes off of her. She is beautiful in a casual, unassuming way, as if it takes no effort. And in her case it doesn't. I have seen her after an exhausting run, after a shower, after making love, after a night's sleep, after a tearful conversation, after a long day in the office, and even after a physical confrontation with a violent suspect. These observations have convinced me that they haven't invented the "after" that could make Laurie look anything but wonderful.

But if I'm looking at Laurie, then I can't be looking at my tiles. This is an effective part of her plan, but it's not nearly the most daunting part of her game. She is a woman with no Scrabble morals whatsoever; she'll do anything it takes to win, and the rules are for her opponents to worry about.

I usually lose by about fifty points, but tonight I'm actually ahead by seventeen. We're about three-quarters of the way into the game, which means she simply will not take her turn unless and until she comes up with a great word. She will ponder and agonize over her decision until August if necessary, but will under no circumstances make anything other than the perfect move.

About ten minutes have gone by, and I'm about to doze off, when she finally puts down her word. It lands on a triple word score, totals forty-eight points, and, if left unchallenged, will put her well into the lead.

The word is . . . "klept."

Now, there is no reason I should let her get away with this. Well, there's one. She gets really aggressive when I put up any resistance at all.

"Klept?" I say very gently. "I'm not sure that's a word, Laurie dear."

"Of course it's a word. Klept. It's what kleptomaniacs do."

"A kleptomaniac *steals,* sweetheart," I say.

Laurie sits up a little straighter, poised and ready to pounce. "No, the run-of-the-mill losers that you represent *steal*. The real sickos *klept.*"

I look around for the dictionary that we keep in the box with the game. It's nowhere to be found.

"Do you know where the dictionary is, my little honey-bunch?" I ask.

"I looked for it before, but it's gone," she says, a razor-sharp edge in her voice. "I guess somebody must have klepted it."

The game rapidly heads downhill after that. I start to make moves too quickly, she slows down even more, and she beats me by sixty-seven points.

That's the bad news. The good news is it means we can go to bed, and bed with Laurie is much better than Scrabble with Laurie. Bed with Laurie is better than Scrabble with anybody. Though I'm speaking from a rather limited database, I think it's very likely that bed with Laurie is better than bed with any-body.

I wake up at six-thirty in the morning and turn on the television to the local news. Laurie is still sleeping, but the sound doesn't wake her. The sound of an enormous asteroid hitting Hackensack wouldn't wake her.

There is almost nothing of consequence on the local news. It's traffic, weather, boring banter, light features, and then back to the traffic and weather. Today is no exception. It's raining, so they have the poor weatherman out on a street corner, giving his report from under an umbrella. He's predicting that it's going to rain. All that money spent on meteorology school obviously paid off.

Laurie wakes up at seven and says something that sends a bolt of agony through me. "Weren't you going to the gym this morning?"

I've gained a few pounds lately and noticed a slight gut. Even worse, Laurie has noticed it. I announced that I was going to start going to a gym, and she made no effort to talk me out of it. Today was to be the first day. I had genuinely forgotten about it, though I would certainly have faked forgetting about it if I thought I could get away with it.

I get up, walk Tara, then throw some things in a bag, and go. I'm not yet a member of a gym myself, so for this initial foray into future fitness, I've chosen to be a guest of Vince Sanders. If I can't keep up with Vince, I'm going to stop off at the embalmer on the way home and turn myself in.

Vince is the city desk editor of the *Bergen Record*; it was a young reporter working for him that Willie Miller was accused of murdering. He helped me on that case, and we've become pretty friendly since. Vince is the single largest consumer of jelly donuts in New Jersey, with the gut to prove it.

I'm ten minutes late getting to the gym; it would have been longer if not for the fact that there's valet parking. Vince is a little grouchy about my late arrival.

"You here to work out or you here to be late?" he snarls.

It's not the most coherent of questions, so I just shrug my apology, and he flashes his guest pass and gets me in. The place is a spectacular modern facility, with state-of-the-art exercise machines, a fashionable workout clothing boutique, a fancy hair salon, and a restaurant/snack bar area that could host a debutante ball.

It's the restaurant that's our first stop. Vince orders a large fruit smoothie, banana nut muffin, and fruit salad. I get an orange juice, and by the time I'm finished drinking it, he's already eaten his tray clean. He orders a raisin scone and another smoothie and takes it with him as we head for our workout.

"Where are we going?" I ask.

"The treadmills. Best workout you can have."

"How come?"

He sighs, as if he can't believe he's been saddled with this fitness novice. "Because it's the closest to everyday life. I walk in life, so I walk on the treadmill."

I nod. "If the trick is to imitate life, how come you don't go to the jelly-donut-eating machine?"

He begins a snarl, but it turns into a laugh. "Believe me, if they had one, I would."

We get to the treadmill, where I soon find that preparation is the key. Vince prepares by attaching his stereo headphones to outlets allowing him to hear sound from the large-screen TVs. Then he adjusts those headphones so they won't fall off his head should he ever decide to actually exercise. Then he adjusts the treadmill to the proper speed and elevation, which can best be described as slow and none. Then he hangs his towel neatly on the side bar, in case he should happen to sweat, which I don't think is a serious possibility.

I start my machine at a quicker pace with higher elevation, not too strenuous but enough to be of some possible value. Five minutes later Vince gets off, explaining that "this aerobic shit is good, but you don't want to overdo it." Ever the accommodating guest, I follow him into the locker room, where we take a whirlpool bath, in order to soothe our exhausted muscles.

While Vince may not qualify as a gym rat, he's as good a newspaperman as there is. His most valuable asset is his amazing knowledge about what is going on in the communities he covers. When it comes to northern New Jersey, he knows what is happening, who is causing it to happen, and whom it's happening to.

"Do you know a guy named Geoffrey Stynes?" I ask.

Nothing registers on his face. "Nope," he says. "Who is he?"

I shrug. "Just a guy."

"Oh, just a guy? You sure? I figured he was just a fish, or

just a tennis racket. You asked about him, now who the hell is he?"

I'm sorry I brought it up; but my curiosity got the better of me. "It's privileged," I say.

Vince is incredulous. "He's your client? He's your client and you're asking me who he is?"

"Forget I asked."

He nods and goes back to enjoying the water churning around his blubbery body. After a few minutes of silence, he asks, "You want me to check him out?"

"I do."

"What's in it for me?" he asks.

"I promise not to tell anyone that I get more exercise using the TV remote control than you get in your entire workout."

He thinks for a moment. "Deal," he says.

We head back to the locker room to shower and change. According to the mirrors, I haven't lost any weight as a result of the workout, even though I'm sure I burned off at least eight or nine calories.

The locker room is as fancy as the rest of the place, and there are three or four televisions positioned so they can be viewed from anywhere. They are tuned to a local news show, and as I walk by one, I hear Alex Dorsey's name mentioned.

I look up and see a newscaster sitting at a desk and speaking. Behind him is a photograph of a man, and the type legend below his face is, "Arrested in Dorsey Murder."

I don't know who the man is, but he sure as hell is not Geoffrey Stynes.

• • • • •

LAURIE IS WAITING FOR ME when

I arrive at the office. It is no surprise that she is fully briefed on the media's version of the arrest; when it comes to Alex Dorsey, she is command central.

The arrested man's name is Oscar Garcia, a twenty-seven-year-old Puerto Rican immigrant living in Passaic. He is described as a handyman by trade and is said to have a few drug arrests, though no convictions, in his apparently less-than-illustrious biography.

While Laurie's awareness of the news was to be expected, her take on it is not. "There's no way Garcia did it, Andy," she says. "I know this guy."

"You do?"

She nods. "He's a small-time dealer who hangs out in Pennington Park introducing kids to the glories of cocaine. I busted him once."

"The radio said he's been arrested but not convicted."

She nods, unhappy at the memory. "As moments go, that was one of my lowest."

"What happened?" I ask.

"A friend of mine, Nina Alvarez . . . I went to high school with her. Garcia got her fourteen-year-old daughter started on pot first, then a quick move to crack. Nina tried everything, even had her in a lockdown facility for a while. Finally, she decided to try and deal with the source, and she came to me."

"To get Garcia?"

She nods. "Right. It took a while . . . the creep was pretty careful. Then one day I was in court testifying on a case, and that's the day my partner caught him carrying. We booked him, and I thought that was the end of it."

"But it wasn't," I say, fulfilling my function to wander the earth, stating the obvious wherever I find it.

"He walked two days later. His lawyer convinced the judge there was no probable cause for the search."

"And you never got him again?"

"No," she says. "The Dorsey thing blew up, and I left the force."

"What about your friend's daughter?"

"She ran off a few months later and seems to have never looked back. No doubt learning the joys of life on the street. Fourteen years old . . ." She struggles to get the words out without crying, and the look of pain in her eyes is tangible. On some level she feels responsible for her friend's losing a child in this horrible manner.

This incident is obviously something that has incredibly strong emotional importance to her, yet I knew absolutely nothing about it. What else is there about her that I don't know, what deep personal pains that she hasn't seen fit to mention on Monday, Wednesday, or Friday nights? And how could I be feeling shut out for not having been told something that I've just been told?

I move the conversation back to the matter at hand. "Why can't you buy Garcia for the Dorsey killing?"

"Dorsey worked undercover for fifteen years, Andy. I was with him after that time, but I got to know him very well. He was a tough, dangerous guy who could see any kind of trouble a mile away. I can't picture anyone killing Dorsey, but there is no way a little twerp like Garcia could have done it. If you tied Dorsey to a tree and gave Garcia a bazooka and a tank, Dorsey would skin him alive in thirty seconds."

What I want to say is, "Congratulations, you're right again, Laurie! The guy who's really guilty sat in that chair yesterday! Show her what she's won, Johnny!" The fact that I can't say it is frustrating, but obviously something I'm going to have to get used to.

"I assume the cops know what you know," I say, "but they must have something on him, or he wouldn't have been charged. Maybe he's graduated to the big time since you were after him."

She shakes her head. "He hasn't."

The conviction in her voice surprises me. "You *know* that?"

She looks me in the eye and says quietly, "I *know* that."

There are implications here that I decide not to go near. Our conversation eventually expires from lack of new information, so Laurie goes off to gather some more. It leaves me alone to think, which in this situation is not a particularly good idea.

I must at least perceive a client as innocent in order to take on his defense. This rigid attitude tends to reduce my caseload, but I've accepted that reality. Of course, I almost never really know that a client is innocent. All I have is a distrust of the facts the prosecution presents, and a faith and belief that the client is telling me the truth. And, with the Willie Miller case as a notable exception, even in a best case I can't prove innocence; I simply hope to establish reasonable doubt of guilt.

This situation is far different. I can be positive that Garcia is innocent because I know who is guilty. Which leaves me with a lot to think about, and the way I best do that is by taking Tara to the duck pond. That is what I am about to do when Edna tells me that my eleven-fifteen meeting is here. Since I have no clients, her designating it as the "eleven-fifteen meeting" is overkill. Just "meeting" would suffice. In any event, I had no idea I had any meeting scheduled, never mind an eleven-fifteen one.

It turns out that my eleven-fifteen is with Edna's stockbroker cousin, Fred. Agreeing to meet with cousin Fred was one of those things that I say I will do, as long as it's in the future, and I somehow assume it will never come about. But here it is, and I'm trying to figure out if I can make it out the window when in comes Edna and the man she considers the perfect caretaker for my twenty-two million dollars: cousin Fred.

It's no surprise that Edna has a cousin up to this task. She seems to have the largest extended family in the Western Hemisphere; they cover every occupation ever invented, yet somehow have managed not to overlap jobs. Cousin Fred handles the financial markets.

Fred is about my age and decked out in a three-piece suit. He shakes my hand, and I have a vision of the scene from Woody Allen's *Take the Money and Run,* when Allen's convict character is caught attempting to escape. As punishment, he is locked in a cellar with an insurance salesman from Dayton, and they shake hands as they descend into the hole.

This meeting would be a form of torture in any event, but right now I want to get away and think this Dorsey thing through, and it's going to be tough doing that while talking puts and calls with cousin Fred.

Much to my surprise, Fred turns out to be a normal human being, and one who shares my general distrust of people who claim to understand the stock market. My view is that no one has any idea whether the market will go up or down. Commentators come up with coherent, logical reasons for the market's behavior at the end of the day; it's the morning's pre-opening predictions that are a tad less reliable.

Fred and I talk the same language. As much as I like to gamble on football and basketball, in the stock market I want to be careful, cushioning myself against disaster. Fred advocates the exact same strategy, and most important, he voices that opinion before I do. That is how I know he is not just telling me what he thinks I want to hear.

Even though I'm conservative on these financial decisions,

I'm also quite impulsive. Fred seems as good as anybody I've met, so I agree to let him handle eleven million dollars of my money. I expect him to grab on to my leg and whimper his thanks, but he handles it as if it's good news but nothing he didn't expect. I tell him to coordinate everything with Sam Willis, then I call Sam and alert him that Fred is going to be stopping by. Moments after Fred leaves my office, I hear Edna shriek with glee; she's not quite as reserved as her cousin.

I am finally free to leave, so I pick up Tara and take her to the duck pond in Ridgewood. It is a wonderfully peaceful place, especially since it's still chilly, so parents and their screaming children aren't out in force. Tara is always mesmerized by the ducks; she can sit quietly and stare at them for hours. We bring a loaf of bread to feed them, and Tara knows it's theirs and doesn't compete for the food. Tara and I both do some of our best thinking here.

I feel like I am facing a dilemma, yet it is totally of my own creation. Ethically, there is nothing I need to do; in fact, there is little if anything I am allowed to do. The rules of my profession call for me to behave as if Stynes never sat in my office and confessed. All I should be doing is feeding the ducks, petting Tara, and trying to come up with a charity to support, just in case cousin Fred doesn't lose all my money.

Garcia is a slime. Laurie said so, and I totally trust her judgment. The problem is that our system doesn't and shouldn't convict an innocent suspect of a crime just because he must have committed other crimes, which couldn't be proved. Make-up calls are for NBA refs, not our courts.

So an injustice may be committed. So what? I'm aware of injustices all the time, which I can't do anything about. The world is full of them; putting away Garcia is a fairly mild example.

And who said he'll be put away? If he didn't do it, which he didn't, then how strong can the evidence be? The prosecution won't be able to prove its case, he'll walk, they'll catch the real murderer, and all will be right with the world. My job is to feed a couple of dozen ducks and have a nice afternoon with Tara.

I've just got to drop this Garcia thing. Wipe it from my mind.

I can't.

I leave Tara back home and go down to the courthouse. The court clerk, Rita Golden, is on a lunch break that her secretary tells me should be over in ten minutes. I position myself in the hallway outside her door, and she comes back two minutes ahead of schedule.

I like Rita. She lets you know exactly where you stand, all the while doing her job with total efficiency. That job is to keep the court schedule running smoothly and protect the judges from pain-in-the-ass lawyers like me.

Rita talks about two things: the court and sex. She does this simultaneously and creatively and lets me participate. For instance, when she sees me standing by her door, she says, "Andy, is that a gavel in your pants, or are you happy to see me?"

"I'm always happy to see you, you hot little clerk you." She's clearly better at this than I am.

"Then why don't you come into my office, and I'll conduct a direct examination?" she says. "I'll be the aggressive lawyer, you can be the hostile witness. There won't be anyone around to object."

"Alas, my heart belongs to another. But you can have everything else."

She laughs, then gets down to business. "What's up?"

"I want to know if Garcia has representation," I say.

She enters the office and I follow her in, talking as we go.

"That would depend on who Garcia is," she logically points out.

"The guy they arrested for Dorsey," I say.

"Oh, right, another of the wrongly accused." She reaches her desk and looks for the information on the list. "PD," she says, which means the case has been assigned to the public defender.

"Thanks, Rita," I say, and turn to leave.

"Don't tell me you're scrounging around for clients," she says. "Not with your money."

"Money isn't everything."

She nods. "You're right. Sex is everything. And if the money's right, I'll prove it to you."

I barely get out of there with my male dignity intact, and I head down to the public defender's office. Movies generally portray public defenders in one of two ways. One version has them as courageous defenders of our precious rights, fighting on despite a horrible work overload, a woefully inadequate budget, and working conditions straight out of *Oliver Twist*. The other view has them as incompetent hacks who couldn't make it anywhere else and who guarantee their poor clients a life in prison due to miserable representation.

In this jurisdiction, neither portrayal is accurate. For the most part, PDs are tough, competent lawyers who do a damn good job. They are in fact overworked, but the system provides them with an adequate budget to represent their clients. It wouldn't fund the dream team, but if an expert witness is needed, it gets paid for. As far as office space goes, it's a hell of a lot nicer than mine. Of course, as Edna would point out, that ain't saying much.

The head of the Public Defender Division is Billy Cameron, nicknamed Bulldog, not because of his considerable tenacity on behalf of his clients but because he played wide receiver for the University of Georgia. Legend has it that he caught eleven passes for four touchdowns to beat Auburn. I would have been about five years old at the time, so of course, I don't remember the game, but I probably bet on Auburn.

"So, Andy," he says when I walk in, "I hear you've got three dollars more than God."

"Only because he's made some bad investments lately."

He nods, having reached his rather low banter tolerance already. "What the hell are you doing here?"

"I've come to offer my humble services as a barrister," I explain.

He's immediately distrustful. "Why?"

"Why? Doesn't the word 'civic responsibility' mean anything to you?"

"That's two words," he points out.

"All the more reason for you to accept my gracious offer." He looks dubious, so I push on. "Come on, Billy, the big firms send you their inexperienced losers for pro bono work, and you lick their faces. I'm giving you a chance to get the one and only Andy Carpenter. So what's your problem?"

"Because they're doing it to look good in the community by impersonating decent human beings. Your motive isn't quite as clear."

"You've got a client I think is innocent," I say, "and I thought it would be nice for all concerned if I proved it."

"And this client is . . . ?"

"Oscar Garcia."

He looks up sharply. "Oscar Garcia?"

"The very one." I can see Billy's mind working. Oscar is someone no lawyer in his right mind would want as a client, yet here I am applying for the job. Billy knows I can get as many clients as I want. So if I want Garcia, he's thinking, then he should want him as well, but he has no idea why.

"And you think he's innocent?" he asks. "How did you come up with that theory?"

"Somebody told me there's no way he could have done it," I say. "That he never could have gone up against Dorsey."

Billy laughs a short, put-down laugh. "That's it? That's your evidence? Who told you that?"

"Laurie Collins."

Billy stops laughing. He knows Laurie very well and is fully aware that her opinions about matters like this are to be taken very seriously. But he has to stand his ground. "I don't think the 'Laurie defense' will hold up in court."

"I'll try and come up with something else just in case," I say.

I can see that he is weakening, so I up the pressure a little. "Come on, Billy, you know every lawyer you have is hiding in the closet when you walk by so you can't dump this on them. And I won't use your resources. Everything comes out of my office."

He can't think of a reason to say no, so he doesn't. "And you'll keep me informed?"

"Every step of the way," I say.

"Andy, you know how many of these cases I've seen? Don't count on this being another Willie Miller."

"I won't," I say. "It's Oscar Garcia all the way."

He reaches down and picks up a file off his desk. He hands it to me. "Here's all we know so far. Read it and then go see your client."

I take the file back to my office and read what Billy found in the police reports. They had received an anonymous tip phoned in to 911 by a woman claiming that Garcia was involved. They were then able to match his fingerprints to those found on the door to the warehouse where Dorsey's body was found. Witnesses also claimed to have seen Garcia near that warehouse on a number of occasions, including the morning of the murder.

I'm sure the case is stronger than this, and I'll have to direct my efforts toward finding out what more they have. The 911 call is intriguing, since the information given was wrong. It could simply be a mistake, but it more likely seems to be an indication that someone, most likely Stynes, is trying to frame Garcia.

I'm about to go visit with my potential client when Laurie comes in. She is obviously upset, and it takes about a fraction of a second for me to find out why.

"Is it true you're taking on Oscar Garcia as a client?" It's a question, dressed up like a demand.

"I haven't met with him yet," I reply rather lamely.

"So you are meeting with him? You want to take his case?"

I nod. "I'm on the way over there now."

"Incredulous" doesn't quite go far enough to describe her reaction. "Let me see if I understand this," she says. "You were turning down every client in town for six months so you could hold out for Oscar Garcia?"

"Laurie, I'm late. Can we talk about this if and when he hires me? He might want a different lawyer." The fact is, I'm hoping he turns me down. My conscience will be clear.

She laughs derisively. "Yeah, he's a real prize. There'll be a roomful of lawyers trying to win him over. Andy, how the hell could you do this to me?"

"I'm not doing anything to you, Laurie."

"You know how I feel about him, you know what he's done to my friend, yet of all the people you could represent you pick him."

"Laurie, I know how this might seem. But believe me, it's not about you. It has nothing whatsoever to do with you."

It's clear that she isn't close to being convinced. "Then why are you doing this? Just tell me why."

"There are reasons that I can't go into, I truly can't go into."

"Yeah, right."

I try a different approach, because this one obviously isn't working at all. "Okay, you tell me why I would be taking on a client to get back at you. I love you, I care about you, but I would do this to punish you? To hurt you? Does that make sense? Did we have a fight I forgot about?"

She takes a moment to weigh my argument, and I think I have a chance until I can see the reject button go off in her brain.

"Don't do it, Andy." It's a combination plea and command.

"I'm sorry, but I have to."

She shakes her head. "No, you want to."

She turns and leaves. I feel bad that she is hurt, but I feel much worse that she believes I would intentionally hurt her.

• • • • •

BEING PUT IN COUNTY JAIL is

like signing a first baseball contract and reporting to the low minor league team they assign you to. You're in professional baseball, and while you know you might someday find yourself in the big leagues, for right now this seems pretty significant. Of course, if someday you do make it to the majors, you realize just how small the minors were.

County jail is the flip side of that. When you're sent there, you know you might find yourself in state prison if you get convicted, but for right now this seems pretty awful. Of course, if you do wind up there, or in a federal prison, you realize just how easy you had it back in County.

The thing is, when you're in County, at least things are happening. You're getting the lay of the land, seeing your lawyer, preparing for trial . . . it's a new experience. When you're convicted and sent to State, it feels like the system has forgotten about you, and in fact it has. Your life is not only miserable, it's also boring, and there is no end in sight.

I guess my point is that, all in all, county jail is a pretty super-duper place to live. But for some reason, Oscar Garcia doesn't see it that way. Oscar thinks it's an outrage—a "motherfucking joke" is the homespun way he puts it—that he should be in this position.

He rants and raves for two or three minutes, then finally realizes that, since I am sitting there, I just might have a role to play in all this. "Who the hell are you?" he asks.

"My name is Andy Carpenter. I'm an attorney working for the public defender's office on your case."

He stares at me for a few moments, as if trying to remember something. "Don't I know you from somewhere?"

I shrug. "Maybe. I went to NYU. What fraternity were you in?"

Oscar's sense of irony doesn't seem that well developed, and I've got a hunch he's not going to be a master of self-deprecating humor either. He ignores my comment, mainly because he's just remembered where he's seen me.

"You're that lawyer, right?" He points at me, no doubt to make sure I know he's not talking to the table.

"That's what I just finished telling you."

He shakes his head. "No, I mean the guy that was on TV."

I nod. "That's me. The TV lawyer."

He sort of squints at me, checking me out. "What do you want with me?"

He's suspicious, the first sign of intelligence I've seen. I decide to tell the partial truth, which seems to be the most I can manage these days. "I thought you might need my help."

"I don't need nobody's help."

"Then I'll find someone who does." I stand up to leave. "See ya around the campus."

I reach the door and I'm halfway out when I hear, "Wait a minute, man." I can pretend I don't hear it and keep walking, or I can turn around and continue with this self-destructive insanity. I turn.

"What is it, Oscar?"

"I didn't do it, man. I've done some pretty bad shit, but this ain't me."

"Did you know Dorsey?" I ask.

"A little bit, no big deal. He hassled me a few times. Nothing I couldn't handle."

"How did you handle it?" I ask.

"I just let it slide, went about my business."

"And just what is your business?" I ask.

"What the hell is the difference? This ain't about my business. My business is my business."

I pull up a chair and sit down less than a foot away from him. "Listen to me, Oscar, because I'm only going to say this once. Your business is my business. Everything about you is my business. And every question I ask you, every single one, is one you are going to answer as best you can."

He can tell I'm pissed, and he's afraid I'm going to walk away. "Okay, man," he says. "But you can't tell nobody, right? It stays between us?"

I nod. "It's called attorney-client privilege, and you can't imagine the shit I go through to maintain it."

He proceeds to tell me about his drug dealing and prostitution activities. It's fairly small-time, but like Danny Rollins, his small territory has been bestowed upon him, and he pays a substantial portion of his earnings to his patrons. The days of Al Capone are over, but the mob influence, at least in this area, is surprisingly substantial.

Oscar adamantly refuses to talk about the mob people that he deals with. He pathetically considers himself "connected," even though the truth is that the only people below him on the mob food chain are the victims. I don't press him on it, since there is little possibility his connections had anything to do with his facing these charges.

I move the conversation to the specifics of the case. I don't want to ask too many questions at this point; I'll save that for when I know more about the police's evidence. I concentrate on the warehouse where the body was found.

"Of course my prints were there," he admits. "That's where I operate out of."

He goes on to explain that because the warehouse was adjacent to the park, he would occasionally hide merchandise in there and have certain customers meet him inside when the police were in the area. He considered the warehouse his corporate headquarters.

And besides that, as he so eloquently puts it, "Prints don't mean no damn shit anyway."

"Write that line down. I'll want to use it in my closing argument."

He doesn't respond; there may be no bigger waste of time than using sarcasm on someone who has absolutely no understanding of it. "Now, this is important," I continue. "Someone called the police, a woman, and told them that you killed Dorsey. Do you have any idea who that could have been?"

"Shit no, man."

"What about one of your girls on the street?"

He shakes his head vigorously. This he is sure of. "No way. No fucking way. They know what would happen."

Every time he opens his mouth I dislike him more. "There's no one you can think of who might want to frame you?" I ask. "No one who has it in for you?"

"I got some enemies, my competitors, you know? It's part of business."

We clearly have a Macy's/Bloomingdale's situation here. "Make a list of everyone who dislikes you," I say.

He nods. "Okay."

"How many reams of paper will you need?"

"The guard'll get me paper."

What I think, but don't say, is, "Oscar, I'm insulting you. I'm your lawyer and I'm insulting you! Fire me!" Instead, I mentally vow to swear off sarcasm for the duration of this case. I'm not sure if I can do it; my addiction goes way back. I wonder if they make a sarcasm patch that I can wear to wean me off it.

For now I confirm that Oscar wants to plead not guilty, and I tell him that I'll see him again tomorrow at the initial court appearance.

I turn and leave. The only thing I've learned in this visit is that Oscar is a really easy guy to leave.

As I walk to my car, I reflect on how depressing this situation is. A lawyer-client relationship, particularly in a murder trial, is close and often intense. Unfortunately, I would rather have warts surgically implanted all over my body than be close and intense with Oscar Garcia. But he's been wrongly charged, and since I'm not willing to risk my legal career by breaking Stynes's privilege, the only way I can right that wrong is by defending him.

When I get in the car, I make a couple of phone calls to determine where my next stop should be. In that regard, I come up with two significant pieces of information. First, I learn that the dry cleaner closes at six. This is good news because I have only three suits and they've all been sitting there, no doubt hanging in plastic and feeling abandoned, for weeks. Getting there by six will be no problem, which means I won't have to wear sweatpants to the hearing tomorrow.

The next thing I find out is that the assistant DA assigned to the Dorsey case is Dylan Campbell. This takes me out of the good mood that the dry cleaner news had put me in. Dylan would have been my last choice as an adversary on this case, which may well be why they don't let the defense attorneys choose the prosecutor.

I know every assistant DA in the county; in fact, more than half had been chosen by my father when he ran the office. To generalize, they are tough, hard-nosed prosecutors whom I can't stand in a courtroom but like drinking beer with afterward.

Dylan Campbell does not fall into this category. While his colleagues and I will bend the legal rules and watch the other side bend them back, Dylan bends them until they break and then throws them in your face. He's smart but unpleasant, and I would much prefer to go up against dumb and affable.

I call Dylan, and he agrees to see me right away, which means he probably wants to make a deal. I find that plea bargains are most likely to be made either at the beginning of a

case or just before trial. Early on, the accused is often scared
and shaken, while the prosecutor is standing at the foot of the
enormous mountain of work that preparing a case represents.
It's a likely time for compromise.

Just before trial, the possibility of a bargain being struck
again increases, mainly because both sides know that soon it is
going to be out of their hands and into a jury's. That threat of
imminent repudiation of one's position is a major motivating
factor toward dealing.

When I reach Dylan's office, he catapults himself out of his
chair and rushes over to greet me, hand extended. This uncharacteristic and transparent graciousness is another sign he
wants to deal. "Andy, good to see you. Good to see you. Here,
sit down. Sit down."

I'm not sure why he is saying everything twice, but it's probably to show me how sincere he is. "Thanks, Dylan. Thanks,
Dylan."

I sit down, and Dylan's next act as the perfect host is to go
to his little refrigerator and ask me what I would like to drink.
He's something of a health nut, so it basically comes down to
whether I want American, Swedish, or Belgian mineral water. I
shrug, and wind up with Swedish.

He sits back behind his desk and smiles. "I've got to ask you
a question," he says. "Everybody in the office is wondering—I
mean, no offense—but how in God's name did you wind up
with a loser slimeball like Oscar Garcia? Did you lose a bet or
something?"

"Oscar Garcia is godfather to my children." I say this quietly,
with as straight a face as I can manage, and I see a quick flash
of fear in Dylan's eyes, as his mind processes the possibilities.
It takes three or four long seconds for his look to switch to nervous relief, as he realizes it just couldn't be.

"Hey, buddy, you had me going there for a second. But only
for a second."

I grin. "Can't fool you, you old rapscallion you."

He's a little uncomfortable with this, so he decides to get

back on firm ground, which unfortunately for me is his case. "So I assume you're here to do a little business?" he asks.

"Well, I was hoping you could bring me up to date. I just officially took the case a few minutes ago."

"You want me to do your homework for you?"

"You don't have to. I can just ask the judge for a delay." A delay is something he most certainly does not want. The court system is like a conveyor belt in an assembly plant, and the prosecutor is the foreman, charged with keeping it moving. Delays are like coffee breaks: The belt stops and the system grinds to a halt.

Dylan pauses for a moment, considering his options. "You looking to deal?"

I'm not, of course, but I don't want him to know that. "I sometimes find it helpful to know what my client is up against before I advise him on what to do."

He sighs; there's no way around this. "Okay. I'll have the file copied and sent over to you with the police reports."

"Good. I'd like it today. Can you also give me the shorthand version?" I ask.

"What do you know so far?"

"About the 911 call and the fingerprints at the warehouse. Unless that's all you have . . ."

"Come on, Andy, if that was all we had, your boy Oscar would be out in the park peddling dope, and you wouldn't be sitting here. Dorsey's gun was found in Garcia's house."

I'm surprised by this, but only because I know Oscar is innocent. "You think Garcia murdered Dorsey, then took his gun and left it in his house?" I ask, trying to exaggerate my incredulity at the stupidity of such a move.

He shrugs. "You visited with Garcia, right?" he asks. "You see any diplomas hanging in his cell?"

I ignore that. "What about motive? That seems to be in short supply."

"We're not there yet. Dorsey was into some bad things, maybe Garcia was a partner, or a competitor. We'll get to motive, but if not?" He throws up his hands. "So what? We don't have to prove motive. Even you public defenders know that."

Dylan has opened up an area I had planned to get into: Dorsey's illegal activities. I nod and say as casually as I can, "I also should look at what the department had on Dorsey."

The fake affability immediately vanishes. He shakes his head firmly. "No can do."

"Why not?" I ask.

"I don't have it myself," he says. "They tell me it doesn't relate in any way to this case."

"Let me see if I understand this," I say. "Dorsey takes off and goes into hiding because the department had something on him, he gets murdered a week later, and what they had isn't relevant? Earth to prosecutor, come in please, come in please."

His look turns cold as he changes the subject. "It's time to make this case go away, Andy. Twenty-five to life, Garcia can be out in ten."

"He can also be in for fifty." I shake my head. "I'll talk to my client, Dylan, but the answer is going to be no."

"I might be able to do better," he says, then sees my look of surprise. He explains, "Dorsey is not a person the department brass wants to read about every day."

Warning bells are going off in my head. The offer of twenty-five to life was actually very generous on his part for the brutal murder of a cop. If he's going to try to better that, it's more than just a desire to get the conveyor moving, or to appease the higher-ups in the police department. There's something here that's interesting and waiting to be discovered.

"Do the best you can," I say. "But my guess is that the day Garcia gets out is the day the jury comes back."

He shrugs his disappointment. "Then I guess we're finished here."

"Not according to the Seventh Circuit Court of Appeals," I say.

"What is that supposed to mean?" he asks.

The fact is that it doesn't mean anything; it's simply a

significant-sounding non sequitur of the kind I occasionally drop to get the other side curious and thinking unproductively.

"You want me to do your homework for you?" I ask, and then turn and walk to the door. He doesn't stand up as I leave. I guess pretending to be pleasant can really tire a person out.

On the way home I call Edna, who is still in a state of shock that I would turn down a prize like Stynes and take on a loser like Garcia. I tell her to call Kevin Randall, who was my second chair on the Willie Miller case, and ask him to meet me in the office first thing in the morning. I ask Edna if Laurie has called, and the answer is no. It wasn't the answer I was hoping for.

Then I call Lieutenant Pete Stanton and ask if I can buy him dinner tonight. He says that's fine, as long as he can pick the restaurant. When I say it's okay with me, he tells me he'll leave the choice on my machine, after he prices a few out and comes up with the most expensive one.

By the time I get home, he has already left the name of a French restaurant which, in his tortured attempt to pronounce it, sounds like La Douche-Face. There is no message from Laurie. I call her, but she's either out or screening my call, so I leave word on her voice mail that I'd like to talk to her. Our last conversation has left me with a sort of throbbing emotional ache, which my work-related activities haven't been able to mask.

The restaurant Pete has chosen looks like a French villa, and when I arrive, he is at the bar drinking from an old and no doubt very expensive bottle of wine. Pete is generally a meat-and-potatoes kind of guy, unassuming and easily able to get by on a lieutenant's salary. Imported beer is usually too fancy for Pete's taste, so it's obvious that his intent is to reduce my financial level to his own.

Pete and I have gotten to be pretty good friends. The relationship began when I helped get his brother out of a legal situation brought on by drug use, and his brother has since turned his life around. Pete and I started playing an occasional game of racquetball, though we haven't played in a while. We still refer to ourselves as racquetball partners, but that's only to maintain the guise of exercise.

Our friendship takes occasional hits, most notably when we're on the opposite sides of a case, but we seem to get through it. The Garcia case presents no such danger, because Pete is not directly involved in the investigation.

We get the menus, and after a quick glance I assume the prices are not just for the food but also for a down payment on the property itself. Or maybe they charge so much because they have to pay for the twelve different forks that are provided for each of us.

The menu is in French, but that doesn't really concern Pete, since he's only interested in the numbers on the right. Pete points to what he wants, and when he gets to the chateaubriand, the waiter explains that it is for two. Pete shrugs and says, "That's no problem, I'll bring what I don't eat home for my dog."

Once the waiter has left, I waste my time by pointing out, "You don't have a dog."

He nods, acknowledging that truth. "It'll give me incentive to get one." He looks around. "I think we need another bottle of wine."

"I can get information cheaper from paid informants," I complain.

He looks up, surprised. "You're looking for information?"

"I agreed to come here, didn't I?" I ask. "What did you think I was going to do, propose marriage?"

"Information about what?"

"Alex Dorsey."

He laughs. "I'm not on the case, asshole. You could have found that out at Burger King."

"I'm not talking about the Garcia case. I'm talking about Alex Dorsey. I'm talking about whatever he was doing, and why he wasn't busted for it back when Laurie turned him in. And why he was going to be busted now."

"I don't know," he says.

"What do you mean you don't know? You're a hot shit lieutenant, plus you're a nosy son of a bitch. You know everything
that goes on down there."

He shakes his head. "Not this. This is buried deep." Then he
adds, "Besides, 'down there' may not be where you think it is,
or want it to be."

"What the hell does that mean?"

He puts down one of his forks, I think the third-smallest
one, and stares at me. It is the kind of stare that has made felons
confess for the last twenty years. "I'm going to tell you something, but if anyone ever learns that it came from me, I'm going
to beat you to death with your wallet."

"Trust me, if there's one thing I've learned this week, it's that
I can keep a secret."

Pete nods. The truth is, he knows this without my having to
say it. "The Bureau is involved."

This surprises me. "The FBI?"

"No, the bureau in my bedroom, bozo."

I ignore the insult; this is too significant a development.
"What about Dorsey makes this federal?"

"I have no idea," he claims, and I'm sure he doesn't. "All I
know is that there was talk that the feds got the department to
lay off. I assume they were covering the same turf with an investigation of their own."

"Then why would that have changed? Why would Dorsey
have had to run?"

Pete doesn't know the answer to that, so I ask him if he's
ever heard of Geoffrey Stynes. He hasn't, but agrees to check
him out. I haven't heard back from Vince yet, so it makes sense
to put Pete on the case as well.

I'm ready to leave, but Pete makes me wait while he tries
both the crème brûlée and the cherries jubilee. Both meet with
his approval, though he considers the crème brûlée "a tad
lumpy." I tell him that if he ever picks a restaurant like this
again, I'm going to introduce him to a different kind of "lumpy."

I start planning some strategy on the way home. What I

need to do is try the case as if I wasn't aware of Garcia's innocence, and that means learning everything I can about the victim, Dorsey. If Pete is right about the FBI's involvement, and he
is rarely wrong about such things, then there's a great deal to
learn, and most likely great benefit in learning it.

When I get home, I am treated to as nice a sight as I can remember in a very long time. Laurie is sitting on the porch with
Tara, with Laurie in the role of petter and Tara in the role of
pettee. I park and walk toward them, just as they come off the
porch and walk toward me.

Laurie hugs me as Tara sits by, waiting her turn. The hug
lasts a while, which is good. I'm in no rush. Finally, she breaks
it off and looks in my eyes.

"I know you wouldn't take this case to hurt me," she says.

"I wouldn't."

"I know you have a good reason for taking it," she says.

"I do."

"I know you can't tell me what that reason is," she says.

"I can't."

"I know that you love me," she says.

"I do."

"I know you're thinking you want me to stay with you
tonight, even though it's not Monday, Wednesday, or Friday,"
she says.

"I am."

"I know that if you give another two-word answer, I'm
going home, and you will have missed out on a warm, loving,
wildly exciting sexual experience," she says.

"I understand that completely and I guarantee you I have
absolutely no intention of ever giving a two-word answer again.
I know long answers are important to you, and since I adore
and worship you, I will keep speaking until you tell me to shut
up."

"Shut up," she says.

• • • • •

I ARRIVE AT COURT well before the preliminary hearing is scheduled to begin. I'm simultaneously feeling dread at having to handle this case and excitement about being back handling any case at all. The excitement must be winning out, because I usually barely make it to court on time, and today I'm so early I could tailgate in the parking lot.

Oscar isn't here yet, so I call Kevin Randall at the office and apologize for not being able to meet him there. I quickly bring Kevin up to date on the situation, and he has the decency not to verbalize his surprise that I took this case at all. I give him the task of going to see the coroner who handled Dorsey's body and to find out whatever relevant details there are, including the estimated time of death.

Kevin has a whole bunch of positive qualities, but the one I appreciate most is his total reliability. When he takes on an assignment, I can check it off my list; he will get it done and done well.

Kevin is a topflight attorney with loads of experience on both the defense and prosecution sides. Unfortunately, both caused him conscience problems. As a prosecutor, he was afraid his considerable talents might cause an innocent person to go to prison. As a defense attorney, he feared he might be helping dangerous criminals return to the streets.

He finally resolved this by quitting the law and opening the "Lawdromat," where customers can wash their clothes and get free legal advice. Laurie knows Kevin well, and on her advice I took him on as second chair on the Willie Miller case. He's been coming in a couple of days a week ever since, with the understanding that he'll help me on future cases, providing there's no fabric softener crisis that demands his time.

I meet with Oscar in an anteroom for a few minutes to explain the procedures. He has some experience in this field, so he catches on pretty quickly. This appearance is basically a formality, strictly done to inform him of the charges, register his plea, and consider bail. Dylan has already impaneled a grand jury to formally charge Oscar, and as always, the grand jury will do the prosecutor's bidding. Oscar's sole responsibility for this appearance is to sit up straight, look respectable, and say firmly and clearly, "Not guilty," when called upon to give his plea.

When the guards come to escort Oscar into the courtroom, I walk with him. We are almost at the defense table when he says—to himself, I think—"What the hell is that bitch doing here?"

I look in the direction that Oscar is looking, and he seems to be staring toward Laurie, who is standing in the back of the room. "Who are you talking about?" I ask as we continue walking.

"The bitch in the blue dress." There is no question he is talking about Laurie.

"Watch your mouth when you're talking about her," I say. It is a silly, unnecessary, but involuntary act of verbal chivalry.

We reach the defense table and sit down. "You mean you know her?" he asks.

"I do."

"Well, let me tell you something, man. You know that list

you wanted from me, of my enemies? People who would
frame me? Well, she's number one, right on top."

"You're dreaming, Oscar."

"Yeah, well, she's been following me, watching me all the
time. Like I can't get rid of her. And a friend of mine said she
was hanging near my apartment the other day when I was
out."

I trust Oscar about as far as I can throw Mount Rushmore,
but I instinctively know that he is telling the truth about this.
He has no real reason to lie, and it fits in with Laurie's cryptic
comment about having knowledge of Oscar's criminal progress
since she left the force.

I don't have time to reflect on the possible implications of
Oscar's comment, because I find myself staring at the sweaty
hand of Dylan Campbell, who, for the benefit of the assembled
media, has come over to wish me luck.

I wouldn't describe today's event as a media circus; there is
much more press here than usual, but the crush is far from
overwhelming. The reason for whatever newsworthiness the
hearing has rests in the victim's being a cop, however discred-
ited, and the brutal nature of the crime.

The judge, Susan Timmerman, enters, and the bailiff calls
the proceedings to order. Judge Timmerman will be handling
only this hearing; the case hasn't yet been assigned. It's unfor-
tunate, because she is a fair judge who doesn't show any bias
toward the prosecution, and we have gotten along fairly well
in the past.

The charges contained in the case of *New Jersey v. Oscar
Garcia* are read, and counsel are identified. Oscar is asked
how he pleads and he performs his part correctly, saying, "Not
guilty," with conviction and a trace of indignation. In Oscar's
case, a trace is all the indignation one can stomach.

The not guilty plea creates the need for trial, and that is
what the court must consider next. Timmerman does not have
all the judges' schedules, and doesn't know who the judge will
be anyway, but she can at least tentatively set a date. We agree

on July 14, about four months from now, and Judge Timmerman asks if there is anything else she must consider.

I jump up. "Discovery, Your Honor."

"What about it?" she asks.

"I've discovered that opposing counsel doesn't seem to believe in it. I've requested reports that have not been turned over."

Dylan looks mortally wounded. "Your Honor," he complains, "the request was made just yesterday."

I'm having none of this. "I'm sorry, Your Honor, but we are talking about the copying of reports. That takes minutes, not days. I would be happy to walk with Mr. Campbell to his office and do it myself. Secondly, the timing of the request is not important; it's not even necessary at all. The prosecution should be aware of their discovery obligations with or without a specific request. Documents should be copied and turned over as they are received, without editing."

The judge nods and issues the order. "The state will turn over copies of whatever reports it has in its possession by close of business today."

She slams her gavel, effectively adjourning the proceedings. The courtroom empties quickly, and with the press having dispersed, Dylan forgets to exchange parting pleasantries.

I arrange to meet with Oscar later to discuss the case in detail for the first time. I'm particularly interested in his whereabouts on the night of the murder. I'm hoping he was having dinner with the secretary of state or being interviewed by Ted Koppel on *Nightline*.

Laurie is waiting for me in the back of the courtroom, and Oscar doesn't take his eyes off her the entire time he is being led off. Those eyes are not ogling; they are hating and fearing.

Once Oscar is out of sight, I go back and meet Laurie.

"You pissed Dylan off," she points out.

I nod. "Had to happen sooner or later."

"This is sooner. Listen, Andy, I want to work on this case."

This surprises me. "You don't have to do that. I know how you feel about Oscar."

"That doesn't matter. I'm a professional and I have to act like it," she says.

I find myself thinking, "I'm not so sure this is a great idea." I find myself saying, "Great."

"We starting right now?" she asks.

"Nope. Tomorrow." I look at my watch. "I'm due back in high school in twenty minutes."

Paterson Eastside is the high school from which I graduated. The school's claim to fame is that it was the subject and setting of the movie *Lean on Me*, starring Morgan Freeman. It told the story of the then principal, Joe Clark, and his heavy-handed method of getting the chaotic inner-city school under control.

My high school career could best be described as undistinguished, at least in the things important to me: girls and sports. My sports mediocrity was the more painful of the two, because at least with girls I had the good sense to give up trying early on. In sports I had perseverance, a trait that is not all it's cracked up to be.

Eastside's football field, adjacent to the school, was actually placed on an old cemetery, after the graves had allegedly been moved. Thus the school had two nicknames, the Ghosts and the Undertakers. It was on that field that I suffered my greatest indignity. As I sat on the bench, the starters were out on the field making awful play after awful play. The coach turned to me and said, "Can you imagine how bad you are if you're playing behind them?"

But I've returned to Eastside today in triumph. I'm endowing the school with a yearly scholarship, given in the name of my father. An assembly has been called to commemorate the occasion, and the principal tells me that my recent media exposure has actually created some student interest in the event.

My speech is a combination of self-deprecating humor and sincere exhortation to the students to make their lives productive. I don't build myself up too much, because even though I'm a pretty good lawyer, the truth is that the only reason I'm standing here today is that my father died and left me a truck-load of money.

When I mention my father's nonfinancial influence on me, I get a little choked up. It's been happening a lot lately. I've noticed that as I get older, I get more and more sentimental. I also notice some other things as I age, like a couple of hairs growing on each of my ears. Now that I think about it, there could be a cause-and-effect relationship at work here. Maybe I should fund some medical research into studying the effect of ear hair on human emotional response.

The question-and-answer session afterward is surprisingly lively. Most of the students want to know about the Willie Miller case, though their interest seems centered on what it was like to visit Willie on death row.

The Garcia case is of less interest. Some of them know Oscar or know of him from the neighborhood, and to know Oscar is to be unconcerned about his fate.

But a decent round of applause sends me off, and I head down to the jail to meet with my client. He's agitated and somewhat scared; for some reason his appearance in court this morning provided a sense of reality to his situation that the arrest and incarceration did not.

Oscar is not the type you make small talk with, so I ask him if he has any questions about what took place in court today.

"That guy Campbell, he seemed out to get me."

It wasn't a question, but it's close enough. "He wants to send you to prison for the rest of your life."

"Son of a bitch . . ."

"You've obviously met him before," I say. "Now, tell me everything you did the night of the murder, minute by minute, as best as you can remember. Don't leave out a thing, no matter how small or unimportant it might seem."

The sullen Oscar becomes even more so. "I hung out," he mutters.

"That's not quite the detail I need."

"Hey, what do you want me to say, man?" he asks, clearly annoyed with my persistence.

"I want you to tell me where you were that night. Because if you don't cooperate with me, I can tell you where you're going to spend every night for the rest of your life."

"I was doing business," he mutters.

"Where? In the park?"

"No."

It's my turn to get annoyed. "Dammit, Oscar, where the hell were you?"

He proceeds to tell me a rather uneventful tale of retail drug peddling in and around the park, with a little pimping thrown in. All of this took place until about one A.M., and he claims that some of the people he mentions would testify if called upon, but even without meeting them I can safely assume that none would have any credibility before a jury.

After one A.M. the rendition gets fuzzy. Only through repeated questioning am I able to piece together that he went to make a payment to the entity that grants him permission to function. In other words, he had to pay his mob bosses their standard piece of the action, and he was doing just that after one A.M.

"I need names, Oscar. Of the people you saw while you were making this payment."

Oscar actually laughs at the absurdity of the request. "Forget it. No fucking way. I give you those names, and you're defending a dead man."

I could give him another lecture on attorney-client privilege, and how the information would be safe with me, but I know it won't help. So I try to get at it a different way. I ask him to tell me the neighborhood, the street, that he was on during this business transaction. Eventually, he does, though he doesn't want to take any chances, so he narrows it to within a two-block radius. The area is a neighborhood that even I am aware is considered by organized crime to be home base.

"How long were you there?" I ask.

" 'Bout three hours."

"To make a payment?" It seems like an inordinately long time.

"They were busy," he explains. "They kept me waiting."

"Is that unusual?"

"Usually, it don't take as long," he says, then qualifies it with, "When *I* go to *them*."

"You mean there are times they come to you?"

I can see him regain a measure of pride. "Sure. Most of the time."

I take him through the three hours he spent in the neighborhood in question. Basically, he hung out in the cellar of the house he was visiting, except for about a half hour when he went out to get something to eat.

"Did you eat at a restaurant?" I ask.

"Nah, I went to one of those big supermarkets—Food Fair, I think it's called. They make these really good sandwiches."

"Did you pay with a credit card?"

"A credit card?" he asks, indicating how absurd the question is. I might as well have asked if he had paid with a walrus.

He doesn't think anybody in the store would remember him, and the truth is, it's not as if Brad Pitt had come in that night for the sandwich. Oscar is a number of things, but memorable is not one of them. I let him off the hook with no more questions for now and tell him we'll be meeting again in a day or two.

As I'm leaving, he asks, "Man, I got things to work on. Am I gonna be stuck in here long?"

"I think it makes sense to go ahead and order furniture and drapes, if that's what you're asking."

It turns out that wasn't what he was asking.

• • • • •

GEOFFREY STYNES is nowhere to be found.

Not that I'm spending a lot of time looking for him. But I've more than half expected him to look me up, to complain about my taking on Garcia as a form of breaking privilege, or at least a conflict of interest. I don't think such claims would have merit, but I did expect him to make them.

These kinds of thoughts are running through my mind as Laurie and I are having dinner at my house. She mentions that I'm being quiet, but doesn't push to find out what's on my mind.

We are just finishing dinner when Vince Sanders calls. "I checked out Geoffrey Stynes," he says.

"And?" I ask.

"And I also checked out the tooth fairy, Rumpelstiltskin, and Tinker Bell. They don't really exist either."

"You're losing me."

"That must happen to you a lot," he says. "Maybe you should wear a bell around your neck."

"What the hell are you talking about?" Vince can be somewhat difficult to chat with.

"There are two registered Geoffrey Stynes with that spelling," he says. "One was born four months ago Wednesday, and the other is ninety-two and in a rest home. In addition to that, none of the sources I checked, and I checked a shitload of sources, have heard of him. Which causes me to wonder why the hell you're wasting my time."

I can't say too much, because Laurie is sitting right near me and I don't want to answer a lot of questions. "Interesting" is all I can muse out loud.

"You sure you want to share a major piece of news like that?" Vince asks. "What if I got captured and tortured? They might force out of me the fact that Andy Carpenter thought it was interesting."

"Hold out as long as you can. Your country needs you."

"Don't forget," he says, "if there's a story here, it's mine."

"You know, for some people, doing a favor for a friend is payment enough."

"Then you should have asked *them*," he snarls, just before he hangs up.

The rest of the evening is quiet. Laurie reads, and I pretend to read while all the time thinking about the case. It's uncomfortable for me that there is a great deal I can't share with her; it's the first time I've had this experience. My sense is also that there are things she isn't sharing with me, most of them centering around Oscar Garcia.

In fact, for all I know, she might also be pretending to read. If she is, then she's more intellectual than I am; she fake-reads higher-quality stuff. Tara is more honest than either of us; she doesn't just pretend to chew on a toy, she actually chews on it.

It's about eleven o'clock when I get tired of fake-reading and Laurie and I go to bed. Once we get into bed, we go to sleep. We have passed the point in our relationship where we have sex at every opportunity. We're still up in the eighty percent range, but sometimes I find myself longing for the good old days.

I get up earlier than Laurie, because I had arranged to meet with Kevin at eight in the office. When I arrive, he is polishing off his standard breakfast: one bagel, toasted, with cream cheese, one bagel, not toasted, with butter. There are people who can stuff their faces and not gain a pound; Kevin is most definitely not one of those people. The main eating difference between Kevin and Vince Sanders is that Vince overeats only fattening, unhealthful foods. Kevin will eat anything: put a barrel of wheat germ in front of him and he'll inhale it.

Kevin and I are alone; Edna isn't in yet. We could have met at ten and we'd still be alone. Since Edna doesn't do any actual work, she doesn't see the need to put in long hours. There's an irrefutable logic to that which I have given up trying to refute.

Kevin met with the coroner yesterday, and even though there isn't much information of value, he is confident that he got all there was to get. The condition of the body makes it impossible to be definitive in the findings, but it appears that the cause of death was the decapitation, that Dorsey was alive when it was done. The lividity, and the resulting effects of the fire, make the coroner quite confident that death came within an hour before the fire. This fits in neatly with my knowledge that the murder took place behind Hinchcliffe Stadium, which is about forty-five minutes from the warehouse.

Since the police know when the fire was set, they can make their estimate of the time of death unusually precise: Dorsey was murdered between two-thirty and three A.M. Right in the middle of the time Oscar says he was all the way on the other side of town, making his weekly payment to the mob.

It is there that Laurie and I meet to begin the process. I am the attorney and Laurie is the investigator; I have no illusions about our roles and no desire to reverse them. But I like to be present at the scene at the beginning of each investigation; it connects me to the case in a way that feels helpful.

The area itself is reminiscent of an earlier Paterson. The houses are modest and very well kept, and the streets have maintained their neighborhood feel. Kids play on the street in a carefree fashion; any criminal who would ply his trade by victimizing the people on these streets would have a built-in insanity defense.

The head of northern New Jersey's version of what may or may not still be called the family is Dominic Petrone. I've met Petrone at various boring city functions which I've been coerced into attending. He's a gray-haired, well-mannered, obviously intelligent man who looks like a typical corporate CEO, which is exactly what he is. His corporation's products and services include drugs, prostitution, loan-sharking, money laundering, and an occasional murder or two. It's not easy work, but hell, somebody's got to do it.

I've brought along a picture of Oscar, and I show it to some people on the street, asking if they recognize him. It's counterproductive; it makes them think we're part of law enforcement, which means we're anti-Petrone, which means we're the enemy. These people have no need or use for the police; all the protection they need lives right in their neighborhood. They would sooner rat out God than Dominic Petrone, and asking them questions only causes them to view us with suspicion.

Of course, there is no chance that the person Oscar came to see was Petrone. Petrone is far too high on the totem pole for that; he would have people who would have people who would have people who would have people to deal with a roach like Oscar. And even they wouldn't be thrilled about it.

Since we don't know which house Oscar came to, and we can't find anybody who remembers seeing him, what we basically do is wander aimlessly about, accomplishing nothing. The investigation is really heating up.

We're about to leave when we see the Food Fair supermarket that Oscar said he had visited. The first thing we do is confirm that a different shift of employees would have been on that night, so there's no chance any of these people would remember him. Laurie will have to come back during the night and cover that base.

We ask to speak to the manager, so that we can see if there

are security camera tapes that covered the evening in question. If Oscar was here that night, he could have been part of a taped record.

The manager is on a coffee break, so while we wait, Laurie decides to do a little food shopping. She goes off to get some things, while I walk over to the cash machine so I can at least offer to pay for it. They actually have a small bank branch right there within the supermarket, with three machines for additional service.

I know from a similar situation on another case that our chances of finding anything on the store taping system are slim. Most stores simply run the tapes on a twenty-four- or forty-eight-hour cycle and then tape over them. But it's worth a try, and when the manager, Wally, comes back, we ask him about it. I know his name is Wally, and I know he's the manager, because above the pocket of his shirt it says, "Wally," and just below that it says, "Manager." These are the kinds of tricks I've picked up by accompanying Laurie on these investigations.

"How long do you keep the security tapes after they're used?" I ask.

"You cops?" Wally asks.

His response isn't exactly on point, and he says "cops" in such a way that, if we were in fact cops, he would try to lead us to our demise in the pesticide department. My sense is that somebody got the word to him that we've been snooping around, asking questions.

"No," I say.

"Then what?"

"Then what what?" I counter. This repartee is on a very sophisticated level; I hope Laurie can follow it. A cashier within earshot is yawning; it's obviously over her head.

"What are you?" he demands.

"Tired of this conversation," I answer, just before Laurie sighs loudly and intervenes.

"He's a lawyer and I'm a private investigator. We can get a subpoena and you can spend an entire day being deposed, or you can answer a couple of easy questions and then go back to stacking cans in aisle seven. Your choice."

"Yeah," I say to add emphasis, but I refrain from sticking my tongue out at him.

He's annoyed, but recognizes the futility of resisting a force as powerful as mine. "We run the tapes for twenty-four hours, then tape over them."

I show him a picture of Oscar. "Have you ever seen him?"

"No," he says immediately. He's not giving anything at all. Had I shown him pictures of Michael Jordan, George Bush, and Heather Locklear, his "no" would have been just as quick.

"Do you wish you could be more helpful, because as a good citizen it's important to you that justice be done?" I counter.

Laurie drags me off before he can answer, which is a shame, because I could tell he was just about to crack.

On the way out, I keep in charitable practice by dropping a twenty-dollar bill in the March of Dimes canister, and then Laurie and I go our separate ways. She is going to snoop around Oscar's neighborhood, while I'm going back to my office for a meeting. Laurie doesn't ask for Oscar's address, which means she knows where he lives. This is curious, since I know from the police reports that he's only lived there two months. This means that Laurie's knowledge can't come from when she was on the force. Oscar had mentioned in court that she had been near his apartment, watching him. I don't ask her about any of this, and I don't ask myself why I don't ask her about any of this.

The meeting scheduled in my office is one I'm actually looking forward to. It's with Willie Miller, and we are going to discuss the lawsuit I have filed on his behalf against my former father-in-law, Philip Gant, and the estate of Victor Markham.

Victor and Philip committed a murder thirty-five years ago, and then committed another long after to cover it up. They arranged to frame Willie for the second murder, and he spent seven years on death row before he was cleared in the retrial.

Philip wound up in jail and Victor took his own life. It was a terrible tragedy for all concerned, especially Willie, but there is one ray of sunshine: Both Philip and Victor were incredibly wealthy.

There is no suspense attached to the winning or losing of this lawsuit, we are going to win. It's a slam dunk, and both sides know it. The only question is how much money Willie will get, and the other side is very concerned about a jury's actions in this regard, since they have asked for settlement discussions. Today Willie and I are going to talk about our position in advance of those discussions.

In the months since his trial, and especially in the first few weeks, Willie became something of a media celebrity. He made the talk show circuit and brought a new twist to it. A street-smart kid who never left the inner city, Willie had no occasion to develop that filter through which most people talk to the media. So in these sessions he was just Willie Miller, and he spoke to interviewers in exactly the same fashion he spoke to friends on the street.

The results were both refreshing and hilarious. Willie interrupted one interview to ask, "Hey, am I getting paid for this?" He asked another questioner about a female camera operator, and when told she was single, he asked her out on the air. She declined, but changed her mind and accepted after the show.

There were embarrassing moments as well, though Willie never seemed to notice. When asked to compare the current world to the one he left seven years ago, he bemoaned the inflated prices of "gas and hookers."

When I get to the office, I walk in on a priceless conversation between Willie and Edna. I pick it up in the middle, but it's immediately clear that Willie has shocked Edna by declaring that he has never seen or even heard of crossword puzzles. She had supposed that there were people in far-off lands, living in caves or trees, who were this deprived. But here, sitting in our office? Impossible.

Willie does not seem the least bit defensive about his admission, probably because Willie is not the least bit defensive about anything. He grudgingly agrees to let Edna attempt to teach him the basics, which only compounds the obvious cultural gap.

"Indeterminate," she says, looking at the newspaper. "Seven letters."

Willie is offended. "I know how many letters 'inde-' whatever has."

Edna shakes her head. "I'm looking for another word for 'indeterminate.' It has seven letters and the third letter is 'u.'"

"Why the hell are you looking for it?" he asks. "You already got that 'inde-' word. Look for one you don't have."

"The word is 'neutral.'"

"I thought you said it had seven letters." Willie starts counting on his fingers, softly mouthing the letters as he counts. When he finishes, his look is triumphant. "No way."

I get a momentary nightmare flash of Willie playing Scrabble with Laurie, and then I break up this conference and bring Willie into my office. Willie is a black belt in karate, but I believe that if I hadn't shown up, Edna would have killed him.

Just before Willie and I start talking, Pete Stanton calls. He has come up as dry as Vince Sanders did in the search for Geoffrey Stynes. He assures me that he's checked everywhere there is to check, which leads to the inescapable conclusion that Stynes was in my office under an assumed name.

This complicates the situation considerably. If he signed the retainer agreement using a false identity, then that agreement has no legal standing. The murkier question is whether this relieves me of the constraints of the privilege. I could research this, but I don't, since right now murky works fine while I figure out what I want to do about maintaining Stynes's privilege.

I decide to split the difference. Without revealing what little I know about Stynes's identity, I will utilize some of the information that I learned from him to help my client. I'm on shaky legal ground, but it's ground I'm prepared to defend if I have to.

I call Laurie and carefully tell her that I have received information about some possible evidence in the Dorsey murder. I describe the area behind Hinchcliffe Stadium in the same fashion Stynes described it to me, and ask Laurie if she could check it out. I further tell her that if she finds anything, she should leave it untouched and call the police.

My feeling is that the evidence may be helpful in demonstrating Oscar's innocence. I will not help the authorities by pointing them to Stynes, but if they get there on their own, I can live with it.

Turning back to Willie, I briefly bring him up to date on the progress of the lawsuit. I tell him that both of the other parties have agreed to be represented by the same attorney, and we are to meet with him later in the week. I also reemphasize that which I've told him at least five times before: Any money that he gets from Philip Gant will in effect ultimately reduce the inheritance of my ex-wife, Nicole. Nicole and I have not spoken since her father's arrest, but it still represents a conflict of sorts for me. It is a conflict about which Willie continues to be unconcerned.

I haven't yet discussed the possible award Willie might get, and a jury decision in this area is particularly hard to predict. Based on my initial settlement discussions, however, I think we could be looking at a five-million-dollar offer, and this is the number I tell Willie.

Willie starts to make a noise that is somewhere between gurgling and blubbering. Whatever he is doing, it is not compatible with breathing, and for a moment I consider whether to call 911. Eventually, he recovers enough to commence gasping.

"Five million dollars?" are the first words he can manage.

I nod. "But I recommend that you reject it."

"I should reject it?" He's having trouble processing the words. "You mean turn it down? Turn down five million dollars?"

"Yes. I think you should hold out for in excess of ten, after my commission."

"Ten what? Million?" he asks.

I nod. "Million. We're talking about almost seven years. Isn't your life worth at least a million five per year?"

He slows down, trying to gather his thoughts to deal with what he is hearing. "Damn straight," he finally says. "This is my life we're talking about." Willie is a really good "thought gatherer."

"So we're agreed?" I ask.

"Definitely. We are standing on the same corner, man. Singin' the same tune. Walking the same walk. All the way."

"Good," I say. "One for all and all for one."

He nods in agreement, then: "But what if they don't give us the ten?"

"Then we'll get a jury to give us fifteen."

"My man!" he enthuses, and actually slaps me five twice, so that it will total ten. A while later he gets up to leave, but stops at the door and turns to me. "You're not bullshitting me, right? I mean, no way you are bullshitting me?"

"No way." I smile, and then he smiles a hell of a lot wider than I do.

Minutes after Willie leaves, I get a phone call from Dylan Campbell's assistant asking me to meet Dylan in his office as soon as possible. I can only assume that the police have uncovered more evidence damaging to Oscar, but there's no sense asking the assistant. Dylan takes center stage whenever he can; if there's a bomb to drop on me, he will drop it personally.

I'm ushered into Dylan's office as soon as I arrive, another sign that he's got something to use on me. It's more often his style to make visitors stew in the reception area, but this time he can't wait to get right to it.

Also in Dylan's office waiting for me is Lieutenant Nick Sabonis, the lead detective on Oscar's case. If he shares Dylan's glee at what is about to be said, he hides it well. Nick's a career cop nearing the day when his biggest concern will be what fishing rod to use. He doesn't get into personal stuff with lawyers; he just wants to lock up the bad guys and move on to the next case.

"Thanks for coming down so quickly, Andy," Dylan says. "New evidence has turned up concerning your client."

I just wait for him to continue; coaxing him to hurry up would give him a satisfaction I don't want to provide.

"We got a call from a Wallace Ferro, the manager at the Food Fair supermarket on Riverside. It turns out that there's a tape of Garcia in the store at the exact time that the coroner says the murder was committed."

I'm pleased but puzzled. "I asked him about the tapes."

Dylan nods, a slight smirk on his face. "According to him, you didn't ask too hard. This was a tape above the cash machines at the bank branch in the market. It's a different system, and they don't tape over them for months. For some reason he thought we'd be more interested in it than you would."

Little of what Dylan is saying makes sense, but I'm not really concerned. No matter what Wally the grocery manager thinks of my investigative techniques, my client is about to be freed and so am I. I'm out of the case and clear of conscience. I can go back to saving otters.

"Does Oscar know about this?" I ask.

"He does. He's been released, and he's agreed to voluntarily answer some questions."

Alarm bells go off in my head. "What kind of questions? Why wasn't I informed?"

"Don't worry, Andy, Oscar waived his right to counsel." He smiles. "Especially your counsel."

"What the hell is going on, Dylan? What are you questioning Oscar about?"

My sense of foreboding increases when Nick, not having said a word, walks out of the office. My sense is that while he may be on the same side as Dylan, he doesn't want to associate himself with this performance.

Dylan doesn't even seem to notice him leave. He is taking his time, savoring the moment. "We've made another arrest in the case, Andy. We believe Oscar has information to provide in connection with that arrest."

"Who did you arrest?" I ask, knowing that this is the reason Dylan called me here, and knowing with even greater certainty that I'm going to hate the answer.

"I'm sorry I have to be the one to tell you this," he lies, "but we've arrested and charged Laurie Collins with the murder of Alex Dorsey."

• • • • •

THE PRESS IS OUT IN FORCE by
the time I get to the jail. When it was Oscar Garcia that stood
accused, it was a marginal story. When it's Laurie Collins, ex-
cop and sworn enemy of the deceased, it's page one all the
way.

I work my way through the reporters and camera crews,
making comments as I go. I don't usually like to speak to the
press until I know the facts, so I say only what I know to be
true.

"What's your reaction to the arrest?" I'm asked.

"It's beyond idiotic," I respond.

"Are you going to defend her?"

"The facts will defend her," I say. "I'll just make sure everybody knows them."

I get inside the jail and ask to see Laurie. The bozo at the
front desk tells me that she's being "processed." I know she's
smart enough not to talk to anyone without me present, but I
don't like the fact that she's alone. After five minutes of waiting,
I tell him I'm going to go outside and tell the press I'm being
denied access to my client. Coincidentally, at that very moment
he receives a telepathic communication informing him that the
processing just ended.

I'm led back to an anteroom where I wait for another five minutes, until Laurie is brought in. Her hands are cuffed in front of her, and she is already dressed in jail clothing. I expect to see fear in her eyes, but that's not what is there. What I see is anger. Which is good, because I've got enough fear for both of us.

"Andy, what the hell is going on?"

"I don't know," I say. "I haven't tried to press anyone for information yet. I wanted to talk to you first."

"They've charged me with Dorsey's murder," she says, total disbelief in her voice.

I nod. "Tell me what happened. Don't leave out a thing."

She sits down, resting her cuffed hands uncomfortably on the table. The cuffs are so offensive to me, I want to bite them off with my teeth.

"There isn't that much to tell," she says. "I went out to the stadium, like you said. It took a little while, but I finally noticed something in the shrubbery. I went over and looked at it, but I didn't touch it. It looked like clothing with blood on it. Then I saw the handle of a large knife, as if somebody had tried to cover it with the shrubs."

"What did you do?"

"I didn't do anything. Ten seconds after I saw the stuff, officers seemed to come from everywhere. There must have been seven or eight of them, guns drawn. They read me my rights and brought me down here."

"Do you think they had been following you, or waiting at the site?"

She shakes her head. "I don't know, maybe both. There were a lot of them." She shakes her head again, this time with more sadness. "It was weird; I helped train two or three of them."

I'm silent for a few moments, trying to figure this out. None of these pieces fit together.

"Andy, why did you send me out there?" It's not an accusation, just a need to know.

"I had information that the killer's clothes might be there. I figured that if they were, it would get Oscar off the hook. It should do the same for you."

Laurie speaks quietly, and for the first time I can hear the fear overtaking the anger. "Andy, they were my clothes."

She can't have said what I think she said. "What?"

"The clothes with blood on them . . . they were mine. I don't know how they got there . . . I never even noticed them missing from my closet."

In a flash that feels exactly like panic, I realize that this is the worst of both worlds. We are facing a situation that makes absolutely no sense, yet clearly has been planned and executed with precision.

"Laurie, we will get through this."

"And where will I be while we're doing that?" she asks.

She's talking about the possibility of bail, which I started thinking about on the way over here. It's very problematic. Oscar was charged with first-degree murder, and there's no doubt that the same will be the case with Laurie. It's very difficult to get bail in that circumstance, and I can certainly count on Dylan to oppose it.

"Bail's going to be tough," I tell her. I don't lie to clients, and I'm certainly not going to start with Laurie.

She nods, knowing very well how the system works. "If we don't get it, and even if we do, we need to get to trial as quickly as possible."

"It's way too early to be talking about a trial. We're going to try and end this before we even get there."

"I can't sit in a cage, Andy."

I would love to tell her she won't have to, but it's not within my power. This point is driven home all too clearly when the guard comes into the room to take her back to that cage.

I tell Laurie that I'll be back to see her tomorrow, at which time I'll have learned much more about the situation, and we can talk about it in detail. I tell her again that we'll get through this, that everything is going to be fine. I tell her that I love her and that she needs to keep her spirits up.

Which brings me to the things I don't tell her. I don't tell her that they couldn't have had time to test the blood on the clothing yet, so they can't be sure it's Dorsey's blood. I don't tell her that that means there is other evidence against her, evidence that the police feel independently justifies the arrest. I don't tell her that I know in my gut there are other shoes to drop, that things are going to get worse before they can get better.

I don't tell her that every single cell in my body is scared shitless.

Once Laurie has been led away, I go downstairs to see Sergeant Luther Dandridge, head of the detail that deals with the prisoners. I know him, but not well, and there's no real reason he would do me any favors. I take a shot anyway and ask him to make things as comfortable as possible for Laurie.

It turns out that he knows and likes Laurie, and he tells me he's already arranged for her to be kept away from the rest of the population and treated as well as possible. When I hear him say it, I want to kiss and hug him and maybe give him the eleven million I didn't give cousin Fred.

I've got to get my emotions in check.

It's almost eight P.M. when I leave the jail, and I call Dylan's office. No one answers, which means I'm going to have to wait until tomorrow to get any information. I call my office machine, and there are a bunch of messages, mostly from friends of mine and Laurie expressing their support. Kevin has also called to tell me he's ready to go to work tonight.

The last call is from Dylan, alerting me to the initial court appearance tomorrow morning at eleven. They are moving quickly, confidently. We have got to do the same, but it's hard to move quickly and confidently when you don't know where you're going.

I call Kevin at his house and he answers at the beginning of the first ring. The conversation is exactly what I expect. Even though I know he is outraged and upset, he doesn't voice either of those emotions. Those would be wasted, unproductive words; what we need to do is spend every moment of our time and thoughts on helping Laurie, not bemoaning the unfairness of her fate. I ask him to come right over so we can get started.

I get home and take Tara for a short walk, and by the time we get back Kevin has arrived. I make some coffee and we get down to making whatever plans and decisions we can, given our current limited access to information.

Our first priority is getting that information, and since I will have to prepare for tomorrow's court hearing, I give that task to Kevin. He will be waiting at Dylan's office before it even opens in the morning, and if he gets any resistance at all to our demand for immediate production of discovery material, he will notify me before the hearing. I will then once again embarrass Dylan about it before the judge. I doubt Dylan will want that to happen, so I suspect he'll be generally, and grudgingly, cooperative with Kevin.

We discuss how we will frame our request for bail, and prepare a motion utilizing what favorable case law there is. Kevin thinks we have a better chance than I think we have, which is encouraging, since he's a terrific attorney who has worked both sides of the system.

I tell Kevin about Stynes; my reservations about breaking that privilege have long since disappeared. Since Stynes had to know that they were not his clothes behind the stadium, he was clearly in my office for the purpose of framing Laurie. He played me like an accordion, and paying him back will be a key component of Laurie's defense.

Kevin leaves and I sit up another couple of hours, thinking about the case. I instinctively know that the victim is going to be the key, that understanding the last two years of Alex Dorsey's life is the only way to reveal the truth about his death.

One thing I know for sure: Laurie did not kill him. Stynes's involvement proves that, at least to me, but I would be sure of her innocence even without it. She hated Dorsey, and she could well have wished him dead. Under certain extreme circumstances, I could even imagine her killing him, be it to protect herself or others. But the brutality of the murder, the total disregard for the dignity of human life, clears Laurie beyond any doubt.

I get into bed, but barely sleep at all. I keep thinking of Laurie in that cell, and on some level it feels as if falling asleep in the comfort of the bed we share would be like abandoning her.

I'm up watching the news by five-thirty in the morning, but it isn't until an hour later that I discover the "sunrise scam." The weather guy has proclaimed that six-thirty-one is the moment of sunrise, yet I can now bear witness to the fact that at that exact time it is already light out, and has been light for fifteen minutes.

Does no one check these things out? Do they think the light is coming from another source, perhaps helping our eyes adjust to the upcoming sudden onset of sunlight? Or are we being deceived by someone, maybe the tanning or suntan lotion industrial complex?

And no matter what the reason for the deception, what is the value of knowing when sunrise is? Wouldn't we be better served by knowing when "lightrise" is? And are there any other idiots like me, up at this hour and paying attention to this nonsense, so as to take their minds off of something important, something that's gnawing at their insides?

How the hell am I going to help Laurie? And what if I can't?

I get up and take Tara for a two-hour walk. As always, she can sense my mood and mirrors it. She doesn't do anything to distract me from my thoughts; even when a squirrel passes, she doesn't try to go after it. I'm able to focus on the job ahead, and by the time we get home, I'm ready.

I shower and get to the courthouse at ten-thirty. As I did with Oscar, I meet with Laurie in an anteroom and prep her for the hearing. I tell her basically the same things, but I hug her considerably more than I recall hugging Oscar.

We are led into the courtroom on time, and Kevin is waiting at the defense table. Dylan and his colleagues are already in place, though this time he forgets to wish me good luck. The courtroom is packed with perhaps twice as many people and press as when Oscar was playing the lead.

Judge Timmerman once again handles the hearing. She asks if there is anything to be discussed before we begin, and Dylan immediately demonstrates just how contentious this is going to be.

"Yes, Your Honor," he says, "we believe that it is a conflict for Mr. Carpenter to be representing this defendant, and we ask that he be removed as counsel."

"On what grounds?" she asks.

"As you know, he represented Oscar Garcia when Mr. Garcia was charged with the same crime. Mr. Garcia may well be a witness in this case, which would be a clear conflict of interest for Mr. Carpenter."

As Dylan is speaking, I can feel Laurie tense up next to me, fearful that she will lose me as her lawyer. Kevin slips me a piece of paper, but I don't look at it, since I'm too intent on what Dylan is saying. There is no way I'm being taken off this case.

The judge turns to me. "Mr. Carpenter?"

I stand up. "Your Honor, just three days ago, Mr. Campbell stood before you and told you Oscar Garcia was guilty beyond a reasonable doubt. We told you he was wrong, and he now admits that he was. Now Mr. Campbell is telling you that it is Laurie Collins that is guilty beyond a reasonable doubt. He is wrong again. I don't know what the indoor record is for bizarre and false accusations in connection with a single crime, but he certainly is on a pace to break it.

"Since it is clearly his intention to keep charging people until he finally blunders onto the guilty party, and since there are more citizens in this community than lawyers, eventually some of us are going to be called on for representation more than once. We might as well start now."

"Your Honor," Dylan says, "I object to the frivolous nature of the response. This is a serious matter." As Dylan speaks, I take the time to look at the paper Kevin has given me.

"It is very serious," I agree, "and it was equally serious in *New Jersey v. Clampett,* which is directly on point and favors the defense position." Kevin had amazingly anticipated this possibility and found case law last night.

"But far more serious," I continue, "is the fact that this prosecutor has accused two innocent people of a brutal crime in one week. He has demonstrated a disturbing willingness to rush to judgment without the benefit of facts, and here he is doing it again." I'm being extra tough on Dylan not only because this motion is a cheap, unprofessional shot but especially because the press will lap it up. I can see the smoke coming out of Dylan's ears as I go on.

"Additionally, I am no longer representing Oscar Garcia and I am unaware of any connection he continues to have to this case. Should this ever reach trial, and should he testify, my co-counsel, Kevin Randall, will cross-examine him."

Judge Timmerman thinks for a few moments, then says, "Since the Garcia matter was of such short duration, I see no clear conflict. Therefore, I am inclined to side with the defense and allow Mr. Carpenter to remain as counsel to Ms. Collins. Mr. Campbell, if you choose to, you can take up the matter again with the trial judge."

Dylan nods his resignation that he has lost this motion, at least for the time being. I can feel Laurie sigh with relief.

That relief is short-lived, as Dylan reveals that the State of New Jersey is charging Laurie with murder in the first degree. When it comes to burns, first degree is not that big a deal. Among murder charges, it's real bad. Simply put, if Laurie is convicted, she will never experience another day of freedom.

It would shake up anyone, but when called upon to give her plea, Laurie says, "Absolutely not guilty, Your Honor." She says it with conviction and power and confidence. It's another reminder that she is one tough lady.

The judge then brings up the matter of bail, which Dylan vigorously opposes. "The defendant is financially self-sufficient, and as a former police officer, is familiar with types and means of flight. Additionally, and even more significantly, the brutal nature of the crime is such that freeing the defendant would represent a serious risk to the community. Setting bail in this circumstance would be a substantial departure from precedent, and the facts simply do not support such a finding."

"Mr. Carpenter?"

I stand. "Thank you, Your Honor. Laurie Collins was a decorated police officer who left the department voluntarily when she felt that it was not adhering to sufficiently high moral and ethical standards. She has since distinguished herself as a self-employed private investigator, and I can personally vouch for her continued impeccable ethics and actions.

"Her entire life to this point has been dedicated to serving this community. She has never been charged with jaywalking, no less a major felony. Simply because she is the latest unwilling contestant in Mr. Campbell's prosecutorial game show, *Suspect for a Day,* that is no reason to deprive her of her liberty."

Dylan is back on his feet. "I object to these personal attacks, Your Honor."

"Sustained. Let's tone it down a bit, Mr. Carpenter," the judge says.

"Sorry, Your Honor. But to call Laurie Collins a flight risk is particularly absurd. People with her courage and character don't run from unfounded charges such as these; they stay and fight them."

The judge does not look convinced. "Bail in these situations is very unusual, Mr. Carpenter."

I'm afraid I'm losing her. Kevin nods slightly in my direction; we have an alternative plan if things look like they're going badly, which they do.

"Your Honor," I say, "we would propose a significant bail and house arrest. Ms. Collins could be electronically monitored if necessary. And if you feel that is insufficient, a police guard could be posted outside the house, which if you so ordered, the defense would pay for."

The judge seems intrigued by this, and I can see her tentatively pulling back from the brink of ruling against us. "Mr. Campbell," she says, "what's your response to that? It would seem to eliminate both the risk of flight and any danger to the community."

It is no surprise that Dylan disagrees completely. "Your Honor, we are talking about a vicious and premeditated crime against a police officer. House arrest is simply not a substitute for prison. This is what prisons are for."

I stand again. "Your Honor, I arrived in court a few minutes after Mr. Campbell today. Was there a trial and conviction that I missed? Prisons are for criminals. Mr. Campbell still must prove Laurie Collins is a criminal, and he will not come close."

The judge nods and makes her ruling. "Bail will be set at five hundred thousand dollars. The accused will be subject to house arrest and electronically monitored. If the state wants to post a guard outside the house, it will be at their own expense."

I lean over to Laurie and whisper. "You okay if it's my house?"

She smiles slightly. "Only on Mondays, Wednesdays, and Fridays."

I fight the urge to return the smile, then ask the judge to allow her house arrest to take place at my house, explaining that it will considerably increase her ability to aid in her own defense, and that as a law enforcement officer and investigator, that help is particularly valuable. The judge agrees, and Dylan doesn't bother to fight it.

"You can arrange bail with the court clerk," the judge says, and then adjourns the hearing.

I immediately walk toward the clerk, passing right by Dylan as I do. "Dylan," I say, "you're an expert on this stuff. You think they want cash or a check?"

He doesn't answer, so I guess I'll just have to ask the clerk.

• • • • •

LAURIE ISN'T RELEASED from the jail

until three hours after the hearing. They blame processing delays, and I'm just about ready to burn the place down when I finally see her. A guard is assigned to drive her to my house so he can make sure that she is within the house when he fastens her electronic ankle bracelet.

Kevin wants to come over with the discovery material he got from Dylan's office, but I tell him that we'll start in the morning. Today was a very intense day for all of us, and we could use a breather before jumping into this. Once it starts, there won't be anything else going on in our world.

I ask Kevin to start the process of transferring the office to the house; I want the phones switched over and all the files moved. Even Edna should be alerted to change her late morning destination, mainly because if we didn't tell her, she might continue in the other office for months before noticing we were gone.

Laurie and I have a quiet, early dinner. She's a tough woman, but I can tell that she's shaken by the experience. I can see her gathering her strength, girding for the ordeal that is to follow.

We are in bed by ten, and I hold her until she falls asleep.

I confess that I would be willing to do more than hold her, but my sense is that it is a sign of insensitivity to attempt to make love to somebody on the same night they have been charged with a decapitation-murder. I fall asleep moments after Laurie does; today was an exhausting day for both of us.

We're still sleeping at eight o'clock the next morning when the doorbell rings and I stagger down to answer it. It is then that I see one of those sights that make you rub your eyes and wonder if you're seeing a mirage, or perhaps still dreaming.

Edna.

Up and awake and raring to go to work, at eight o'clock in the morning. Edna! The mind boggles.

"We've got work to do, Andy," she says, then brushes past me and enters the house. I can see that out on the street the press has already started to assemble; I would be surprised if they're not a constant presence, which is fine with me. Laurie will be inside anyway, and in a case like this manipulation of the press is a necessary part of a defense attorney's job. Having them on hand will make it more convenient.

Edna immediately starts to set up a makeshift office in my den. She pauses only to go to the kitchen to make a pot of coffee. Edna making coffee! With my camera upstairs, I'm missing out on a once-in-a-lifetime shot.

Edna tries to explain to me her level of outrage that Laurie has been placed in this situation. She makes me swear that we will all do whatever is necessary to exonerate her, an easy promise for me to make. Laurie comes downstairs, wearing pants to cover her ankle bracelet. Edna rushes to hug her, offering kind words and renewing her vow to do everything she can. I am actually touched by Edna's response to this crisis, and I can tell that Laurie is as well.

Kevin shows up a few minutes later and informs us that the movers will have the office files and equipment here by eleven o'clock. He has the discovery files with him, and we set up in the den to start going through them.

Laurie volunteers to make breakfast for us, and when I

mention that there's really nothing in the house to make it out of, she casually says she'll go to the market. Before I can respond, she realizes that she misspoke, that she must remain in the house at all times. It's a small thing, but a sobering reminder of her situation.

Edna goes to the market, and I can hear her loudly berating the media "leeches" as she leaves. I make a note to explain to her the importance of maintaining good press relations, but it is pretty far down on my list of notes.

Based on my skimming the morning paper and watching some TV news coverage, the press is giving us the upper hand in yesterday's hearing. There is substantial mention of the ridicule I subjected Dylan to, and while I would ordinarily not view this as a positive, in this case I feel otherwise. Dylan will not willingly give an inch anyway, and I think that getting him angry might cause him to make a mistake. I also think it might make him come across as overly aggressive, never a good thing for a prosecutor.

Kevin and I start to plow through the discovery material, though in this case a plow would be substantial overkill. The file is very skimpy, confirming my belief that extracting material from an uncooperative Dylan is going to be a constant fight. Of course, to let anything slip by us is to invite a disaster in court.

Basically, the case against Laurie as outlined in the material has two powerful linchpins. First is her presence at what has now been identified as the murder scene behind Hinchcliffe Stadium, and what the police see as her attempt to retrieve the evidence. Obviously, the most incriminating part of that evidence is her bloody clothing, and I have no doubt that DNA will reveal it to be Alex Dorsey's blood on both that clothing and the knife.

The second very damaging piece of evidence has been found as the result of a search warrant, executed on Laurie's house. In her garage was an empty can with the residue of a fluid that appeared to be gasoline, and which when tested was the exact same mixture as that used to set Dorsey's body on fire. Laurie is stunned when she hears this, and swears that she has never seen that can in her life.

The remainder of the file consists of witness statements. It's very early in the process, but the police are already making headway in this regard. Oscar and others in his neighborhood claim that Laurie was there frequently, apparently following Oscar. There is also a witness who puts Laurie in the area of the warehouse the day of the murder.

A major piece missing from the discovery documents is any reference to the victim's actions, record, and history. Dorsey must have a file the size of South Dakota, but despite our request, nothing has been included. Only by getting those records will we know why they don't want us to have them.

"Pancakes?" It's Laurie, standing at the door, the smell of her prepared breakfast wafting into the room.

A prime factor that the NFL uses for talent evaluation is the player's speed in the forty-yard dash. If instead they measured the time from den to kitchen, Kevin would be All-Pro and a future Hall of Famer.

Edna and I eat one pancake each, and Laurie has two, so including Kevin we eat a total of sixteen. When we're done, we go back into the den, and we plot our initial moves. Kevin will work on getting access to Dorsey's police records, initially by renewing our request for voluntary discovery. We expect Dylan to again reject it, so Kevin will simultaneously prepare a motion to convince the court to compel him to comply.

The other assignment I give Kevin is to find an investigator to work with us on this case. I'm afraid that Laurie will feel as if she is being replaced, and might get frustrated and upset. I'm wrong again, and she jumps in with ideas for people that we might hire.

When Kevin leaves, Laurie leads me into the bedroom, out of earshot of Edna. Once we're there, she says, "Andy, we need to talk about money."

"What about it?" I ask.

"I've got twelve thousand dollars in the bank," she says.

"That's all? I've got twenty-two million."

"Andy, I've always been self-sufficient. It's how I've defined myself. But right now I can't come close to paying for my own defense, and I don't know what to do about it."

"There's nothing for you to do. I'll pay for it, but first I'll negotiate with myself to cut my hourly rate."

"This case will cost a fortune."

"Then we're really lucky, because I happen to have a fortune," I say. "Look, we bring different things to our relationship, to our friendship. One of the things I bring is money. It's never been that important to either of us, but right now we need it, and there it is. If we spend every penny of it, that's fine."

"Andy—" she starts, but I cut her off.

"I know how you feel, Laurie, but every minute we spend thinking about this is a minute we're not thinking about what's really important. And that is winning this case."

"So this is something I'm going to have to deal with?" she asks.

I nod, and even though she still seems uncertain about her ability to do that, she hugs me. "I love you," she says.

"I love you too." As I said, it's not a response we consider automatic, and there's no obligation to say it, but sometimes it feels right.

I head back into the den, and by that time Edna has worked out phone arrangements. The phone company will be there within the hour to install our office line separate from my home line. Laurie wants to take personal calls on her cell phone, so as not to interfere with our activities. Edna is by now already on another project, though I have no idea what she could be working on. It's possible that some body-snatching work-pod took over Edna's body while she slept last night. Not wanting to disrupt whatever the Edna-pod is doing, and even though I'm still picking pieces of pancake out of my teeth, I go to lunch.

This lunch is with FBI Special Agent Robert Hastings. Pete Stanton, who set it up, told me that Hastings's friends call him Robbie, but that since I'm a defense attorney, I should call him Special Agent Hastings. Pete knows him from a few cases where their paths intersected, and he describes him as a stand-up guy.

The stand-up guy is already sitting at a table when I get there. At least I think he's sitting. Right now he's about half a foot taller than I am when I'm standing. I had asked Pete how I'd recognize him, and he described Hastings as dressing conservatively and balding slightly. Apparently, Pete considered these more distinctive features than the fact that Hastings is in the neighborhood of six foot nine, three hundred pounds.

Hastings is looking at his watch when I arrive. The lunch was called for noon, and a quick check of my own watch shows it to be one minute after.

I reach the table and introduce myself, and then say, "I'm not late, am I?" I say this with the full knowledge that I'm not.

"Yeah, you are," he says.

"Didn't we say twelve o'clock?" I ask.

A slight nod of his massive head. "Yeah."

I decide not to pursue the time issue any further, and I quietly let him take the lead in the conversation. It turns out that conversation-leading is not a specialty of his.

After about five silent and excruciatingly uncomfortable minutes, he says, "Pete tells me you're a pain in the ass."

I smile. "I've been called worse."

"Yeah," he says. "I'm sure."

Hastings goes on to tell me that Pete also said that even though I'm a little runt, there's not a lunch check ever made that's too heavy for me to pick up. He picked this really expensive restaurant to test out that theory.

He's in the middle of ordering enough food to feed the Green Bay Packers when it hits me. "Hey, you're not Dead End Hastings, are you?"

It turns out that he is, in fact, Dead End Hastings, who

spent two years playing for the Denver Broncos and who was so named because when running backs came into his area, they were entering a dead end with no way out. An untimely knee injury cut a very promising career short.

The transformation is immediate. He goes from quiet and surly to affable and gregarious. Fortunately, his mouth is large enough that simultaneous talking and eating presents no difficulty for him at all. He regales me with stories of his playing days and is impressed with my knowledge of rather arcane pieces of football trivia. I always knew that all those Sunday afternoons in front of the television set would turn out to be worthwhile.

We're having dessert when I bring up the reason I wanted to have this lunch in the first place. "I need to know everything there is to know about Alex Dorsey. I'm representing the person accused in his murder."

His nod confirms my expectation that Pete had alerted him to at least this general subject matter. "And why exactly did you come to me?" he asks.

"Because I know the Bureau conducted an investigation that somehow involved Dorsey and that it got him at least temporarily off the hook when Internal Affairs was coming after him. That's all part of the public record."

I'm stretching the truth some: FBI involvement with Dorsey was never publicly confirmed. Hastings doesn't seem to care one way or the other. "It's not my case," he says, "so all I can do is tell you whose case it is."

"That's a start," I say.

"Darrin Hobbs. He's number two man in the eastern region, heading for number one."

"Thanks," I say. "Any chance you can set up a meeting for me with him?"

He shrugs. "I can tell him you want to talk to him. I wouldn't count on it, though. He's a busy guy."

"I understand," I say. "By the way, you said 'is.'"

"What's that?"

"You said it *is* his case. I thought the federal investigation involving Dorsey ended a long time ago. Did you just make a bad choice of words?"

He looks across the table at me with a stare that makes me glad I was never an offensive lineman. "I'm even better at choosing words than I am at eating." That is a significant statement, because based on the size of the check when I get it, Winston Churchill wasn't better at choosing words than Hastings is at eating.

Driving home, I try to focus on that which makes this case unique. In most cases, my view is that my client is wrongly accused and that the real criminal is out there. While that is certainly true here as well, the twist is that Laurie's arrest is not just the result of police error. Stynes's involvement makes it crystal clear that she was set up from the very beginning. It is likely, but not absolutely definite, that the person behind the setup and the murderer are one and the same.

I find it very helpful to sit down with Kevin to just bounce ideas off each other. He has a sharp mind, and while he's emotionally involved in this case, he's far more dispassionate than I am.

We have one of those talks this afternoon, though it's a little hard to hear because Edna is typing like a maniac in the background. Kevin points out that my instinct about Stynes not being disappointed when I turned down his case was right on target. He wasn't in my office for the purpose of hiring an attorney; he was there to plant information in my head. He was betting that my belief in his guilt would cause me to defend Garcia.

"So two people got framed," I say. "First Garcia and then Laurie. But Garcia was always meant to be temporary; he was never meant to take the ultimate fall. He was just there to get me into the case."

Kevin shakes his head. "I don't think so. I think he was there to get Laurie into the case. She works for you, so they had to bring you in first."

In an instant I realize that he is right and that what he is saying has a logical extension. "Which means Garcia was not picked at random; he was chosen because Laurie had a long-standing grudge against him. And now Dylan will use that to say she murdered Dorsey and framed Garcia, thereby removing two people she hated."

He nods. "We're up against somebody pretty smart."

"Lucky we've got Edna the dynamo on our side."

After a while Kevin is about to leave, and together we persuade Edna to leave with him. She vows to be back early in the morning, and I tell her that I'll set the alarm.

Laurie and I have a quiet dinner, trying our best not to talk about the case, while knowing we're each thinking about nothing else. We haven't really had a full-blown attorney-client discussion yet, and I ask her if it's okay if we start the process tonight. She agrees, and we sit on the couch in the den, soft music in the background, sharing a bottle of wine. In terms of the atmosphere for attorney-client conferences, I've experienced a hell of a lot worse.

I start off by telling her that it is important for us to put our personal relationship aside in working her case; that is how we can be most objective and effective. She has to be prepared for me to treat her like any other client.

She nods. "So we won't be sleeping together?"

"Sure we will," I say. "I sleep with all my clients."

That dispensed with, we get down to business. Laurie knows the importance of total honesty in speaking to one's lawyer, but since knowing it in the abstract and living it are two different things, I take pains to remind her.

Laurie tells me that she doesn't know any more about Dorsey's disappearance and murder than I do. Accepting that at face value, I try to focus in on her relationship with Oscar Garcia.

Laurie begins by once again reciting the story of her friend's teenage daughter, who became a drug customer of Garcia's before running away from home. I've heard it all, but

I let her go on. I often find it's better to let a client talk uninterrupted as much as possible; I get more information that way. It's strange to be thinking of Laurie as a client, but I'm getting used to it.

"You made a comment to me the other day," I say. "Something about knowing what Oscar's been up to recently."

She nods. "I've kept my eye on him from time to time."

"What exactly does that mean?"

"It means that when I've had time I've watched him, hoping he would make a mistake. Something that could get him sent away."

"You're not a cop anymore, Laurie."

"No, but I know a few." She can see I'm a little worried about this. "Andy, the guy is a slime. I have the right to watch him."

"Did you catch him doing anything?" I ask.

"Not that I could prove."

"What about personal contact? Did you have any?"

"No."

I feel like she's holding back, although she must know that wouldn't make any sense. The rest of the conversation consists more of her trying to get information from me than the other way around. She wants to know how the case is going, and even though it hasn't had time to go anywhere, I make myself sound upbeat. My goal is to be honest but not depressing. In this case, at least for now, that's not easy.

• • • • •

I'M UP AND SHOWERED by seven o'clock the next morning, which is exactly the time that Edna shows up. I see her through the window; she has brought donuts and coffee for the early assembled press and is outside divvying it up. Obviously, there was no need for press-relations coaching from me; Wonder Woman picked it up on her own.

At nine o'clock I get a phone call from the court clerk informing me that the grand jury has handed down an indictment against Laurie. Dylan has been working fast. She also informs me that a trial judge has been assigned, and I am wanted at a meeting in one hour in his chambers. I start to argue about the inconvenience of this hastily called meeting when she tells me that the trial judge is Walter "Hatchet" Henderson.

I stop arguing. Hatchet could just as easily have given me ten minutes to get there, and held me in contempt if I was late. He is autocratic, obnoxious, and legendarily difficult for all lawyers, though I'm sure he scares Dylan more than me. Hatchet was the judge on the Miller case, and I was pleased— make that stunned—by the competence and fairness he demonstrated while conducting that trial.

Before I leave, Laurie reminds me of her one demand: that

the trial begin as soon as possible. It's a very common feeling among the accused, especially the wrongly accused. This experience is so trying, so frightening, so humiliating, that the need to have it over as quickly as possible is overwhelming.

By the time I get to Hatchet's office Dylan is already there, kissing the judge's ass by marveling about how much weight Hatchet has lost on some diet. Lawyers instinctively try to kiss Hatchet's ass, but even though that ass has in fact gotten smaller during this diet, the tactic doesn't work. Hatchet does not respect ass-kissing attorneys. He also does not respect prosecuting attorneys, defense attorneys, outstanding attorneys, mediocre attorneys, or any attorneys.

"Good morning, Judge," I say.

"Let's do without the small talk, gentlemen. We've got a trial to conduct."

"Oh," I say, "I assumed we were changing defendants again."

"No," Dylan responds, "we're going to put this one away for a long time."

I laugh. "Dylan, I'm going to clean your clock."

Hatchet interrupts and berates us for our unprofessional conduct. He then takes out his calendar and opens the floor to discussion of a start date for the trial.

"I would suggest July fourteenth, Your Honor," Dylan says.

"That is unacceptable to the defense, Your Honor. We wish to invoke our right to a speedy trial. We would be looking at the middle of May."

Dylan is clearly surprised, mainly because he knows rushing is not in our best interest; it's an accepted truth that time is always on the defense's side. And besides, I had already agreed to the July 14 date when the defendant was Oscar. Dylan has no choice but to accede to our demand, however, since we are simply exercising our constitutional rights.

Dylan estimates that the prosecution case might take two weeks, and I say that I doubt we'll even need to mount a defense, but if we do, a week should do it.

Hatchet looks intently at the calendar, then stares at us. "My vacation begins on June twenty-eight."

I nod. "And I hope Your Honor has a wonderful time."

Dylan revisits the issue of bail, as I knew he would. I'm very concerned that Hatchet might revoke the bail and put Laurie in jail.

"I would not have ruled as Judge Timmerman did," Hatchet says. "It is a decision that makes me uncomfortable."

"The decision is wrong," Dylan agrees. "Almost without precedent in this county."

I won't get anywhere by arguing with Hatchet; all I can do is give him another point of view to consider. "I'm not going to defend Judge Timmerman's ruling, though it obviously is one I was pleased with. But there are new circumstances to consider."

He peers at me from behind his glasses. "And they are?"

"Her order has been followed, and there have been no negative consequences. Ms. Collins is safely contained, electronically monitored, and guarded by the police. The community is safe, and will remain so, and there is no risk of flight. Respectfully, sir, altering Judge Timmerman's order provides no benefit to anyone, while hampering Ms. Collins's considerable ability to aid in her own defense."

Dylan starts to argue some more, but Hatchet isn't listening. He is turning the issue over in his mind. My heart is pounding so hard I'm afraid Hatchet won't be able to hear over it.

Finally, after what seems like a couple of months, he nods. "Without a change in circumstances, I'm inclined to let Judge Timmerman's ruling stand." Then he looks at me. "Make sure there is no change in circumstances."

Hatchet dismisses us, and I permit myself a condescending smile at Dylan as I leave. I'm on a winning streak which won't last, but I might as well let Dylan know that I'm enjoying it.

As we had planned, Kevin is waiting for me at the bottom of the courthouse steps. He takes me over to a nearby coffee shop, where I am to meet Marcus Clark. I had asked Laurie and

Kevin to each come up with a list of investigators to join our team for this case, and Marcus's name was the only one on both lists.

Marcus is late arriving, so Kevin uses the time to brief me on his background. Soon after Marcus had become an investigator, Kevin represented him on an assault charge: Marcus had broken a guy's nose in a bar fight. Kevin won the case with a claim of self-defense, which he has always considered one of his greatest victories. He tells me that I'll understand why when I see Marcus.

Marcus comes in moments later, and it's immediately obvious what Kevin was talking about. It is hard to imagine that Marcus could have acted in self-defense, because it's hard to imagine anyone being dumb enough to have attacked him.

Marcus is a thirty-year-old African-American, about five foot ten, with a bald head so shiny you could guide planes to a runway with it. His body is so sculpted, his muscles so perfectly formed, that the clothes he is wearing don't seem to impede a view of his body.

But Marcus's most distinguishing physical feature is his menacing facial expression. Fighters like Mike Tyson and Marvin Hagler were noted for cowing their opponents during the pre-fight instructions with the power and anger in their stares. Marcus makes Tyson and Hagler look like Kermit and Miss Piggy.

Marcus nods a couple of times as Kevin makes the introductions, but it's a few minutes before he says his momentous first words.

"Rye toast."

The waitress says, "Yes, sir," which seems to be the appropriate response to Marcus, no matter what he requests. My guess is that if the coffee shop didn't have any, the waitress would have gone outside, captured a rye, and slaughtered it herself.

I explain Laurie's basic situation to him, and when I finish, he simply says, "She is a good person."

I nod vigorously in agreement, which I would have done had he said the earth was an isosceles triangle. "Yes, she is. A really good person."

"I'll take the job," he says, despite my not having offered it. "A hundred an hour, plus expenses."

"Great," I say. "But just so we're on the same page, tell me how you operate."

He doesn't seem to know what I mean. "My style?" he asks.

"Right, that's right. Your style."

Marcus turns to Kevin. "He serious?"

Kevin, who hasn't said two words during this entire meeting, is surprised to be called in at this point. Marcus and I have to wait until Kevin chews the pound and a half of hamburger in his mouth. I think Kevin actually stores food in his mouth, just in case he should get hungry.

"I suppose," Kevin says with a shrug, a stunning statement clearly worth waiting for.

Marcus matches the shrug and turns back to me. "My style is, you tell me what you want to know, and I find out."

"How?" His stare gets a little meaner, so I soften the question. "I mean, generally . . ."

"I ask people questions," he says, "and they answer them. I'm real easy to talk to."

I accept his explanation, even though I personally would rather be questioned by the SS. I decide to hire him, but I don't have to announce it, since he did so earlier. I have reservations, but Kevin and Laurie recommended him highly, and they know as much about this stuff as I do, in Laurie's case even more.

We bid Marcus a warm and poignant goodbye, then Kevin and I drive to my house. We pull up in front, and Edna comes rushing out to meet us.

"Have you noticed Edna is a little high-energy these days?" I ask.

Before Kevin can answer, Edna reaches the car. "Come inside, quick."

The look on her face says that she's not calling us in for calisthenics, that something is wrong.

"What is it?" I ask, already on my way inside.

"Laurie should be the one to tell you."

Kevin and I break into a run, and Laurie is at the front door when we open it. Her cell phone is in her hand, which seems to be shaking.

"I just got a phone call," she says in a nervous voice.

"From who?"

"Alex Dorsey."

I try not to overreact to this announcement, and Kevin and I take Laurie into the den to talk. There are no rules for situations like this, but I instinctively feel that phone calls from headless murder victims should be viewed calmly and rationally.

Laurie explains that she had answered her cell phone and immediately heard a voice she recognized as Dorsey's say, "Hello, Laurie, it's Alex."

Laurie says she was momentarily too stunned to respond, and Dorsey went on to say that it was payback time, that she'd be sorry for what she did to him, and now was the time.

"Can you tell us his exact words?" I ask.

She shakes her head. "No, I don't know what his exact words were. I was pretty shocked that he was calling. But that's definitely close to what he said."

"What did you say?"

"That it wouldn't work, that somebody would find him, that he should give it up now."

"And his response?"

"All he said was, 'So long, rookie,' and hung up."

"But you're positive it was him?" I ask.

She nods. "As positive as I can be. It sounded just like him, and he used to call me 'rookie' because he knew it irritated me. Andy, I don't understand this. They said they ran a DNA test. The body was definitely Dorsey."

We spend the next hour kicking around how we should

handle this. Laurie's testimony as to the facts would have no practical significance. For the accused to announce that she and she alone knows that the victim is really alive would obviously be recognized as self-serving and suspect. Nor does she have an obligation to report what has happened; it is not up to the defense to provide the prosecution with information of any kind.

But it is obviously in our interest to bring this to the attention of the authorities. The phone call opens up questions that must be investigated. For example, can the call be traced? How could the DNA test have gone wrong? Whose body was burned in that warehouse? Where is Dorsey, and how can we get the police to try to find someone they believe to be dead?

Kevin believes that we should call Dylan immediately and make the judge aware of the development as well. I disagree; Dylan will ridicule our claims and not act on them at all. For me the issue is whether to bring this to the police or the press. At this point Lieutenant Sabonis has not given me reason to mistrust him, so I decide to start with the police. The press will be backup if Sabonis doesn't take action.

Most important is what we have learned from this. Obviously, and most significant, we have learned that Dorsey is alive. And while we have always known that someone was framing Laurie for Dorsey's murder, now we know it is Dorsey himself doing the framing. Dorsey must have sent Stynes.

Making the phone call, though, was a brazen and overly self-confident act on Dorsey's part. It also reveals the depth of his hatred for Laurie. It is not triumph enough for him to ruin her life; he wants her to know that it is he himself who is ruining it.

I call Sabonis and ask to meet with him as soon as possible on a new development. He is surprised and a little uncomfortable with the request, since normal protocol would be for me to go through Dylan.

"This information is too important to get buried," I say.

"Obviously, you can discuss it with whoever you want once I tell you, but it's important to me that you hear it directly."

He agrees, and I ask if he can come to us, since Laurie can answer any related questions he might have. He says that he'll be over in twenty minutes.

I use the time to brief Laurie on how to answer his questions. She has been the questioner, but never the accused, and I tell her that she is to pause before answering anything, so that if I want to intervene, I'll have the time to do so. Having a client answer police questions is uncomfortable for a defense attorney, but in this case it is necessary, as long as those questions relate to the Dorsey phone call.

Sabonis arrives five minutes early. I thank him for coming and bring him into the den, where Laurie proceeds to describe the phone call. He listens quietly and respectfully, not saying anything at all until she's finished.

"I assume you didn't tape the call?" he asks.

She shakes her head. "No, it was on my cell phone."

"Who has that number?"

"A lot of people, mostly my friends. But calls to my home are being routed to it."

"Did you have that phone number when you were on the force? Would it have been in your file?"

She nods. "I think so."

"What do you think, Nick?" I ask.

He pauses a moment, then, "I think you were right in not bringing this to Dylan; he'd throw you out of his office and laugh in your face while he was doing it. My reaction would be the same with typical murder suspects, but Laurie is not your typical murder suspect."

"So," I ask, "will you treat it as a reliable piece of information and keep me posted on what you learn?"

"I'll treat it as information to be investigated. Whether it's reliable or not is still to be determined. As far as keeping you posted, you know that's Dylan's responsibility."

"He'll shut the door on us," I say. "I'll have to go to the judge."

"No skin off my ass." My sense is that he'd be fine if I did that; it might lessen the hassles he has in dealing with Dylan.

Sabonis tries to take advantage of the proximity to ask Laurie some case-related questions, but since they are not about the phone call, I don't let her answer them. He leaves, and Kevin goes off to amend our motion for discovery on Dorsey's department file to include this latest development in the investigation.

I had planned to think about what would be best for Marcus to work on, but this turns that decision into a no-brainer. I call him and tell him that his time should be devoted to finding out whatever there is to find out about Alex Dorsey.

"I want you to find his head and tell me if there's a body attached to it," I say. He grunts, but I think it's an agreeable grunt. And I leave it at that.

Laurie is freaking out, but not from fear. It's only been a few days, but the inactivity and feelings of frustration are really getting to her. Now that she knows Dorsey is out there directing this torture, the desire to get out and find him is overwhelming. I've had to devote more and more time to either calming her down or easing her fears.

I receive a pleasant surprise when I get a call from FBI agent Cindy Spodek, who identifies herself as assigned to Darrin Hobbs's command at the Bureau. Agent Dead End Hastings has been true to his word and told Hobbs, the agent in charge of the Dorsey-related investigation, that I wanted to meet with him, and Agent Spodek is calling to say that Hobbs will be at his Manhattan office that afternoon. I expected to have to wait weeks for this meeting, and there is no way I will not fit this in.

Traffic into the city is light, and I'm there a half hour before the two-thirty meeting. I go in anyway and am greeted by Agent Spodek, a tall, attractive brunet in her early thirties. She very crisply informs me that Special Agent Hobbs is in a meeting, and we can wait in Hobbs's small conference room just outside his office.

Looking around, I have to assume we visitors are often deposited in here first to impress us, as the room is a shrine to Special Agent Hobbs. Hastings had told me that Hobbs was a star within the Bureau, and the decor drives that point home. Hobbs's commendations and newspaper clippings detailing his heroics cover most of the walls and almost obscure the top of every piece of furniture in the room. The only remaining spaces are taken by similar tributes to his exploits in Vietnam. Based on all these chronicled heroic triumphs, it's amazing we didn't win.

"Very humble," I say.

"He's earned it" is Agent Spodek's response.

It seems like my time with her is heading for a conversational wasteland, so I immediately trot out the line guaranteed to turn that around. "By the way, I saved a golden retriever from death row at an animal shelter."

"How nice for you," she says with no enthusiasm, leaving me to wonder where I went wrong. Maybe the line requires Tara to be standing next to me, or maybe it only works outdoors. It's certainly going to require further study, but for now I just nod and look around the room.

I'm holding one of the photos from Vietnam in my hand when the door opens and Hobbs walks in. He's probably fifty years old, not that imposing in size but energetic and fit, the type who hasn't found a room he can't dominate. He sees me holding the photograph.

"Those were dangerous but exciting times," he says. "Were you over there?"

I was a good fifteen years too young for that, but I don't mention this. "No, I missed it," I say, ruing that fact by snapping my fingers. "Just my luck."

"It was no fun, believe me."

I already knew that, so this is not a revelation that throws me off my stride. At least not as much as his handshake, which reminds me of Superman squeezing a lump of coal so hard it turns into a diamond. "Darrin Hobbs." He smiles. "Good to meet you."

I could wait to speak until the circulation returns to my hand, but I don't think he invited me here for a sleep-over. "Andy Carpenter. Thanks for seeing me so quickly."

"No problem." He looks at his watch. "Although I don't have a hell of a lot of time. Hastings said it was important."

"It is. I'm representing a woman charged with the murder of Alex Dorsey."

Hobbs looks over to Agent Spodek, as if realizing for the first time that she is even there. "We'll be fine, Spodek" is how he dismisses her.

Once Spodek has left the room, Hobbs picks up the conversation as if she had never been there. He shakes his head, as if remembering past times. "Dorsey was always a murder waiting to happen."

I nod. "But my client didn't make it happen." I decide not to share with him the fact that Dorsey is still alive and making phone calls. That has nothing to do with what I'm trying to learn.

He smiles. "Another innocent client . . . so what is it you want from me?"

"I know you were familiar with Dorsey's actions a couple of years ago, when he was almost nailed by Internal Affairs. I know you, or at least the Bureau, intervened."

"You know that?" He smiles, apparently amused.

"Are you telling me otherwise?"

He seems about to say that he is, but then shrugs with some resignation. "What the hell, sure. Inside these four walls . . . that's basically what happened."

"Was Dorsey the target of the investigation?"

"No way. We had bigger fish to fry."

"And they were?"

"They were none of your business. Next question."

"Is the investigation ongoing?"

His smile is a sad one. "No, I wish it were. The Dorsey stuff killed it—too much publicity."

Dead End Hastings had indicated the investigation was in fact ongoing, but Hobbs is denying it. Could it be that Hobbs doesn't trust Andy Carpenter, defense attorney?

I continue asking questions, and he continues smiling and answering them, all the while providing me with absolutely no useful information. He may have such information, but I'm sure not getting it out of him. Or he may not.

I leave after about a half hour, with Hobbs wishing me luck and offering to be available should I need more help in the future. I make a note to myself that if I ever want to have another completely unproductive meeting that is a total waste of time, I will give him a call.

I meet Kevin back at the house, and he tells me that Dylan has turned over some information from Dorsey's file, though not anything relating to Laurie's accusation against him or anything about the Internal Affairs investigation.

Before we get started going through it, we eat the dinner Laurie has prepared for us. Since she has little else to do besides worry, she's been spending a lot of time in the kitchen, and the results have been extraordinary. Tonight is a crabmeat salad, followed by *fusilli amatriciana,* followed by freshly baked brownies. It is absolutely delicious, and I match Kevin chomp for chomp. It's lucky we've pressed for a speedy trial, or I would have "Goodyear" painted on my ass by the time we reach opening statements.

Kevin and I roll ourselves into the den afterward to go through the Dorsey discovery material. It's basically a chronological biography, and a very positive one at that. Dorsey grew up in Ohio and earned a B.A. in history at Ohio State. He enlisted and served a long hitch in Vietnam, apparently seeing a good deal of combat and earning several commendations for his service. He returned home and moved to Paterson, where he signed up for the police academy. His rise up the department ladder was rapid and relatively uneventful.

Certain little items are left out, nitpicks like his connections to organized crime, the Internal Affairs investigation and subsequent reprimand, as well as his disappearance and real or faked decapitation. Kevin will file our motion to get access to those facts tomorrow, and it's becoming more and more crucial that we win.

As we are finishing, the phone rings and Laurie answers it. I hear her side of the conversation, mostly consisting of how-are-yous? and I'm-okays.

After about thirty seconds of this, Laurie puts down the phone and says to me, "It's Nicole." She is talking about Nicole Carpenter, my wife of twelve years, from whom I was divorced just a few months ago, and to whom I haven't spoken since.

As I move toward the phone, the uniqueness of this situation flashes through my mind. I've just overheard a conversation between my ex-wife, whose father I caused to be convicted of multiple murder, and my current love, who is facing a decapitation-murder charge. I don't remember what my high school yearbook listed as my future goals, but I don't think any of this was foreseen.

"Hello, Nicole" is my clever opening line.

"Hello, Andy. How are you?"

This brilliant conversation goes on for another minute or so, as we both wait for her to get to the point of her call. Finally, she tells me that she needs to talk to me, in person, tomorrow morning, she hopes.

I don't want to meet with her, I don't have time to meet with her, there is no reason for me to meet with her, I can't be forced to meet with her, there is no way I'm going to meet with her, so I tell her I'll meet her at ten at a breakfast place near her house.

• • • • •

TO SEE NICOLE, you would never know the kind of year she has had. She's been shot and severely wounded by people aiming for me, her United States senator father has been convicted and jailed for multiple murder, and she's gone through a divorce. All this happened to a woman whose largest prior disappointment, at least that I am aware of, was when she got bumped out of first class on an overbooked flight to Paris.

She looks wonderful, with such a deep tan that, if she's spending a lot of her time visiting her father, he must be serving his sentence at Oahu State Prison. She gives me a little hug of hello, and we go to our table.

Mercifully, Nicole seems to know that we used up all our meaningless chitchat on the phone last night, because she comes right to the point.

"My father has cancer," she says.

"I'm sorry," I say.

She nods. "Thank you, but he's not sorry at all. Oh, I guess he's sorry that it's not a massive fatal heart attack, but anything that kills him is fine with him."

She's saying that being in prison is so horrible for Philip that he would rather be dead. What she's not saying, but which we both know, is that I put him there. It's a rather large hurdle to scale in reestablishing a friendship, if in fact that is what we are attempting to do.

It's not. Nicole has contacted me about Willie Miller's lawsuit against Victor Markham's estate and her father. His terminal illness gives her an even clearer connection to the suit: Half of whatever money Willie gets will come straight out of her inheritance.

"I'm frightened, Andy. I'm afraid I'm going to lose everything."

"Nicole," I say, "we shouldn't be having this conversation." That is understating the case; it is completely inappropriate and unethical.

"I've lost so much already."

I don't point out to her that her father is astonishingly wealthy, that the most generous jury verdict imaginable for Willie would still leave her with close to two hundred million dollars. She has to know this; she is not a stupid or uninformed woman. But her fear is so powerful that it is completely blinding her.

Her plea presents me with a curious ethical dilemma. The issue isn't whether I will be less vigorous on Willie's behalf; I will not. But Nicole's revealing her frightened mind-set to me presents me with a clear tactical advantage. To know that the opposition is so frightened is to know how far they can be squeezed. Can I wipe that from my mind? Should I?

"Nicole, you're hurting your negotiating position."

She's offended. "Negotiating? Is that what we're doing? After all these years, we're negotiators?"

"Nicole, talk to me through your lawyer. And my advice is to tell him what you've told me. It's a piece of information he should have."

She shakes her head in disagreement. "Andy—"

I cut her off. "I'm sorry, but this conversation is over. One of us is now going to leave. Do you want it to be you or me?"

She doesn't say another word, just gets up and walks out. I wait five minutes, then do the same.

I'm starting to become more comfortable with my personal connection to Laurie's case, and on the way back to the house I'm able to focus on that case as I would any other. I view it as a competitive puzzle, to be played with strategy and discipline and logic. Always logic.

Actually, my type of logical approach is more appropriate here than in any case I've ever had. I view every detail, every piece of the puzzle, as if it had been planned. In my mental world there is no room for coincidence, or even happenstance. Every fact, no matter how small, must be related to the case and significant. Of course, after analysis much turns out to actually be happenstance and/or insignificant, but it helps me attack the case to assume otherwise.

For instance, Garcia was set up to be the police's first suspect. I agree with Kevin that Garcia was chosen to make Laurie look even guiltier, and Stynes was sent to draw myself and Laurie into his defense, and for this to work, Garcia had to seem guilty. If, say, he had been at a party or restaurant with a bunch of friends when Dorsey was thought to have been killed, he could not have been charged, and I would not have rushed to his defense. Dorsey had to have known with certainty where Garcia would be; it couldn't have been left to chance.

Since at the time of the murder Garcia was paying off Petrone's men, I have to make the assumption that Petrone or his underlings were part of this conspiracy. Garcia had said that they usually came to him to collect, but that night he had been summoned to them. I believe that if the tape from the supermarket had not surfaced, some other fact would have come up, clearing Garcia and opening the way for Laurie to be charged.

Following this to its logical conclusion, Dorsey and Petrone, or people working for Petrone, were in this together. But why? Dorsey benefits in obvious ways. He gets to safely disappear, while at the same time getting revenge against Laurie. But what does Petrone get out of this? Does he have any reason to hate Laurie? How does he benefit from Dorsey's successful escape?

All cases are a series of questions and answers. Early on there are far more questions, and the answers are few and far between. Eventually, the answers start to come, and the questions get fewer. If I can tip that scale far enough, I solve the puzzle and win the game. First prize is Laurie not having to spend the rest of her life in prison.

As I reach the house, it seems as if the press contingent stationed outside has gotten substantially larger. There are at least two additional camera trucks, which make it difficult for me to enter the driveway. I persist trying until they move, since I know if I relent and park on the street, I'll have given up the driveway for the duration.

As I get out of the car, I am swarmed by the reporters, all asking me if it's true that Laurie claims Dorsey is still alive and has phoned her. I decline to comment and with some difficulty make it through the horde and into the house.

Laurie, Kevin, and Edna are in the den watching television. The few afternoon news programs are having a field day with Laurie's claim of having spoken to Dorsey. Despite the seriousness of the situation, the ridicule has already begun. After pointing out that DNA results have confirmed the charred, headless body to be Dorsey's, one amused newscaster takes mock offense and says, "I thought we were the only talking heads around here."

Laurie is furious at the treatment she is getting, and I can't say I blame her. I have little doubt that Dylan leaked the story, and it's a public relations triumph for him. I should have been the one to take this public. Allowing Dylan to frame the issue has the effect of making Laurie look (a) desperate, (b) crazy, (c) guilty, (d) ridiculous, and (e) all of the above. Since the public is by definition the jury pool, it's not a good position for us to be in.

I can go to Hatchet and complain, and since he's not the most media-friendly judge around, he might sympathize with my position. However, it's beyond his power to erase what the public already knows, so all he could do is issue a gag order on the case from this point on. I'm not ready to advocate that; I still think there's more to be gained than lost in the public relations battle. I'm just not doing a very good job of it.

To that end, I conduct a press conference on the steps of the house. My intent is to openly acknowledge Laurie's claim that Dorsey is alive; at this point there is nothing to be gained by denying it. I point out that we did not try to take advantage of it in any way. We simply went to the police to ask for the investigation it deserved. Instead of focusing on that, they've seen fit to release it to the press.

"The district attorney's office is conducting a search for advantage, not for truth" is how I sum it up.

After my impromptu statement has concluded, I invite questions. The first one is from a woman representing the *Newark Star-Ledger*. It begins with, "Assuming your client got this phone call—"

I interrupt her. "She got the phone call. She is a truthful person, as you will come to know. What you should already know is that nothing would be gained by our making this up. There was absolutely no possibility the police or prosecution would believe it without adequate and independent proof. We had hoped and expected they would look for such proof, rather than create a media circus designed to make my client look foolish."

I take about five questions, making sure that every one of my answers includes an attack on the prosecution. I'm hoping to defuse the impact of today's revelation on the evening news, and once I've done the best I can in that regard, I go back into the house.

A couple of hours later we sit around the television and find out that my front porch salvo was too little too late. Lau-

rie continues to take hits and ridicule, and while my protesta-
tions are included, they are given short shrift.

Laurie and I have been going to bed fairly early each night.
For her it seems as if being asleep is considerably less painful
than being awake. When we are awake, we don't want to talk
only about the case, but there's absolutely nothing else that we
can focus on. So we've been in bed by ten, and then, unable
to sleep, I've been getting up at midnight or later to strategize
and figure out my next steps.

Tonight is slightly different. Tonight we make love for the
first time since this nightmare began. Laurie instigates it, and it
is one of the most intensely passionate encounters I have ever
experienced. There is a "deck of the *Titanic*" urgency that is at
the same time frightening and wonderful. And afterward I do
something I didn't think possible.

I sleep through the night.

The most important thing I do when working on a case is
ask questions. I ask them of anybody and everybody. Some of
the questions are informed or even perceptive, but many are
fishing expeditions. I get as many answers as I can and sift
through them in my mind. Sometimes this helps me figure out
the truth, but at the very least it helps me think of more questions to ask, which is fine.

Our situation in this case is so bad that I can't even come
up with people to question. I can't get near Petrone, I can't find
Stynes, and on behalf of the FBI, Special Agent Hobbs smiles
and gives me nothing.

My plan for today reflects that lack of options. I'm going to
go to Oscar Garcia's neighborhood and question some of the
people that identified Laurie as having been in the area. I'm
certainly not going to shake their stories; Laurie has admitted
that she was there, keeping an eye on Garcia. I'm just going to
see if they know or saw anything else, something, I hope, that
can help my case.

An early phone call changes my plans for the day. It's from

a woman who says, "Mr. Carpenter, I know you're very busy, but I saw you on television last night, and I'd like to talk to you about my husband."

"Who is your husband?" I ask.

"Alex Dorsey."

She gives me directions to her apartment, coupled with the disclaimer that she's only lived there for about a month and isn't really sure if the directions are correct. They turn out to be exactly correct, and it takes me about fifteen minutes to get there. It would have been less, but I had Kevin park around the block, and then I sneaked out the back way and took his car. I don't know what Dorsey's wife wants, but I certainly don't want the press or Dylan to know she wants it from me.

Celia Dorsey lives in a small complex of garden apartments. She watches me from the window as I get out of the car, and opens the door before I can ring the bell.

"Thank you for coming, Mr. Carpenter. Please come in."

I enter a one-bedroom apartment a little bigger than your average phone booth. Every square inch of the place is filled with furniture, photographs, and trinkets. She has said she's only lived here for a short time, yet this place already has the meticulously cared-for look of a longtime residence.

She is a petite woman, reserved and quiet. I didn't know Alex Dorsey that well, but I would never have placed them together. He was high-energy, gruff, and dominant in any room he occupied. If you added them up and divided by two, you'd be left with one normal personality. So, on second thought, they'd be perfect together.

She offers me coffee and I accept, mainly because it seems she couldn't handle the disappointment if I said no. Once we're set, coffee cups on coasters and sitting on her couch, she says, "I'm sure you're wondering why I asked you here."

"You said it was about your husband."

She laughs a sad laugh. "I'm not even sure he's still my husband."

"What do you mean?"

"I filed for divorce three months ago. The final papers just came through yesterday, but I don't know if one can divorce a deceased spouse. Of course, now there is very considerable doubt that my spouse is deceased, which seems to complicate things even more."

She starts to cry, softly, as if she's afraid if she lets it out full blast, it would disturb me. Of course, it probably would, so I just wait until she's finished. It only takes a few seconds, and she continues.

"I know the police don't believe your client, but I do. My husband is alive."

"Why do you say that?" I ask.

"Well, for one thing, I simply cannot picture him dead." She smiles. "But you probably are hoping for something more concrete."

"Yes."

"I heard him talking about faking his own death."

Yesss! Finally, a positive development. "When?"

"Two years ago, when he was being investigated by the department."

"Who was he talking to?" I ask.

"I'm not sure. You have to understand, in the last five or so years of our marriage, and perhaps long before that, my husband kept a great many things from me. On some level I was glad he did; I sensed that there were things I wouldn't want to know. But there was one man he spoke to very often, and he got secretive whenever he did. But I overheard things, and one was this conversation with this man."

"How do you know it was a man?"

"Now that you mention it, I can't be sure. But he always called the person 'Lieutenant,' and even though women can certainly rise to that level and higher within the department, I've always assumed it to be a man."

Based on what I know about Dorsey, and the department, the odds are she is correct.

"What exactly did he say?"

"I can't remember exactly, but it was something like 'If they don't back off, they'll never see me again.' And then he laughed and said, 'They'll bury my box, but I won't be in it.'"

"And you never asked him about it?"

She shakes her head. "No, but it was one of the things that changed my perspective on my marriage. It finally helped drive into my thick head what should have been obvious all along: that I had not been an important part of his life for a very long time. I should have left then."

"But you didn't."

"No, and by the time I did he had taken all our money."

"What did he do with it?"

A smile, even sadder this time. "I wish I knew. But if you follow the money, you will find Alex. It's part of what drives him."

"What else drives him?" I ask.

"Power and hatred. And when he can exercise power to get back at those he hates, he is in his glory. I suspect that's what your client is finding out right now."

"Can I ask what drives *you*?"

"What do you mean?" she asks.

"Why did you call me?"

She pauses a moment to think about this. "Alex took the years of love and loyalty I gave to him and treated them like they meant absolutely nothing at all. He hurt people and I stood by and watched, and then I became one of those people. I'm ashamed of how I've acted, and I can't act that way anymore. If there is any way I can help you, I will."

There is a toughness and resolve in her voice that is impressive. This is a delicate, vulnerable woman that I want to have in the foxhole with me when the war starts.

Before I leave, Celia provides me with whatever financial records she has, so that I can try to follow Dorsey's money trail. To that end, I decide to stop off at my office and visit with the best money follower I know, Sam Willis.

Sam is surprised to see me and expresses his concern about

Laurie. He assumes I'm there to see how he's doing with cousin Fred, and he tells me that they've hit it off really well and that I'm soon going to be even richer than I am now. Goody, goody.

"I need you to help me find someone," I say. "Or at least his money."

Sam brightens up immediately. This is his kind of assignment. "Who?"

"Alex Dorsey," I say.

"The dead cop? Or, I mean, the not-dead cop?"

"The very one." I give him the financial records that Celia gave me, and he spends a few minutes looking at them. His expression is that of an orthopedic surgeon looking at a CAT scan, calling on his years of experience to make perfect sense out of what to me is bewildering.

"This guy was a cop?" he asks.

I nod. "Yes."

"This is pretty sophisticated stuff."

He calls Barry Leiter in from the other office, and the two of them eagerly devour the records. Every twenty seconds or so, Barry says, "Wow!"

I'm glad to be able to bring such pleasure into their lives, but I'm getting a little impatient. "If he moved his money, can you find out where it went?" I ask.

"To a degree," Sam says. "We can tell you a lot about it, but we won't be able to identify the city."

"Why not?"

He shrugs. "Because each town looks the same to me, the movies and the factory. And every stranger's face I see reminds me that I long to be homeward bound."

It's a sign of my desperation that I'm sitting here relying on a compulsive song-talker. Well, I'm simply not going to be drawn into it. "How long is this going to take you?" I ask.

"I won't be doing it at all. I'm going on vacation tomorrow. Barry will take care of it."

I turn to Barry. "You can do this?"

He smiles. "Sure, Mr. Carpenter. No problem. I'll start tonight on my computer at home. Whole thing should be wrapped up by tomorrow."

Sam notices my slightly worried expression and reassures me that this is definitely within Barry's expertise. Additionally, Sam will call in from his trip to make sure everything is going smoothly.

"Where are you going?" I ask.

"Puerto Rico. Do a little gambling . . . get some sun . . ."

I can't help myself. "So you're leaving on a jet plane? You don't know when you'll be back again?"

He smiles. "Oh, babe, I hate to go."

● ● ● ● ●

I'M SICK OF STUFFING Pete Stanton's mouth with expensive food, but I do need to talk to him, so I suggest we meet at a Taco Bell. He calls me a "cheap son of a bitch," but since he has a genetic weakness for grilled stuffed burritos, and since I promise him an extra-large Pepsi, he ultimately agrees.

We meet at six o'clock, and I'm finished bringing him up to date on my progress by six-oh-two. He tells me that Sabonis is taking Laurie's report of the phone call seriously and that the investigation into Dorsey's possible whereabouts, as well as the possible misidentification of the body, is proceeding.

"How many lieutenants are there in the department?" I ask.

"Why? You thinking of signing up? You'll have to start a little lower."

"Come on . . . how many?"

He thinks for a few moments. "Including me . . . six."

"Are they the same as two years ago, when Dorsey was being investigated?"

He thinks a little longer. "Well, Dorsey was part of the group then. As far as the rest? Almost the same . . . I think we had five then. I'm pretty sure McReynolds got promoted a while after that. Now you gonna tell me why you want to know?"

I nod. "I have information that Dorsey was working with another lieutenant. They weren't defending the cause of truth and justice. Any idea who it could be?"

"No." His answer is a little too quick, a little defensive. "I don't buy it. Not that group."

"What about Sabonis?" I ask.

He shakes his head firmly. "Nick? Absolutely not possible; Nick's as straight as they come. There's more chance it was me."

Having taken that as far as it can go, I move on. "They identified the body against Dorsey's DNA. Where would they have gotten it from?"

"What do you mean?" he asks.

"Well, I don't keep a bottle of DNA in my medicine cabinet. How would they have Dorsey's?"

"Every cop has to give blood for typing when we join the force," he says. "I assume they used that."

"Where is it kept?" I ask.

He shrugs. "I don't know. Maybe the precinct first-aid room, maybe the lab."

"Could somebody, could a cop, have gotten in there?"

"You mean could Dorsey have gotten in there before he disappeared, and replaced his blood with somebody else's? I don't see why not. Especially if it's in the first-aid room. It's not high-security."

"You think you could find out where the blood is kept?"

"I believe that everybody is put on this good earth for a purpose," he says. "Mine is to carry out whatever assignments you have for me."

"And you're doing a hell of a job."

I get home about eight o'clock, a half hour later than I told Laurie I would. She had dinner prepared, and my being late probably made that difficult, but that isn't the kind of thing that upsets her. She is, however, growing increasingly frustrated that she can't help defend herself, and that frustration translates to isolation. I understand it, but I can't fix it.

Actually, we're living a kind of weird sit-com. Maybe I'll head out to Hollywood and pitch it to some TV executive. "It's about two people who decide to move in together, and they start to get on each other's nerves. But she can't move out, you see, because—get this . . . she's wearing this ankle bracelet . . ."

One thing that I've noticed is how bonded Laurie and Tara have become. Tara is constantly at her side, graciously accepting the petting that Laurie seems comforted to give. Tara might even be more inclined to be near Laurie than to be with me. A less secure person than myself would be jealous, but the way I figure it, whenever I have the chance to be stroked by either Laurie's hand or my own, it's a no-brainer to pick Laurie's. Why should I expect a smart dog like Tara to make a different choice?

Laurie and I have settled into a kind of pattern, where after we have dinner, we sit in the living room and I bring her up to date on the events of the day. Very often she knows a lot of it, since my office is operating out of the house. But in this case I tell her about Celia Dorsey and ask her if she can make an educated guess as to the identity of the other lieutenant who was in cahoots with Alex. It seems as improbable to her as it did to Pete.

We're finished talking at about ten o'clock, and we go upstairs to bed. I'm just falling asleep when the phone rings, and I get it.

It's Barry Leiter's voice on the line, a little tentative. "Mr. Carpenter? This is Barry . . . from Sam's office? I'm sorry to bother you at home, but I found something, and I figured—"

I interrupt. "You traced the money?"

"Part of the way, and then I sort of ran into a roadblock. I wanted to talk to you before I went any further."

"What about?"

"These guys are good—I mean really good. I think . . . well, they were waiting for somebody to try and follow this money."

This isn't terribly surprising news: Once we knew that Dorsey was alive, it became a predictable way to try to follow him. "How do you know that?"

"Believe me, I can tell," he says. "But that's not the strange part. The strange part is they were geared up to trace the tracer. That's what I thought you should know."

"I don't even know what you're talking about," I say.

"I mean they were set up to know who was tracking the money. They know it's me."

Now I'm fully alert and growing uneasy. "Did you give them your name or address?"

He laughs. "Mr. Carpenter, no offense, but this is the twenty-first century. They can get that by pressing a button."

It's amazing how fast unease can turn to panic. "What's your address?"

"Three eighty-three Vreeland Avenue."

"Okay. Barry, lock your doors and turn your lights off. I'm coming right over. Don't let anybody in unless you know it's me."

"Why? What's going on?"

"Just do what I tell you." I hang up the phone and get dressed.

Laurie is asleep, and I wake her. She can tell from the sound of my voice that something is wrong.

"What's going on?" she asks.

"Call Pete Stanton and tell him that there's an armed break-in taking place at three eighty-three Vreeland."

"Is there?"

"Not if I can help it."

I'm out the door and running to my car. I can run really fast when I'm scared, and this is just about the fastest I've ever run.

Barry lives on the other side of town from me. It would ordinarily take me about twenty minutes, but there's no traffic and I'm not stopping at any lights, so it takes me fifteen. It feels like an hour.

As I turn onto his street, I'm glad to see that the police have beaten me there. There's about half a dozen police cars, lights flashing. I see Pete standing in front of Barry's house and I pull up in the driveway. He's going to be pissed at me, but it's a lot better than the alternative.

I get out and walk over to Pete. "Thanks for coming," I say.

He nods. "I wish it could have been a few minutes earlier. You know the victim?"

It feels as though somebody has lifted Barry's house off the ground and dropped it on my head. The pressure literally pushes me to my knees. "Don't say that, Pete. Don't say there is a victim. Please . . ."

"I'm sorry, Andy . . . the guy who lived in the house. He was shot once through the head."

"Oh, no . . . no . . ." I don't think I can stand this.

"We got the perp, Andy. He's on the floor in the kitchen."

I start walking toward the house. Pete yells ahead for the officers to let me through and then follows me. It feels like it takes me an hour to get to the front door, but in truth Barry lived on a small piece of property.

We finally reach the kitchen. There is blood everywhere, obviously that of the murderer, whose bullet-ridden body lies on the floor next to the counter.

"You know him?" Pete asks.

He's lying on his stomach, with his head turned away from me, so I have to walk around toward the counter to get a better view.

I'm struck by how little I'm surprised that I'm looking at the very dead face of Geoffrey Stynes.

Pete mentions the obvious, that he needs me to detail what I know about tonight's incident to him. He drives me down to the precinct, having somebody else follow in my car. I ask him to have someone call Laurie and tell her what happened, and then I don't think either of us says another word the entire way there.

My mind is still something of a blur, and the only clarity that is able to get through is the fact that I am responsible for

Barry Leiter being murdered, as surely as if I pulled the trigger. I brought this craziness, this sickness, into his twenty-three-year-old life, and he paid the price.

We reach the precinct and go into an interrogation room so that Pete can record what is said. I tell him everything, starting with the moment Stynes walked into my office. He raises his eyebrows when he hears that it was Stynes, the man he tried to find at my behest.

When I'm finished, I have a couple of questions for Pete. "Stynes was shot a bunch of times. Did he resist?"

Pete shakes his head. "He committed suicide." When he sees my surprise, he explains. "We had him dead to rights, half a dozen of us, guns pointed at him. We yelled, he saw the odds, and he raised his gun to fire, forcing us to shoot him. He had to know he would die, but in his mind it was better than letting us take him into custody."

"How can you be sure about that?" I ask.

"I saw his eyes," he said. "They weren't scared . . . they were already dead."

It's almost two o'clock in the morning when I leave the precinct, after assuring Pete that I'm okay to drive. He promises to update me on whatever he learns about Stynes, and tells me I'll probably have to answer more questions from Sabonis in the next day or two. He's also going to track Sam down and tell him what happened, and ask where Barry's family is.

Laurie is waiting up for me when I get home. She heard from Pete's underling what happened. The numbness I felt is wearing off, and the pain is changing from a dull throb to a piercing agony. Laurie has a million questions, but she hardly asks any of them. She just holds me, and Tara nuzzles against me, until it's morning.

It doesn't make me feel better, but it doesn't make me feel worse. Nothing could make me feel worse.

• • • • •

MARCUS CLARK SCARES Edna half

to death when he comes to the house to give his first weekly report. I assure her that he's on our side, but I don't think she can reconcile his menacing presence with the fact that he's one of the good guys.

Then Laurie comes into the room, and the transformation is immediate. She and Marcus hug warmly, and he inquires as to her health, her mental outlook, anything she might need, etc. Edna grudgingly accepts him as one of the team, though she occasionally glances over at him, as if to make sure he doesn't turn on us.

Marcus essentially has made no progress, which in his eyes is in itself a sign of progress. He has not found a trace of Dorsey, and since he firmly believes he can find anyone, he considers his failure a sure sign that Dorsey is dead.

"I spoke to him," Laurie points out.

"Or somebody trying to sound like him" is Marcus's response.

She pushes back. "It was him."

They kick around this unresolvable issue until finally Marcus allows as how it's possible Dorsey is alive, but with a lot of help powerful enough to keep him totally hidden. We all agree that only somebody like Dominic Petrone has that kind of power, but Marcus doesn't believe that Petrone would have let Dorsey make the phone call. That was the act of a man with intensely personal motivations, and Petrone would look at this as strictly business.

The court clerk calls to announce that Hatchet has reviewed Dorsey's files and set a meeting for tomorrow morning in his chambers to discuss our motion to receive them in discovery. Hatchet likes to resolve these matters without a formal hearing, and that's fine with me. I'm glad he didn't call it for this morning, because I've got the meeting with Willie Miller and the attorney representing the estates we are suing.

The easiest way for me to explain how Willie is reacting to his impending wealth is to say that he asks me to pick him up at a Mercedes dealership. He's standing out front when I pull up, and he gets in the car.

"How come you weren't inside kicking the tires?" I ask.

"They weren't taking me seriously. They don't think I can afford one of those pieces of junk. Shows what they know."

"How much do you have in your checking account?" I ask.

"I don't have no checking account," he says, and then he smiles his broad smile. "But I'm gonna."

The conversation during the rest of the drive to the lawyer's office involves Laurie. Like everybody else who knows her, Willie is concerned, and he has a better idea than most how unjust the justice system can be.

We arrive at the law firm of Bertram, Smith, and Cates, a respected civil litigation firm in Teaneck. I have spoken a couple of times to Stephen Cates, the attorney representing the defendants, and he has been properly noncommittal as to his position, pending this meeting.

He greets us cordially, sits us at a conference table with a large fruit bowl, offers us something to drink, and gets right down to business.

"I understand you've been approached by the daughter of one of my clients," he says, referring to Nicole.

I nod. "I have."

"I apologize for your being put in that position. I, of course, had no idea until after the fact."

"No problem," I say.

He then launches into a long-winded recitation of the position of his clients, and their desire to bring this unhappy matter, or at least this portion of it, to a close. They recognize the negative impact their actions have had on Willie's life, and they have concocted a formula that they believe accurately assigns a financial value to it. He is so busy explaining the formula, he neglects to mention what that value is.

After twenty minutes that seem like two hours, he reaches the end and says, "Do you have any questions?"

Willie, who has had three oranges, two apples, a banana, and a bunch of grapes during this presentation, doesn't waste any time. "How much?" he asks.

Cates seems somewhat taken aback by Willie's directness, but decides to meet it. "We're looking at in the neighborhood of four point three seven million dollars, paid out over seven years."

Willie almost spits up three grapes at the absurdity of the offer. "That may be the neighborhood you're lookin' in," he says. "But not us. We're lookin' uptown." By "us" Willie means he and I, although my intention is to keep him functioning as chief negotiator. He's doing fine, and I prefer to spend my time mentally beating myself up over Barry Leiter's murder.

But Cates turns to me, obviously looking for a weaker link than Willie. "What exactly is your position?"

I look to Willie and he nods, in effect giving me the floor. "Eleven point seven million, paid out over five minutes."

He doesn't blink. "May I ask how you arrived at that figure?"

"Gut instinct," I say. "We consider it a fair figure, and as such it is nonnegotiable. I believe we can get considerably more at trial."

"I see. I'll convey this to my clients."

I tell him that'll be fine, and with Willie grabbing a final orange on the way out, we say our goodbyes.

Willie asks if I can drop him off at his girlfriend's house, which is in a rather depressed area of downtown Paterson. Paterson is a city of over a hundred thousand people and can match any other city blight for blight. Yet whenever anyone in the area refers to "the city," they are talking about New York.

We are about ten blocks from our destination when we almost hit a dog running loose on the street. It looks to be a Lab mix, skinny, worn-out, and frightened from life on the street.

Willie and I are both shaken by the near miss. "Damn, that was close," he says.

"Poor dog. They'll catch him and take him to the pound," I say.

"And then what?"

"And then they'll kill him."

"What?" Willie yells, outrage in his voice. "Stop the car!"

I barely have time to pull over when Willie jumps out, chasing the dog down the street and calling, "Here, dog!"

The dog demonstrates his intelligence by running away from the screaming Willie, so I pull the car up ahead and try to cut him off. I jump out of the car and start chasing him back toward Willie, but again the dog is clever enough to run down an alley.

The chase is on, as Willie and I spend the next twenty minutes running up and down streets and in and out of alleys, all in pursuit of this poor dog. We execute a number of maneuvers to cut him off, but he outsmarts us each time.

The workout in the whirlpool at Vince Sanders's club hasn't quite prepared me for this kind of running. I'm gasping for air and my insides are burning, but Willie handles it like he's out for a walk in the park.

After a few minutes more I lose sight of both Willie and the dog, and they are going to have to handle this on their own. I stagger up and down a few alleys, hoping to find one of them, although my first choice would be to stumble upon an oxygen tent.

And then, at the end of an alley in front of a dirty garage, I see Willie. He is sitting on the cement, back against the wall, cradling the dog in his lap and petting him gently on his head. The dog contentedly rests that head on Willie's knee. They look so relaxed that the only thing missing from this picture is a pond and a fishing pole.

When I'm able to breathe and walk again, the three of us go back to the car. Willie keeps the dog on his lap in the front seat and announces that he is now his dog, and his name is Cash, for obvious reasons. I check and see that there is no collar or tag on the dog, which makes it far less likely that there is an owner somewhere looking for him.

Willie promises to put up signs in the neighborhood with pictures of the dog, but I'm not sure he'll follow through on it. Whatever. A dog has found a loving owner; there are worse things that can happen in this world.

I get back home and am surprised to see Pete Stanton waiting to update me on the early stages of the investigation of Stynes. He could have done it by phone, but I think he wanted to see Laurie and offer additional moral support.

The report on Stynes is stunning in its brevity. "So far Stynes doesn't seem to have existed," Pete says.

"What are you talking about?" I ask.

Pete proceeds to tell me that they have run his prints everywhere, military, federal, and state, and come up with nothing. They've circulated his picture to every law enforcement agency in the country on a priority basis and came up empty as well.

"How is that possible?" I ask.

"I don't think it is," Pete says. "A guy like that, he had to have a record, or been in the military, or applied for a gun permit . . . something. If there's no record of him, then that record had to have been erased."

"By who?"

Pete shrugs. "By some record eraser—how the hell should

I know? Anyway, we're still looking, but I don't think we're going to find anything."

Pete leaves and I spend the rest of the night preparing for the meeting in Hatchet's chambers tomorrow to discuss our request for all of Dorsey's records. It's not a motion we can afford to lose.

The morning is sunny and bright, but as always, Hatchet's chambers are cloudy and dark. Once again, Dylan is there before Kevin and me, which annoys me. The judge should not be talking to one counsel without the other present. I could lecture Hatchet on this point, or I could decide to keep living.

It becomes instantly apparent to me that their pre-meeting was by Hatchet's design. "Mr. Campbell has decided not to oppose your motion" he announces to me.

"Good," I say.

"You will have the file by close of business today."

"Good," I say.

"That will be all, gentlemen."

"Good," I say.

Dylan hasn't said a word, and I've only said one, although it's a word I like and I've gotten to say it three times. Within moments Kevin and I are back in my car.

"What the hell was that about?" Kevin asks.

"Hatchet obviously read him the riot act before we got there," I say.

Kevin is incredulous. "And Dylan just caved?"

"You've obviously never had Hatchet read you the riot act. Giving up on the motion was easy; if Hatchet had really put on the pressure, Dylan would have sacrificed his firstborn."

I call Edna and she tells me that there's an important message from Marcus, asking me to meet him at an address in a very depressed area of town. Kevin agrees to go along, and within twenty minutes we're at the location, which seems to be an abandoned apartment building. It is next to an abandoned movie theater and across the street from some abandoned stores.

We get out of the car and start looking around. After a few moments we hear a voice.

"Up here."

Looking down at us from one of the few unboarded windows in the building is Marcus. "Come on up," he says. "Sixth floor."

I moan, since the elevator in this building would obviously not be running, and I'm still sore and barely catching my breath from yesterday's dog-chasing jaunt with Willie. But ever the trooper, I march into the building with Kevin and we trudge up the steps.

When we reach the sixth floor, I instantly know that my instinct that the elevator would not be running was a correct one. I know this because hanging above the empty elevator shaft is a human being. He's hanging from a shoulder harness, his eyes bulging in fright and trained on Marcus, who stands nearby with a large knife in an apparent threat to cut that harness and send the man six stories to his demise.

I'm speechless, but Marcus is calm and relaxed, as if we were meeting him at the pool to have piña coladas. Ever aware of the social graces, he performs the obligatory introductions. "Andy Carpenter, Kevin Randall, this is Asshole. Asshole, this is Mr. Carpenter and Mr. Randall."

When I first walked in, I couldn't understand how a person could find himself hanging over an elevator shaft. Now I understand that most of the fault lies with his parents. When you name your kid Asshole, you are pretty much preordaining his being treated with a lack of respect as he grows older.

Marcus informs us that the hanging man has something to tell us. I think Kevin is going to have a stroke at being part of this scene, and I'm not terribly comfortable with it either, so I convince Marcus to bring the man onto safe ground. Marcus grudgingly agrees, after the man croaks a promise to speak just as candidly standing as he would have hanging.

Once he gets out of the elevator shaft, the man calms down some, and I learn that he has another name. Mitch. Mitch is apparently a small-time hustler, part-time informant, and full-time slimeball, who keeps his ear to the ground in the hope of gathering information he can sell. Marcus, persuasive fellow that he is, has prevailed upon Mitch to share some information with us for free. He has even prepared the special harness as a show of support for Mitch in that effort.

Mitch is able to shed some light on Dorsey's illegal activities, but it is a slightly different light than we had pictured. Dorsey was, as we suspected, heavily involved in the criminal activities of the Petrone family. But according to Mitch, Dorsey was merely a glorified bagman; the real power and protection for Petrone came from above Dorsey on the totem pole. Mitch doesn't know the identity of the man or men above Dorsey, but he's sure that Dorsey's main function was to collect money and pass a good chunk of it up the ladder.

This angle certainly fits in with what Celia had to say about the other lieutenant that Dorsey was involved with. Whether that lieutenant was in fact above Dorsey in the Petrone operation, or just working alongside him, it's becoming very clear that someone in the department has an interest in Laurie getting convicted.

We send Mitch on his way with our sincere thanks and our admonition to him to keep his ears open and report back to Marcus if he learns anything else. He promises that he'll do just that, but my guess is that Mitch will choose not to remain in the same hemisphere as Marcus.

Hatchet Henderson is the kind of judge whose orders are followed, and Dylan is not about to be the lawyer to buck that trend. When Kevin and I get back to the house, the remainder of Dorsey's file has already been sent over, and Kevin and I immediately start to pore over it.

The interesting period in Dorsey's record starts with Laurie's accusations against him, which are documented here. There is a report from Internal Affairs which, while not exactly on the scale of the Warren Commission, nevertheless confirmed Laurie's charges and expanded upon them.

Dorsey was in business with Dominic Petrone in various areas of his operation, mostly loan-sharking, prostitution, and drugs. His role in those businesses was essentially to provide protection—actually insulation—against the police. Occasionally, his role was even more active and direct, but it is clear that his value to Petrone was in his capacity as a police lieutenant.

The FBI did in fact intervene to save Dorsey's job two years ago, and the specific intervener was Special Agent Darrin Hobbs. Amazingly, Hobbs provided not much more information to the police than he provided to me; he simply said that there was an important FBI investigation that would be compromised if Dorsey's role were to be revealed. Hobbs said that the operation had nothing to do with Dorsey but was directed at "elements of organized crime." The fact that the Paterson authorities caved in to this federal intervention is not exactly something they should be proud of and is most likely the reason they resisted turning the information over to me.

In return for receiving the incredibly mild punishment of a reprimand, Dorsey promised to desist from his unlawful activities in the future. There is some evidence that he kept that promise, but only for a short time. About six months ago, Internal Affairs became aware that Dorsey was at it again, and that charge was also confirmed.

Hobbs was made aware of the situation before action was taken, but this time neither he nor anyone else in the FBI intervened. Dorsey was about to be arrested when he disappeared, and a week later the body that they believe to be Dorsey's was discovered.

It is rather depressing for us to get the information that we have been seeking and discover that it is not particularly helpful. It opens up no new areas to investigate or strategies to formulate.

The next nail in our legal coffin is a phone call from Nick Sabonis. He informs me that they have turned up zero evidence that Dorsey might be alive. It will remain an open investigation, but as far as he and the department are concerned, Dorsey is dead. He allows that he is not saying Laurie is lying about the phone call, simply that she must have been deceived by a fake or crank caller.

My frustration is reaching the boiling point. "Mind if I ask you a question, Nick? How is it you came to be on the Dorsey case?"

He pauses for a moment, considering the implications of the question. "Why? You think I'm this mysterious 'lieutenant' that Dorsey was working with?"

"Somebody was," I say. "At this point I'm not ready to eliminate anyone."

"Be careful who you're accusing," he says, his tone even more ominous than his words.

"Are you going to answer my question, Nick?"

"I asked on the case."

"Why?"

"I didn't like Dorsey or what he was doing. But I like cop-killers even less."

• • • • •

TIME IS THE ULTIMATE pain in the ass.
It consistently, absolutely, and obnoxiously does the exact opposite of what one wants it to do. This is my theory and I'm
sticking to it. In fact, it is just one of the profound theories I
am able to come up with in situations such as this, lying in bed,
unable to sleep, at three o'clock in the morning.

The weeks leading up to the trial, set to begin later this
morning, represent a perfect example of my premise. For Laurie the calendar has moved excruciatingly slowly, as she
awaited the day when her confinement would be at least partially relieved and, more important, she could be on the way
to legal vindication.

For Kevin and me today's trial date approached like a
speeding, out-of-control freight train. We spent every moment
of every day trying to prepare, to figure out a defense strategy
that we could have confidence in, and yet haven't come close.

I fall asleep around four and wake up at seven, adrenaline
starting to pump. Laurie seems more excited than nervous. The
prospect of actually getting out of the house holds such great
appeal that it has temporarily overpowered the natural fear that
she should and will feel. But that's okay; right now I'm afraid
enough for both of us.

A bailiff arrives at nine to accompany Laurie to court, and she has her first experience wading through the gathered press outside. The questions called out to her mainly refer to her feelings as the trial is about to begin. Some ask about our personal relationship, which has made for considerable fodder in the press in recent days. There has been open speculation that Laurie broke up my marriage, and veiled criticism about the propriety of mixing our private lives with our professional ones.

I have responded openly and directly, completely acknowledging that I am and have been in love with Laurie, starting after my marriage had ended but before she had become my client. But for Laurie it is difficult and embarrassing to take, especially since she has no choice but to take it.

The press crush is far greater at the courthouse than at home, but we are given a special entrance through the back, so as to avoid it. Before long we are seated at the defense table, as Hatchet goes through the formalities involved in opening the proceedings.

At the defense table with me are Kevin and Laurie. Across the aisle Dylan sits with two other prosecutors. He is dressed in his Sunday best; I'm surprised he doesn't have a flower in his lapel. He has an air of confidence about him, confidence that I wish were misplaced.

The gallery is packed, as expected, and according to the bailiff, the public won their coveted seats through a lottery drawing that will be held each day. The group today, while they might consider themselves lucky winners, is about to be bored out of their minds by the tedium of jury selection.

I've consulted two jury consultants on tactics but ultimately decided to go it on my own. One of the few things we have going for us is the incongruity between Laurie's appearance and demeanor on the one hand and the brutality of the crime on the other. The consultants felt that female jurors would have the most trouble believing Laurie could do such a thing, but I don't agree. I'm going to listen to my gut instincts, although it would be nice if my gut would stop churning and allow me to hear them.

It is conventional wisdom to say that jury selection is perhaps the most important phase of a trial, a process during which cases can be won or lost before a single witness is called. In theory this is true, but in practice it is rarely that decisive.

Competent lawyers have become sophisticated enough at jury selection that it is very unusual for one side to gain a decisive advantage. It's like in a football game. The mechanics of the game, the x's and o's, are vital to a team's success, but modern coaching staffs have become so knowledgeable that it is usually in other areas that a team develops a winning edge.

Every chance Dylan gets, he publicly describes Laurie as a tough-as-nails former cop, while my goal is to have everyone view her as a delicate flower. In the real world she's both, so it makes our little game more challenging.

Laurie hates when I refer to a trial as a game, but that's how I see it, that's how I have to see it to perform at my best. And it is a game in the sense that it has strategy and luck, peaks and valleys, ebbs and flows, and winners and losers. The stakes are not what make a game a game; you play to win and then you cash in your chips, whatever they are worth.

For me to be effective, I must depersonalize the case, view it only from the perspective of proper strategy and tactics. That is my greatest danger here, other than the fact that the prosecution has a seemingly airtight case. It is a constant struggle for me to step back and look at the game, without looking at the people and the incredibly high stakes.

I am scared that I will not do well enough to win, but I will not do well enough to win if I am scared.

Hatchet is in good form. I've always suspected that he carries a "glower meter" with him. The more significant the occasion, the more momentous the moment, the more he glowers and threatens. Today the meter is hitting approximately a seven, which is to say he would certainly chew a lawyer up, but might not spit him out. It's a sign that he considers this an important trial. He's right about that.

After about an hour Hatchet turns to me. "Is the defense ready?"

"Yes," I lie, and we're under way in the case of the *State of New Jersey v. Laurie Collins.*

One hundred prospective jurors are brought into the room, and Hatchet gives them his standard lecture on the importance of jury service to society. He thanks them for being good citizens, but he knows as well as I do that they are here because, unlike the majority of their fellow good citizens, they couldn't figure out how to get an excuse from serving.

The jurors are given questionnaires to fill out, answering many of the questions that the lawyers would ask. This is designed to reduce the repetition and time necessary to get through this process, as the written responses often disqualify people without us having to take the time to question them.

It takes two and a half days to empanel the twelve citizens, plus four alternates, who will decide Laurie's fate. Seven men, three African-Americans, one Hispanic. There's not a brain surgeon in the group, but for a jury I would say they're above average in intelligence and apparent open-mindedness. That's important, since they're going to have to be receptive to our defense, should we happen to come up with one.

The last juror is sworn in at three o'clock in the afternoon, and Dylan takes Hatchet up on his offer to delay opening statements until tomorrow morning. That's fine with me; I can use the extra time to prepare. I ask Kevin and Marcus to be at the house at six o'clock, and we can once again go over where we are and where we have to go.

Laurie makes dinner, then sits with us in the den. Marcus is very frustrated; he feels he has never done so little to advance a case, yet for him this is the most important case that he has ever worked on. Stynes's real identity and his connection to the murder are still a complete mystery, as are Dorsey's whereabouts.

I'm disappointed that Laurie has not received any more communications from Dorsey. I was hoping that he would have a need to continue contacting her so that he could twist the knife even further. We've even set up an elaborate taping system on her cell phone so that we could nail him. No such luck.

Marcus has had success in cataloguing a list of missing persons who might be the actual decapitated body found in the warehouse. After narrowing it down by height, weight, and time of disappearance, there are seven possibilities. Unfortunately, every possible cross-check has not yielded a connection between any of these people and Dorsey.

Marcus leaves about nine o'clock, and Kevin and I go over the parameters of my opening statement. I don't like to write openings out in advance; even detailed notes seem to cut down on my spontaneity and effectiveness. So we go over general areas, points to be made, and then I send him on his way.

Laurie and I get into bed at about eleven, and we lie there talking for an hour or so. She's a realist; she knows how difficult the situation is. The tension I am feeling is overwhelming, and it must be that much worse for her. At least I have some control over the events of the next few weeks; she can only watch and then face whatever consequences those events cause. Even Tara seems to be on edge, uncharacteristically barking out the window at street noises.

Once Laurie and Tara go to sleep, I can focus on Barry Leiter and perform my nightly self-flagellation. I will always consider myself to blame for his murder, and I will always be right.

It's a really long night.

We've been studiously avoiding television coverage of the case, and this morning is no exception. It's very difficult for Laurie to watch people openly calling her a murderer, and the few that are on her side represent small consolation.

Today, however, she will hear Dylan give his opening state-ment, and it will be far worse than anything she might hear on television. She will have to listen as he tells the jury that she decapitated Alex Dorsey and set fire to his body, and she will hear him ask that jury to send her to prison for the rest of her life. I restate to her what she already knows: that she must sit there stoically and unemotionally, not reacting in any way.

Outside the courthouse today, it is even more chaotic than usual, and inside, the tension level has been ratcheted up con-siderably. All of this is due to the start of opening statements. The prosecution gets to present its road map of the crime, telling the jury exactly what it is they will prove. They promise only what they believe they can deliver, and in this case that is quite a bit.

Before Hatchet brings in the jury so the statements can begin, he asks if there are any last-minute things we need to go over. We had included my name on our witness list, since I'm the only one who can testify to the meeting I had with Stynes. Dylan attempts to get Hatchet to rule that I should be prohibited from testifying, since Stynes is not relevant to the case. The canons of legal ethics frown on lawyers as witnesses and preach that efforts should be made not to take on cases in which the lawyer will have to testify. But it is not prohibited, and I'm not backing out.

I stand and argue that Stynes is completely relevant, that he in fact is the sole reason Laurie was out behind the stadium. Hatchet decides to defer his decision until the defense case is set to begin, and he calls in the jury.

Lawyers, start your mouths.

"Ladies and gentlemen," Dylan begins, in a tone reflecting his sadness that we have to be here at all, "over the next few weeks you are going to hear different points of view about the incidents that brought us here today. But let me make one fact very clear right at the start."

He walks over toward the defense table and stands a few feet away from Laurie, pointing at her. "This is the person on trial. This is the person whose actions you are here to judge. Now, that may seem obvious now, but soon it won't be. That is because Mr. Carpenter is going to stand up here and try to make Alex Dorsey the person on trial. That's right, he is going to make the victim the criminal, and the criminal the victim.

"Make no mistake about it, Mr. Carpenter is going to pull some tricks that would make Houdini blush. You'll watch as he makes a man rise from the dead, you'll be shocked as he turns a murdered man into a conspirator, capable of concocting grand schemes, and you'll shake your head when, for his next trick, he turns a brutal murderer into an innocent, victimized woman.

"It will be amazing, and it will be amusing, but it will all be nonsense. Because fortunately, there will also be facts that even a magician like Mr. Carpenter can't make disappear, and those facts, every single one of them, will lead you to the conclusion that Laurie Collins brutally murdered Lieutenant Alex Dorsey of the Paterson Police Department."

He points toward Laurie again. "Doesn't look the part, does she? Not who you envision when you think of a person who could decapitate a human being and set the body on fire. The very idea of it seems almost beyond comprehension. But I've prosecuted a lot of horrible criminals, ladies and gentlemen, and let me tell you something: They come in all different shapes and sizes. I've seen mothers that killed their children, I've seen schoolchildren that killed their friends, and none of them looked the part of killer.

"Laurie Collins was a police officer until she left the force after a dispute with Alex Dorsey. She carried a grudge against him and against another man, Oscar Garcia. So she concocted a plan, to murder Lieutenant Dorsey and to frame Mr. Garcia for that murder. Two birds with one stone. And it almost worked."

He shakes his head, both for effect and to demonstrate his own amazement at the brazenness of Laurie's crimes, and repeats, "It almost worked."

Dylan then gets into the meat and potatoes of his case, describing the crime and the prosecution's theory of how it was accomplished. "And I say to you today, there is nothing we will claim that we will not prove. Nothing. By the time Judge Henderson sends you off to deliberate, you will have no trouble understanding that we have proved not just beyond a reasonable doubt but beyond any doubt that Laurie Collins committed one of the most heinous crimes this county has ever witnessed. And I know, I am absolutely positive, that you will bring her to justice."

The eye contact Kevin makes with me tells me that he agrees with my assessment that Dylan has done a strong job. It was clear, concise, persuasive, and it had the jury's attention throughout. It also maintained and took good advantage of the presumption of guilt.

There is a myth going around, something about the Constitution granting everyone the presumption of innocence. In the real world, that is total nonsense. Juries go in thinking that the accused is most likely guilty, or that person would not be on trial.

That leads right into the second myth, which is that the prosecution carries the burden of proof and that the defense bears no burden at all. The burden is absolutely on the defense, starting with the opening statement, to aggressively attack that presumption of guilt and plant in the jury's mind that this defendant just might, wonder of wonders, be innocent. If the defense does not meet that burden, the defendant will be eating off of tin plates for years to follow.

Hatchet asks me if I want to make my opening statement now or reserve it for the conclusion of the prosecution's case. It's a no-brainer; it's time the jury came to understand this is not going to be a walk in the park for Dylan.

"Ladies and gentlemen of the jury," I begin, "that was a heck of a speech, wasn't it? That Mr. Campbell can really turn a phrase."

I look directly at Dylan. "I'm such an admirer of his words, in fact, that I'd like to read some more, if I may. I'll make sure I quote him directly so I don't mess things up."

I walk over to the defense table, and Kevin hands me a piece of paper. "Here goes . . . these are words that Mr. Campbell said about this case," I say, as I start to read. " 'Your Honor, the State of New Jersey will prove that on May thirteenth of this year, in the City of Paterson, New Jersey, the defendant did, with malice aforethought, willfully murder Mr. Alex Dorsey, a lieutenant in the Paterson Police Department.' "

I hand the paper back to Kevin and turn to the jury. "A little drier than his speech today, but it summed things up pretty nicely, wouldn't you say? The defendant murdered Alex Dorsey. Very simple."

I walk over and point to Laurie. "The only problem is, this wasn't the defendant he was talking about. He was talking about a man named Oscar Garcia, and Mr. Campbell at that time said that Oscar Garcia was guilty, beyond a reasonable doubt, of the murder of Alex Dorsey. Now he says that Oscar Garcia is innocent and that Laurie Collins is guilty of that same murder, also beyond a reasonable doubt.

"So here's a riddle: How many people, not working together, can be guilty beyond a reasonable doubt of the same crime before those doubts become totally reasonable?"

I look at Dylan and shake my head, as if saddened by his transgressions. "In our justice system, a prosecutor should be certain before he brings charges like these, and Mr. Campbell claimed to be certain that Oscar Garcia was guilty. He was totally wrong then, but he asks you to believe he's right now. And he wants you to send somebody to prison for the rest of her life based on that belief.

"I said he was wrong then, which makes me one for one. I'm telling you he's wrong now, which you will soon see makes me two for two.

"But when the State of New Jersey brings a charge of murder, however unfounded, it must be vigorously defended. So let's look at what Mr. Campbell would have you believe. He claims that Ms. Collins carried a grudge against Mr. Dorsey for two long years, never once during that time attempting to cause him physical harm. Then the police discover that she was right about him all along, and he is forced to go on the run. So according to Mr. Campbell, this was the time she chose to make her move. She found him when the entire police department could not, and then she brutally murdered him, even though she could have gotten total vindication and revenge just by turning him over to the department.

"In other words, when he was free and clear, she didn't go after him. When she had won, when he was a destroyed man, that's when she chose to put her own life in jeopardy by committing murder.

"Doesn't make a lot of sense, does it?"

I go on a while longer, extolling Laurie's record as a public servant and her extraordinary character as a human being. Kevin and I have debated whether to introduce in the opening statement our belief that Dorsey is alive. He is opposed, and I'm on the fence, but I decide to go ahead.

"I talked to you a little while ago about reasonable doubt. I told you that before long, you will be knee-deep in reasonable doubt about the charge that Ms. Collins murdered Alex Dorsey. But I'll take it one step further. You will have reasonable doubt that Alex Dorsey was murdered at all.

"Because, ladies and gentlemen, it is very possible that the murder victim in this case is alive and laughing at all of us."

• • • • •

EVERY MINUTE IS CRUCIAL during

a trial. I try to avoid spending any time at all on anything not directly related to our defense. It requires self-discipline, not something I have in abundance, but I'm able to summon it when I need it.

What I do most often is read. I read and then reread every scrap of paper we have, no matter how obscure. I sometimes find that it can be on the third or fourth reading that the significance of an item becomes clear.

I file things according to subject matter, and then I keep shuffling the files and going through them whenever I get the time. Tonight I take the file labeled "Tomorrow's Witnesses," which Kevin will update daily during the trial, into the den to go through. I also bring the Stynes file, since I haven't been through it in a while.

Dylan will be calling foundational witnesses tomorrow, none of whom will directly implicate Laurie, but who will "set the table" for the later witnesses to do just that. I go through the discovery related to their testimony and roughly plan out my cross-examination. I won't be able to do significant damage to them, but it's important that I make my points so that the jury does not see the prosecution's case as an uninterrupted juggernaut.

The Stynes file is short and depressing. We have all the police reports on Barry Leiter's murder and on their fruitless efforts to determine Stynes's real identity. I feel the now-familiar stab of pain that the real culprits, the people who sent Stynes to kill Barry, are likely never to be discovered.

The reports written by the individual officers on the scene at Barry's house that night basically echo Pete Stanton's statements to me. Stynes essentially ensured his own death by raising his gun when he was completely surrounded by gun-pointing officers. The problem is that no one, certainly including myself, can say why.

The autopsy report on Stynes is interesting but ultimately unenlightening. He was shot eleven times, six of which could have by themselves been fatal. The coroner describes Stynes as being in outstanding physical shape, with almost no body fat. However, at the same time, he writes that Stynes's body was "worn beyond his apparent chronological age." There was significant joint damage in his knees, elbows, and shoulders and an inordinately large amount of old scarring and scar tissue. This is not a guy who spent much time behind a desk. The coroner wryly noted that Stynes had a single tattoo on his right arm in just about the only area on his body that had not been previously damaged.

I'm just finishing the file when Laurie enters along with her traitor companion, Tara. "How are we doing?" Laurie asks.

It's probably the thousandth time she's asked me that question since this nightmare started, and my insides cringe when I hear it. She wants me to tell her that I've just come up with something, a breakthrough, that is going to bring us a quick, decisive, and startling victory.

"We're getting there," I say without much enthusiasm, and then I try not to listen to the sound of her heart hitting the floor. "It's a process."

"I know, Andy, I know it's a process," she says, partially

venting her frustration. "You've told me a hundred times that it's a process, and I've got it down pat. It's a process."

I can get annoyed, start an argument, and we can add "hurt" and "miserable" to our mental state, which alphabetically would follow smoothly after "depressed" and "frustrated." Instead, I put my arm around her shoulder and draw her to me.

"I can say two things with certainty. Number one, this is not a process. Never has been, never will be. In law school that's the first thing they tell you: If you want a process, go to business school."

She smiles, and I can see the anger melting away. "You said you know two things with certainty. What's the other one?"

"That we are going to win. I'd be lying to you if I said I knew exactly how, but we are going to win."

She starts to formulate a question, then changes her mind and rests her head on my shoulder. I know she doesn't fully believe in what I'm saying, but I hope she's getting there. It's a process.

Dylan's first witness is a fourteen-year-old boy, one of a group that saw the smoke coming out of the warehouse that night and called the fire department. Dylan takes twenty minutes when he could have taken two, and since the kid never even saw the body, I don't bother to cross-examine.

Next up is a rookie police officer, Ricky Spencer, who was the first to realize it was a body that was smoldering.

"Did you immediately realize it was a body?" Dylan asks.

"Well, it was dark, and I wasn't really sure. I couldn't see a head . . . a face." He seems shaken by the recollection, which most people would be. "When I shined a light on it, there was no doubt what it was."

"Other than the fact that there was a body, was there anything else unusual that you noticed about this fire?"

Spencer nods. "Yes. The fire seemed localized around the body, and there was a mostly empty gas can about ten feet away. It appeared to be arson, with the body the only target."

"If you know, did subsequent tests show that the same material that was in the can was involved in the fire?"

"Yes, it was. I saw the reports."

I could object to this as hearsay, but the facts are true, and Dylan could bring the same information in with other, more polished witnesses.

I rise to cross-examine. "Officer Spencer, that night at the warehouse must have been an upsetting experience for you."

He nods hesitantly. Dylan has told him to be wary of the evil defense counsel, but this seems harmless enough. "It was. I've never . . ." He catches himself. "It was."

"You said, 'I've never.' Did you mean you've never seen anything like it before?"

He's caught, and he nods sheepishly. "I never have."

"But you weren't so upset that your recollections might be incorrect, were you?" I ask.

"No, sir. I remember everything very clearly."

I nod. "Good. Now, before you knew it was a body that was burning, what did you think it might be? Any ideas?"

He considers this. "Well, I thought it might be a mattress. Or maybe an old sofa. It sounds pretty awful to say that now, but . . ." He lets his answer trail off.

"No, it's okay. I'm sure everybody understands." I look at the jury, and they are clearly joining me in sympathy for what this young man went through. "Now," I continue, "you say it seemed like a mattress, or a sofa . . . so whatever was on fire seemed fairly large?"

"Yes. He was a big man."

"Right. Now, the gasoline can . . . was that near the wheelbarrow?"

"I didn't see any wheelbarrow," he says.

"Really? Then where was the gurney?"

"There wasn't any gurney."

Now my surprise is showing through. "How about a cart or wagon of any kind?"

"No."

"Let me see if I understand this. Mr. Campbell said in his opening statement that the murder was committed behind Hinchcliffe Stadium, and then the body was brought to the warehouse. If that's true, are you saying that somebody carried it into the warehouse?"

"It's possible."

"How far was the body from the nearest door?"

"About forty feet," he says.

I back him further into the corner. "So the murderer is somebody strong enough to carry dead weight the size of an old couch more than forty feet?" I walk toward Laurie, to make it seem even more absurd that someone her size could have done this.

"I assume the murderer had a cart of some kind and then took it with him when he left. Or when she left."

"Then why would *he* leave the gas can?" I ask.

Dylan objects that the witness couldn't possibly know the murderer's internal reasoning, and Hatchet sustains.

"Did you see any wheel marks, or any tracks made by anything other than human feet?"

"No, but you should ask the forensic people that."

I smile, knowing that there were no such tracks. "Oh, I will. Believe me, I will."

Dylan has a couple of questions on redirect, trying to repair whatever damage I may have caused.

"Officer Spencer, do you know what kind of flooring there is in this particular warehouse?"

"I believe it is cement."

"So you wouldn't expect a gurney or a cart to leave tracks?"

"I wouldn't think so, no."

Dylan lets him off, and after Hatchet adjourns court for the day, I head home for what will become a nightly routine. Kevin, Laurie, and I have dinner, discussing the events of the day in court. Marcus will join us when he has something to add, which I hope will be soon. After dinner we move to the den, where we discuss our plans and strategies, and then they both leave me alone with my reading and preparations for the next day's witnesses. It's a grind, but experience has shown that it works for me.

It's eleven o'clock, and I'm sitting on the couch surrounded by paperwork, when Tara comes into the room. She walks over to me and stands a couple of feet away, as if waiting for me to call her over.

"It's obvious you're here only because Laurie's asleep," I say.

She responds by jumping up on the couch, but sitting about six inches away from me. "I need two hands to read, so there's no way I'm petting you," I say.

She tilts her head, as if puzzled by what I'm saying. It should be noted here that Tara has the cutest head tilt I have ever seen. If "head tilting" had been an Olympic sport in the eighties, even the East German judge would have given her a ten.

Tara's next move is to come closer and snuggle up against me, her head resting on my thigh. It's a blatant attempt to receive pleasure, and I can see through it from a mile away. "Nice try," I say, "but I'm not buying it."

She licks my hand, so I spend the next hour reading and petting her until we both fall asleep.

I meet Kevin at the courthouse at nine in the morning, and we again go over how we're going to handle Nick Sabonis, the first witness to tie Laurie to the crime. It's important that we make a real dent in him.

Dylan takes him through his being called to the warehouse the night of the murder, and the actions that he took. They're standard and proper, which is fine, because it has nothing to do with Laurie.

Dylan then moves to the meat of the testimony, which covers the afternoon when Laurie, at my request, went to check out the evidence Stynes had said he left behind Hinchcliffe Stadium.

"She was only there a few seconds before she went towards the clothing and the knife," Nick says.

"So it seemed as if she knew where it was?" Dylan asks.

Nick nods. "Seemed like it to me."

"Have you determined whose clothing it was?"

"It was the defendant's clothing. Ms. Collins." I could argue this point, but the prosecution has fiber evidence and sales receipts, so it would seem like a losing battle to attempt to disprove that these were Laurie's clothes, especially since they were.

"And the bloodstains? Were they the defendant's blood?"

"No, the DNA report showed the bloodstains to be Alex Dorsey's."

Dylan covers the gas can found in Laurie's garage, then starts to introduce the Oscar Garcia side of the equation, getting Nick to talk about the grudge Laurie had against Oscar. He will supplement this later with witnesses to confirm the grudge and to speak about Laurie being spotted near Oscar's apartment.

Dylan, and Kevin for that matter, seem surprised that I'm not objecting more, since a good portion of this is hearsay, but my feeling is that this is all information that the jury will come to realize is true. I don't want to be seen as trying to bury the truth, especially since I can't.

Dylan finally finishes with Sabonis and turns him over to me. I've always believed that a trial doesn't begin until there's a contentious cross-examination. If that's the case, the curtain's about to go up.

"Lieutenant Sabonis, you knew Alex Dorsey fairly well, didn't you?"

"We worked together."

"That would be a really good answer if the question were, 'How did you and Alex Dorsey work?' You could say, 'We worked together,' and then we could move on. The problem, and I do hope it's not a recurring one, is that wasn't the question." I pause. "Am I going too fast for you?"

Dylan objects to my tone, but Sabonis lets the insult roll off his back. He's an experienced witness; he's not going to be drawn into a fight with me. "I knew him fairly well, yes," he says.

"So when you saw the body that night, you were upset that this person you worked with and knew so well was dead?"

"I didn't realize it was him. He had been decapitated and his body badly burned."

I nod. "So he couldn't be identified from the condition of the body?"

"Not by me. It took the DNA tests." I can tell by Sabonis's self-satisfied expression that he's pleased to have gotten in the mention of the DNA. He no doubt thinks it makes my questioning about the body seem unimportant.

"Yes," I say, "we'll get to that. So if there were no subsequent scientific tests, you still wouldn't know who that poor soul was?"

"He was wearing that distinctive ring, which I noticed at the morgue. I've seen Alex wear that ring before."

"You're not saying that you can identify a man's body by the ring on his finger, are you?"

"I'm saying it makes it much more likely that it was him."

I take the ring, which Dylan had introduced into evidence, and hand it to Nick. "Do you recognize this as the ring he had on that night?"

He nods. "I believe so, yes."

"Would you try it on, please?"

Nick puts the ring on his finger and looks up at me, as if waiting for the next command.

"Alex, we were so worried about you," I say, wiping my brow in mock relief. "They said you were dead."

Hatchet admonishes me even before Dylan objects.

"I'm sorry, Your Honor," I say, then I turn back to Sabonis. "You *are* Alex Dorsey, aren't you?" I ask.

Dylan jumps up. "Objection, Your Honor, this is frivolous. Counsel knows who the witness is."

"Sustained," says Hatchet, staring a hole through my fore-head. "Be very careful, Mr. Carpenter."

Undaunted, or at least only partially daunted, I try again. "Does it make it more likely that you are Alex Dorsey because you're wearing that ring?"

Dylan objects again and this time Hatchet overrules him.

"No, it does not."

"But putting Alex Dorsey's distinctive ring on his otherwise impossible-to-identify body would be a good way to make you believe it was him, isn't that right?"

"There is no evidence that happened. And we have the DNA results."

It's my turn to be annoyed. "That's twice that you've mentioned DNA, just like Mr. Campbell asked you. Did he promise you a lollipop if you did what you were told?"

I can see a flash of anger from Sabonis, which makes the question worthwhile, even though Hatchet sustains Dylan's immediate objection.

I change the tempo and throw some questions at him in rapid-fire fashion. "Did you run the DNA test, Lieutenant?"

"No."

"Are you an expert on DNA?"

"No."

"Would you know a piece of DNA if it walked into this room, stood on the prosecution table, and sang, 'What kind of strand am I?' "

Dylan objects again, and I move on. I like to jump around, moving from subject to subject, to keep the witness off balance. "You said that Ms. Collins didn't like Oscar Garcia, that she had a grudge against him. Do you know why?"

"I was told it was because Garcia got the daughter of a friend of hers hooked on drugs."

"When?"

"I'm not sure. I think about two years ago."

"Has Mr. Garcia ever filed a complaint that Ms. Collins attacked him? Tried to kill him?"

"No."

"So she carried this terrible grudge for two years, yet never cut off his head? Never set him on fire?"

"No."

I press on. "Was Oscar Garcia protected during those two years? Any police unit assigned to make sure Ms. Collins couldn't get to him?"

"He wasn't under police protection."

"Do you know if Ms. Collins is licensed to carry a gun?"

He nods. "She is."

A quick change in attack. "How did you happen to be there when Ms. Collins showed up in the area behind Hinchcliffe Stadium?"

"We received some information linking her to the Dorsey murder. We initiated surveillance, and she led us to the stadium," he says.

I react as if surprised by his response, though of course I'm not. "Information from who?"

"It was a phone call from an anonymous informant."

I nod. "You testified earlier that you received information from an anonymous informant initially linking Oscar Garcia to the murder. Is there an 'anonymous informant fairy' looking down on this case?"

Dylan objects and Hatchet sustains; it's getting to be a pattern.

I rephrase. "Was the extent of your investigative efforts in this case to sit by the phone and wait for someone to anonymously call you?"

"It is not uncommon to get such information. People often know things, but don't want their identities to be known."

"And sometimes the information is right, and sometimes it's wrong?"

"Yes."

"Lieutenant Sabonis, did I ask you to go over Ms. Collins's internal police records before you testified today?"

"Yes. I did so."

"Thank you. Would you please tell the jury how many times the then-*Detective* Collins was found to have committed any form of police brutality?"

"None that I could see."

"Any times that she was accused but not found guilty?"

"No."

"Is there anything in her record that could in any way have predicted she could be capable of a brutal act like this murder?"

Sabonis looks at me evenly. He's pissed and he could waffle, but he doesn't. "No, there isn't."

I end the cross there, and Dylan tries to patch up the holes I punched. Afterward, we break for lunch, and Laurie, Kevin, and I are all feeling pretty good about the Sabonis testimony. We cast some significant doubt in an area where there should automatically already be doubt: the question of whether someone like Laurie could have committed such a horrendous act.

Kevin and I do some quick preparation for Dylan's next witness. It's the head of the police lab, Phyllis Daniels, who will be testifying to the DNA typing. She is our key to establishing doubt that the DNA evidence is reliable, and I think we've got a shot to do just that. Marcus, with some off-the-record help from Pete Stanton, has come up with some good information on lab practices to help me in that effort.

Twenty years ago, Phyllis Daniels was a police lab technician, not particularly accomplished, who had the foresight to recognize the incredible implications the infant science of DNA would have in forensics. She successfully set out to make herself an expert, thereby putting herself on the fast track, or at least the fastest track a scientist in the Paterson Police Department can be on.

I have come up against Phyllis on cases before. She can be long-winded and proud to show off her expertise, but her basic knowledge and honesty come through. In Dylan's hands she is an outstanding witness, leaving no doubt in anyone's mind that the DNA from the body absolutely matched the blood labeled as Dorsey's in the police lab. This testimony comes as no surprise, nor do I have any intention of challenging it.

"Ms. Daniels, you testified that Lieutenant Dorsey's blood sample was in room 21 of the police lab. How is that room guarded?"

"There is always a person sitting at a reception desk at the entrance to the room. Twenty-four hours a day."

"Is that person armed?"

"No, it is a civilian job. But everyone entering must sign in."

"If you know, is the evidence room entrance handled the same way?"

"No," she says. "The evidence room has an armed officer assigned to it."

"So an armed officer is considered more effective than a civilian sign-in monitor?"

"I would say so, yes."

"Who is allowed to enter room 21, after signing in?"

"Police officers who need to access material in the room."

"Thank you," I say. "Now, you testified that the DNA in the blood listed as Lieutenant Dorsey's matched that of the body in this case. Correct?"

"Yes."

"Allow me to present a hypothetical. If the blood in the lab had been changed or incorrectly marked—and in fact wasn't Lieutenant Dorsey's?—then the body also could not be his. Correct?"

"That's certainly correct. But I saw the vial myself when I ran the test."

I introduce a sign-in list from the lab into evidence and ask her to read a specific part of it. It shows that Alex Dorsey had entered the lab twice in the three weeks before his disappearance.

"It is not unusual for him to have been there," she says. "Officers enter all the time."

"If he entered for the purpose of substituting a different vial of blood for the one in his file, could he have done so?"

"I guess it's possible" is her grudging response.

"*Reasonable* to assume he could have?" I ask. It's a loaded word, since if I can establish reasonable doubt that the blood was Dorsey's, we're home free. How can Dylan prove Laurie murdered Dorsey if he can't even prove beyond a reasonable doubt that Dorsey's dead?

"I'm not sure I know the answer to that" is the closest she will come to a concession.

"What if you were to hear Lieutenant Dorsey's wife testify that he planned to fake his own death? Would that make it reasonable to believe he could have changed the blood?"

"I suppose that it would."

"Thank you. And just so we're clear: If that blood were changed, if it were not Dorsey's blood, then that would mean that the body was not Dorsey? Correct?" I'm repeating myself for effect.

"Yes."

I let her off the stand while barely stifling my desire to yell out "Game, set, and match." We have had a hugely successful day, and the evidence of that is etched on Dylan's face.

I stop outside long enough to conduct a mini–press conference, during which I allow myself some gloating. The questions demonstrate just how successful a day we have had, as the reporters want to know if I believe Hatchet will dismiss the charges once the prosecution rests. I don't believe that he will, but I certainly do nothing to discourage the speculation.

We have our evening meeting as usual, and I try my best to temper the group enthusiasm. Laurie and Kevin completely understand intellectually that we won a battle today but that victory in the war can only be declared by the jury. Nevertheless, we have become so used to depressing news that it is only natural we overreact on the positive side.

Laurie proposes a toast at dinner to her "wonderful attorneys," and since it is bad luck to refuse to toast an obvious truth, I join in. I throw in a toast to Barry Leiter, partially as a sobering device. Kevin is as happy as I've ever seen him, and it takes me a while to get them both to calm down so we can start planning for tomorrow's witnesses.

Just when I think I have them sufficiently wary and depressed over what lies ahead, Willie Miller shows up. He explains that he was going to call to find out if there's been any counteroffer on his case yet (there hasn't), but when he heard today's good news on the radio about the trial, he decided to come over. And with him is Cash, the Wonder Dog.

Cash goes everywhere with Willie, and Willie has determined that Cash is the smartest, most amazing dog in the history of the universe. Since it is a known fact that Tara is the smartest, most amazing dog in the history of the universe, I am aware that his claims are overblown, but I let him continue in his blissful ignorance. Besides, Cash is a pretty cool dog, and Tara seems to like him.

Unfortunately, Willie also brings along his infectious enthusiasm. Without the benefit of any knowledge at all, he confidently tells Laurie that she is just days from vindication. In the process, he pretty much eradicates my efforts to get the group back to thinking cautiously. Just when Laurie is about to bring out the party hats, I convince Willie to take Cash and Tara outside in the yard to play, so that we can get back to work inside.

Willie obliges, grabbing a couple of tennis balls and a Frisbee and leading the dogs out to the yard. Kevin and I get started on the files, but after a few minutes I see Laurie looking out the window and shaking her head in disapproval.

"Look what they're doing to my vegetables."

I sigh and go to the window. Cash is out near the back of the yard, digging furiously in Laurie's vegetable garden. I don't think it's such a big deal. "Looks like we're back to buying basil like the city folk," I say.

"Come on, Andy. I put a lot of work into that garden," Laurie complains.

I'm annoyed at the interruption, but I've got little choice but to deal with this vegetable crisis. I tell Kevin that I'll be right back, and go out to the yard.

As I exit the house, I'm surprised to see Willie coming toward me, looking uncharacteristically upset. He's holding on to Cash by the collar, and I can still see the dirt on Cash's nose from his digging.

"Andy," Willie says, "you'd better get your ass over here."

My initial instinct—make that panic—is that something has happened to Tara. But Willie turns and runs back to the garden, and Tara is standing there, looking none the worse for wear.

Willie points down to where Cash was digging, and I see why he is so upset. Something is buried there, in clear plastic and well preserved.

Alex Dorsey's head.

●　●　●　●　●

AS LONG AS I LIVE, I will never see as disgusting a sight as that severed head in that plastic bag. I only look at it once, but it will forever be etched in my memory.

I turn and walk back to the house, asking Willie to stay by the garden and secure the area. I go in and tell Laurie and Kevin what I've seen, and we basically sit there speechless, waiting for Pete to show up.

Within five minutes, it is as if a police convention has convened on my lawn. Pete is there, as well as Nick Sabonis and just about every other cop of every rank in the department. Dylan shows up as well, acting as if he is in charge. His look is somber and serious, in an attempt to conceal his total glee at this turn of events.

I tell Nick what happened, truthfully disavowing any knowledge of how the head got there. I remember that Tara had barked out the window facing the garden a few nights before, and that might be when the head was buried. They don't believe me, and they don't even attempt to question Laurie, no doubt fully aware that I would not allow it.

The forensics people spend a couple of hours out there, and the detectives fan out to interview my neighbors. The head is actually taken away in an ambulance, though I think it's too late to save it. I can't speak for the EMS people, but I'm certainly not about to give it mouth-to-mouth.

Just before Nick leaves, he tells us that the coroner is going to be examining the severed head tonight, and Kevin goes down to the morgue to get the results of that examination. Once everyone is gone, Laurie and I stay up to wait for his call.

The call from Kevin comes in less than an hour. "We've got a problem," he says. "The official determination is that the head was from the body in the warehouse, and that obviously means the time of death is the same. He also says that the cut was made from the back, so the murderer probably snuck up on him."

That is all the information he has, and I ask very few questions. We are both aware that our case is in shambles. All our success so far has centered on creating a reasonable possibility that Dorsey's death was faked, that the body in the warehouse may not have been his. We staked our credibility with the jury on this, and the resulting loss of that credibility is devastating, and most likely impossible to recover from.

Just as bad is Laurie's claim that Dorsey called her, at a time long after he was dead, as has now been shown. The jury can logically conclude that she lied about this and can thus doubt anything else she or her lawyer has to say.

It is a disaster.

I tell Laurie what we've learned, and she receives the news quietly, almost with a sense of resignation. She's smart enough to know what it means to our case and to know what Dylan will do with the revelation.

It's only as we get into bed that she reveals what she's been thinking about. "Andy, why don't you ask me if I did it?"

"Laurie—," I begin, but she cuts me off.

"You say that everything in the case fits perfectly into our claim that I was framed. Wouldn't it fit even more perfectly if I actually did it?"

"Laurie, this is not a conversation worth having. We need to focus on what's important. I know that you didn't do it."

"How?" Her eyes are boring in on me like a laser beam.

I sigh, a tactic that turns out to be pitifully ineffective against laser beams.

"Andy," she presses, "how do you know I'm not guilty?"

"Because I know you."

She shakes her head. "Not good enough," she says. "I want to hear facts—facts that prove my innocence to you."

I'm not going to put her off, so I might as well play this out. "Okay. Did you send Stynes to hire me?"

I keep going before she can answer; the questions come out in a barrage, and there's no prosecutor to object. "Did you send yourself to find your own bloodstained clothes? Did you ask me to represent Garcia? Did you murder Barry Leiter? The damned facts are on your side, Laurie. I'm just the only one who knows them."

She's quiet for a moment, then says, "Thank you for that. We're going to be okay." She kisses me, rolls over, and goes to sleep.

Women.

I'm not as good at getting to sleep these days as I used to be, and this is a tougher night than most. Instead of counting sheep, I count evidence, and I apply my "nothing is coincidence theory" to the latest developments.

I had always wondered why someone would decapitate a victim and then bother to set the body on fire. In light of today's events, I can now make the assumption that it was done so that we would have reason to doubt that the body was Dorsey at all.

That might not have been accomplished by the decapitation alone, since there may well have been marks on the body capable of identifying Dorsey. Perhaps scars, perhaps a distinctive tattoo—

I jump out of bed, rush down to the office, and then rummage through the case files until I get to the Stynes file. I find what I'm looking for—the autopsy records. And, more important, the autopsy photographs.

The coroner had made reference to a tattoo on Stynes's body, and I look to see if I can find it on the photographs. Sure enough, there it is, on the upper right forearm, where the coroner said it was. Even with my magnifying glass, though, it's too small for me to make out details.

At a key moment in the Willie Miller case, I called upon Vince Sanders to utilize the sophisticated machinery at his newspaper to blow up a photograph so that I could read a license plate. He was a pain in the ass about it, and that was at six o'clock in the evening. This is two in the morning. I'm going to call him, but if he has the technology to murder me over the phone, he'll do it.

I call Vince at home, and he answers on the third ring. "What the hell do you want?" are the first words out of his mouth.

"How did you know it was me?" I say, though I realize he must have caller ID.

"Next question," he says dismissively.

"Would you meet me at the paper? I know it's late, but I need your help."

"Not as much help as you'd need if I met you at the paper," he snarls.

I play my only trump card. "Vince, it could be crucial to Laurie's defense."

"Twenty minutes," he says. "Take Market Street."

"Why?"

"When you get to the corner of Market and Madison, you'll know," he says, and then hangs up.

I quickly get dressed, leave a note for Laurie in case she should get up, and head for Vince's office. Since my life is important to me, I stop at the Dunkin' Donuts at the corner of Market and Madison. And since it should only be a twenty-minute meeting, I pick up six jelly and six glazed.

The fact that Vince is meeting me at this hour reflects his feelings about Laurie. Vince Sanders, Pete Stanton, Kevin Randall, Marcus Clark, Andy Carpenter . . . we know who Laurie is and what she's about. And if we have any power at all, she's not about to spend a goddamn day in prison.

Vince stuffs a donut in his mouth, takes the picture, and brings it into a room filled with large machines and people to run them. Within a few minutes the job is apparently accomplished, and he brings the enlarged photograph over to me, laying it out on a table.

The tattoo on Stynes's arm is now at least three times the size of the entire original photograph. I'm not sure what I was hoping for, probably a name or something that could become a clue to his identity. It's still hard to make out, but it doesn't seem as if my hopes are realized.

"What the hell is that?" I ask.

Vince shakes his head in disgust. "What are you, one of those hippie, draft-dodging, limousine liberal, pinko, defeatist, chickenshit, pacifist bastards?"

I nod. "Pretty much . . ."

"Those are crossed arrows. Your boy was Special Forces. Green Beret time."

This, if true, could be helpful. "Are you sure?"

Vince snorts and points to his right knee. "Of course, I'm sure. If I didn't have this trick knee, I would have been fighting commies right alongside him."

I point to his other knee. "I thought your left knee was the trick one."

He nods without embarrassment. "That's part of the trick."

I thank Vince, and in an uncharacteristically gracious gesture, he offers me a jelly donut on my way out. The bigger they are, the nicer they are.

I go home, grab three hours' sleep, and get up at six to call Kevin. I tell him that we need to find a way to track Stynes, or whatever his real name was, back through his army record.

"No problem," he says. "I'll call my brother-in-law."

It turns out that Kevin's brother-in-law is Lieutenant Colonel Franklin Prentice, stationed at Fort Jackson, South Carolina. Not only does Kevin get along great with him, but he has done him some legal favors in the past, which Lieutenant Colonel Prentice would love to reciprocate. It is a stroke of luck, the first that we have had on this case.

We agree that Kevin will spend the day following this lead and leaving the courtroom action in my so-far-incapable hands. And if there is a trial day to miss, this is as good as they come.

Dylan is emboldened by last night's news and loaded for bear. Before the jury comes in, he informs Hatchet of the developments and requests permission to revise both the witness list and the order in which they are called. He wants to make sure that the jury is immediately informed of the defense's disaster. I object, but I don't have a prayer of success, and Hatchet blows me away.

Dylan calls the first officer to arrive at my house last night, who describes what took place. The jury doesn't look terribly surprised, which is evidence that they have been ignoring Hatchet's repeated admonitions to avoid media coverage of the case. The discovery of Dorsey's head on my property was the lead story this morning.

Next up on Dylan's list is a neighbor of mine, Ron Shelby, who semireluctantly testifies that he had seen Laurie digging in the garden. I start off on cross by getting him to admit that he's only seen Laurie planting seeds, not heads.

Moving on, I ask, "Do you remember when you saw the defendant digging in the garden?"

He thinks for a moment. "I can't be sure. Maybe a couple of months ago. It's hard to remember. I mean, at the time it didn't seem unusual."

"Was it daytime?" I ask.

"Yes, absolutely. And I work during the week, so it had to be on a weekend." He's trying to be helpful.

"Was Ms. Collins acting secretive? Like she was hiding something?"

He shakes his head. "No, she waved to me, and then we talked a little."

"Was she behaving at all strangely? Did you sense anything was wrong?"

Shelby is picking up on where we're going. "No, sir. She was as nice as can be. She's a really nice person."

Dylan objects and Hatchet overrules. I conclude with a hypothetical. "Mr. Shelby, if you were trying to hide something very important, do you think you would do it in broad daylight on a weekend when everyone in the neighborhood could see you?"

Shelby allows as how that is not how he would behave at all, and I let him go. I made a little progress, which Dylan doesn't seem too concerned about, mainly because his next witness is the coroner, Dr. Tyler Lansing.

Dr. Lansing is approaching retirement age, which will conclude what can only be described as a thoroughly distinguished career. He has no doubt spent more time in courtrooms than I have, and if there is such a thing as a truly unflappable witness, he's the one.

Dylan takes him through his findings concerning the time of death and the likelihood that the severed head and the burned body are a match. He also brings out the fact that the murderer struck from behind, making it more credible to the jury that Laurie could have done it without having to overpower Dorsey in the first place.

Anybody in the courtroom with a brain knows that what he is testifying to is accurate and correct, and the jury would no doubt frown on anyone trying to get them to believe otherwise. Which is okay, because I'm not dumb enough to attempt it.

"Dr. Lansing," I begin, "you've testified that the head that was dug up last night was severed from its body almost three months ago."

He nods. "That is correct."

"Was the face recognizable as Alex Dorsey?"

"Yes, it was."

"Why had there been so little decomposition?"

"It was buried in an airtight plastic wrapping," he says.

"A plastic bag?"

"No, there was considerably more effort taken here. It was a thick plastic that was stapled and sealed at the edges."

"So the purpose of that effort would have been to prevent decomposition? To preserve the head?"

Dylan objects. "Your Honor, the witness cannot possibly be expected to know the murderer's purpose in doing this."

"Sustained," says Hatchet.

I try again. "Are you aware of any effect the plastic wrapping would have other than preservation?"

He shrugs. "It would keep it clean."

"Would all of this keep it recognizable?"

"Yes. Certainly."

"So let me sum up, and tell me if you agree. The murderer decapitated and burned the body, which had the effect of leaving the identity in some question. Then the murderer wrapped the head in airtight plastic, thereby preserving the identity. Is that fair?"

"Yes."

"And the body was left in a place that could not be tied to the defendant, but the head was left in a place that could directly be tied to her?"

Dylan objects, saying that this is beyond the scope of the coroner's expertise. Hatchet sustains, but my point has been made. Even so, I try to drive it home.

"Dr. Lansing, how well did you know Ms. Collins when she was with the police force?"

"Reasonably well, I would say."

"Seem like a good cop? An intelligent cop?"

He nods. "In my dealings with her, yes."

"Assuming she has a normal amount of common sense and a good knowledge of police procedures, wouldn't you say that the prosecution's theory as to her actions would make her self-destructive and stupid?"

Dylan objects, but Hatchet lets him answer. "It would seem

so. On the other hand, though this is not my area of expertise, I would say that some people who commit terrible crimes want to be caught and punished."

"Good," I say. "We agree."

He is surprised. "We do?"

"Yes. We agree that whoever did this wants Laurie Collins to be caught and punished."

• • • • •

LIEUTENANT COLONELS have a

large workforce to call on when they want to get something done. Which is why Kevin's brother-in-law, Lieutenant Colonel Prentice, is able to call him back with our information just six hours after we had requested it.

Kevin reports that since all identification records of Stynes had mysteriously been erased, our favorite LC had his minions compare his face with that of every known member of the Special Forces during the Vietnam era. A positive match was made, and Stynes's real name is Roger Cahill. He was a sergeant in the 307th Division, Delta Company, and served in Vietnam for three years, distinguishing himself and winning three combat medals.

Kevin asked him to run a military report on Alex Dorsey, but unfortunately Dorsey and Cahill were not in the same division. At first glance, nothing in Stynes/Cahill's record matches Dorsey, but we put Marcus on the case to try to dig something up. The bottom line is, we have new information but don't yet know enough to benefit from it.

I put in a call to Darrin Hobbs, the FBI special agent who deflected my earlier attempts to get information about the FBI's intervention into the Dorsey matter. I'm told he's in a meeting, and I wind up speaking to Agent Cindy Spodek, Hobbs's underling, heretofore best known for successfully resisting my conversational charms when we last met.

This time she's just as aloof, but I'm not trying as hard. I don't really care if she likes me or not; I'm looking for information. I tell her what I've learned about Cahill and that I want access to the FBI investigative files to see if he is included in them, under either "Cahill" or "Stynes."

To my surprise she seems interested by what I am saying, and asks some clarifying questions. But ultimately, she says, "You understand that I can't authorize the release of our confidential information. That will be up to Special Agent Hobbs."

This is what I expected. "When can I speak with him?"

"I'll be talking with him before the end of the day."

I give her my phone number and tell her I'll be waiting for his call.

"One of us will call you back," she says. "But I must tell you, I think you should pursue any other avenues you have. It is not the kind of information Special Agent Hobbs is likely to share."

I again ask that he call me, and she promises to do her best. She seems sympathetic to my request but cognizant of the inclinations of the person for whom she works. My guess is that she is right, and I doubt that I'll hear from him.

It takes ten minutes to again be proved wrong. The phone rings and Hobbs himself is on the phone.

"Andy? Darrin Hobbs here. What's this about you needing more information?" His tone is friendly but on-the-run, as if he's really busy, but he'll take a few seconds to rid himself of this annoyance.

"That's right," I say. "There's a new piece added to the puzzle. A guy named Cahill."

"Never heard of him," he says dismissively.

"It's not the only name he uses. I need to know if he turned up in your investigation of Petrone and Dorsey."

"That road is closed. I told you that."

The guy is on my nerves, but it won't pay to antagonize him. "Yes, you did," I say. "I'm hoping you'll reconsider."

He laughs a short laugh at the absurdity of my hope. "It's not going to happen."

There's no sense beating around the bush. "Hopefully, the judge will have a different view of that."

The temperature of his voice drops fifty degrees in the blink of an eye. "I don't know how much you know about me, Carpenter, but if you know anything, then you know I can't be threatened."

"I'm defending my client," I point out, my voice reflecting my annoyance.

"Good for you." *Click.*

Within thirty seconds of the time he hangs the phone up, my anger switches from being directed at Hobbs the pompous asshole to Carpenter the idiotic, counterproductive defense attorney. I've just permanently pissed off the only guy who might have information that could help Laurie.

Good job, Andy.

I call Kevin and give him the job of preparing a motion asking Hatchet to compel Hobbs to turn over the FBI investigation files. Kevin is happy to do it; motions like this are undoubtedly one of his strengths, and this will prevent him from having to be in court tomorrow morning. It would be depressing to watch me spend another day playing legal rope-a-dope, lying back as Dylan pummels us with witnesses.

Actually, the rope-a-dope analogy isn't quite accurate.

Ali, in using it in his fight against Foreman, was doing it intentionally. I'm not.

Ali had a strategy. I don't.

Ali had the masses chanting *"Ali bomaye! Ali bomaye!,"* which when translated means "Ali, kill him! Ali, kill him!" I have the press, writing columns and going on TV, essentially saying, "Carpenter, you're a moron! Carpenter, you're a moron!," which when translated means "Carpenter, you're a moron! Carpenter, you're a moron!"

Dylan's first punch/witness of the day is a neighbor of Oscar Garcia, who recounts having seen Laurie hanging out near Oscar's apartment on a number of occasions. I make the point that "apartment hanging" is not a felony, but it remains an effective small piece of Dylan's puzzle.

Next up is Laurie's ex-partner on the force, Detective Stan Naughton. He looks like he would rather be anywhere else than here and occasionally looks over at Laurie, his eyes apologizing for what his mouth is saying.

Naughton recounts the story of Oscar providing drugs to the daughter of Laurie's friend and how Laurie was determined to nail Oscar for it. It provides motive with a capital "M," at least concerning the initial framing of Oscar for the Dorsey killing.

With Naughton obviously friendly to the defense, it's simply my job on cross-examination to lead him where he already wants to go. I take my time doing so, prompting him to talk about Laurie's exemplary record on the force, his feeling that she is a levelheaded, decent human being who abhors violence and who never came anywhere close to committing police brutality.

Kevin shows up, motion in hand, and I tell Hatchet that we have an important matter to bring up before the court. We file the motion, providing Dylan with a copy, and Hatchet schedules argument for nine A.M. tomorrow.

Kevin and I are going to be up late tonight going over our position on the motion. We will have to convince Hatchet that the Cahill/Stynes involvement in the case is relevant and presents a credible alternative to Laurie's guilt. At the same time, we also have to make him believe that there is at least a reasonable chance that the FBI files contain information that could be exculpatory to Laurie.

I arrive home before Kevin, and Edna hands me the mail that has built up over the last three days. It's mostly solicitations for charitable contributions, and I have a quick pang of

guilt that I have been neglecting my philanthropic blundering during the trial.

There is also an envelope from Stephen Cates, the opposing lawyer in the Willie Miller civil lawsuit. It's surprisingly thick, and when I open it, I see why. It is a one-page letter attached to a long legal document. The letter informs me that they have agreed to our demands and that when Willie signs the attached settlement agreement, they will forward a check in the amount of eleven million seven hundred thousand dollars.

I'm thrilled for Willie, but I'm so obsessed with the trial that my first reaction is to view this as a distraction. Nevertheless, it wouldn't be fair to Willie not to tell him about it immediately, so I ask Edna to call him and have him come over.

Willie arrives so quickly that I think he must have been waiting on the front lawn for Edna to call. With him, as always, is Cash, who is probably delighted at the prospect of digging up another head.

"What's up?" Willie asks.

"We received an official response from the other side."

"We did?" he asks nervously. "You got any beer?"

"You want a beer before you hear their answer?"

"Every time I've ever gotten good news in my whole life I've had a beer in my hand. Every single time."

"Really?" I ask. "What about the time the jury found you not guilty and you got off death row?"

That time had slipped his mind. "Okay, forget the beer. What did they say?"

I hold up the settlement agreement. "That if you sign this paper, they'll give you a check for over eleven million dollars."

Willie looks at me, not speaking, for about twenty seconds. Then he leans over, picks up Cash and holds him right up to his face, and says, "Did I tell you? Did I tell you?"

And then he starts to cry. Not huge sobs, but serious sniffles and definite tears. Cash seems far less upset, no doubt rec-

ognizing that he has gone from roaming the streets eating garbage to a future filled with designer biscuits.

Willie turns back to me, apparently wanting to explain his reaction. "This doesn't make up for what I went through, you know? But it's pretty damn good."

I had long ago told Willie I would handle his case for ten percent, which is far lower than customary. Even at that, I've just earned more on this one case than I've made in the totality of my legal career.

I laugh at the realization and turn to Kevin. "Do you realize that we just made over a million dollars in commission?"

"What do you mean 'we'?"

"You're in for half," I say.

Ever honest, Kevin says, "Andy, you pay me a hundred and fifty an hour."

I shake my head. "Not on this case. On this case you get half a million. You can buy those triple-load washers and dryers you've had your eye on." I turn to Edna. "And you get two hundred."

"Dollars?" she asks.

"Thousand," I say.

Laurie comes into the room, and I give her the rest, which she can put toward her legal fees. Within a few moments we're all laughing, out of control, a brief but welcome respite from the ongoing pressure we've been under for months.

Edna calls cousin Fred, making appointments for him to talk to both Willie and herself about investing their windfalls. Kevin and I adjourn to the den to plan for tomorrow's hearing. Based on what we come up with, I probably should have saved Kevin's half million to offer to Hatchet.

We're joined in court by Darrin Hobbs, Cindy Spodek, and Edward Peterson, the U.S. attorney representing the FBI's position. Hobbs, certainly still angry about my supposed threat to do exactly what I've now done in bringing him to court, ignores me. Spodek does the same, no doubt taking the lead from her boss.

Hatchet calls on me first, admonishing me to be brief, since he's already read our motion papers. I recount what I know about Dorsey's involvement with organized crime, and the FBI's intervention with Internal Affairs on his behalf. I then talk about Cahill/Stynes, starting with his visit to my office, his "admission" about the bloody clothes behind the stadium, right up to his murder of Barry Leiter.

I think my story is intriguing, if not compelling, but rather weak regarding relevance to the FBI files. It is difficult to conceal what is the essential truth: We have no idea what is in those files, and our seeking them is nothing more than a fishing expedition.

Dylan is quick to see it for what it is. "Your Honor, this is a fishing expedition," he says. "The defense counsel is telling an uncorroborated story to help the defense. Even if the court were to take it at face value, which I am certainly not suggesting, the link to this FBI investigation is just not there."

Hatchet then turns to Peterson, the government lawyer, who presents a stipulation from Special Agent Hobbs that there is nothing in the files regarding Dorsey that would be helpful to either side in this case and that there is no mention at all of Cahill/Stynes. Peterson takes great pains to point out that Hobbs is a highly decorated military officer, who has earned similar praise in his career with the Bureau. There should be no reason, according to Peterson, to question his word.

Peterson doesn't stop there. "The details in the file are of little consequence to the government," he says. "Its insignificant revelations would have no impact on this case, but the act of releasing it could have widespread ramifications on other cases. By their very nature, these investigations must be cloaked in secrecy; many who cooperate do so with that secrecy as a condition. If that trust is violated, the inhibiting effect on future investigations could be devastating."

Hatchet, bless his heart, seems unmoved. "We are not talking about publishing this in the *New York Times*," he says, "we are talking about my looking at the material *in camera* to determine probative value to this case."

"Respectfully, Your Honor," Peterson counters, "Agent Hobbs has stipulated that there is none."

"And he may be correct. But he's a war hero, not a judge. Which balances things out quite well, since I'm a judge and not a war hero. I assume you brought the file with you?"

Peterson nods. "As you ordered, Your Honor."

"Good. Turn it over and I'll review it."

Peterson just nods in resignation, and Hobbs turns and walks out, with Spodek behind him. It's a victory for us, but whether it will turn out to be a meaningful one will depend on what Hatchet finds in the file.

• • • • •

DYLAN HAS SOME finishing touches to cover before he rests his case. These take the form of fact witnesses, basically noncontroversial, who will provide information to round out and support the prosecution's theories.

First up is the 911 operator who received the anonymous tip alerting the police to Oscar Garcia's guilt, information that proved erroneous.

The tape is played in court, though I've of course heard it many times. It's a female voice, masked somewhat by some computer or electronic technique. Dylan's theory is that the caller was Laurie, and he buttresses his contention by pointing out that the caller referred to Oscar as a "perpetrator." It's a term, in Dylan's view, that a cop or ex-cop like Laurie would be likely to use.

I have an expert prepared to testify that, computer enhancement techniques being as advanced as they are, the original voice could be female, male, or a quacking duck. There's no sense questioning the prosecution's witness about it at this point, so I let her off the stand with no cross-examination.

Next up is the police officer who found Dorsey's gun in Oscar's house during the execution of a search warrant. Since Oscar has been cleared, and since Laurie has been placed near

Oscar's apartment, this supports the theory that she planted the gun there as part of her frame-up of poor Oscar.

Once again there's little I can do with this witness, other than to get him to confirm that Laurie's fingerprints were not found anywhere in the apartment. I'm sure the jury would consider Laurie, as a former cop, too savvy to have left any prints, so I don't accomplish much.

The parade continues with Rafael Gomez, a police officer who found the gas can in Laurie's garage and who testifies that the gas/propane residue in it is the same mixture as that used to set Dorsey's body on fire. While that is no doubt true, his testimony at least gives me an opening to score some points.

"Officer Gomez, were there any fingerprints on the gas can?"

"No, sir. Wiped clean."

"Really? So you think she was stupid enough to leave this terribly incriminating piece of evidence in her own garage but smart enough to wipe off the prints?"

"Well . . ."

He's unsure, so I push the advantage. "Maybe she figured the police wouldn't be able to figure out whose garage it was?"

He thinks for a moment and comes up with a pretty good answer. "Maybe she didn't wipe it. Maybe she was wearing gloves. To keep the gas off her hands."

"Is the gas dangerous to touch?" I ask.

"No, but some people—"

I interrupt, and Dylan doesn't object, even though he should. "Where did you find the gloves?"

"We didn't find any gloves."

"But you said you conducted a full search of the premises," I point out.

"We did, but there were no gloves. Maybe she threw them away so we wouldn't find them."

"Under the theory that Ms. Collins would get rid of the gloves but keep the can of gas?"

"I can't say what she would do" is his fairly lame response.

"Is that what you would do?" I press.

"I wouldn't murder anyone."

"You and Ms. Collins have that in common," I say. "No further questions."

I've done with Officer Gomez exactly what I've done with many of Dylan's witnesses, no more and no less. I've shown that if, after the murder, Laurie had done the things Dylan has alleged, then her behavior was illogical. The problem is that there is no reason a jury should expect someone who has decapitated and set fire to a police officer to act logically. In effect, I am saying, "She couldn't have committed this bizarre crime because if she did, look how strangely she acted afterwards." In this case, strange behavior fits neatly with the crime and could be taken as an indicator of guilt, rather than as exculpatory.

Dylan's last witness is retired Paterson police captain Ron Franks, probably Dylan's best friend on the force. Though Franks retired more than a year before the Internal Affairs investigation that Laurie instigated, Dylan's purpose in calling him is to present the positive side to the victim.

It makes sense. We have been tearing Dorsey down as best we can, and Dylan certainly knows that will be a big part of our defense. The worse Dorsey looks, the less compelled the jury might feel to avenge his murder.

Franks is only on for fifteen minutes, but he talks warmly and admiringly of Dorsey's years of public service, both in the military and especially with the police department.

My cross-examination is brief, honing in on the fact that Franks knows nothing about the Internal Affairs investigation or the facts that caused Dorsey to go on the run. The man seems to sincerely have been a friend of Dorsey's, and it will do me no good to attack him.

Dylan rests his case, I move for a dismissal, and Hatchet denies my motion. Since it's late, and it's Friday afternoon, he excuses the jury and tells me I can start our defense Monday morning. Unfortunately, he means this coming Monday.

As we're about to start one of Laurie's perfectly prepared dinners, a phone call comes in that certainly has the potential to ruin it. It's from Hatchet's office, setting up a conference call between Dylan, Hatchet, and myself. Dylan is already on the line, but I'm not in the mood for chitchat, so I just wait for Hatchet.

After a few minutes His Majesty gets on the line. "Gentlemen, I have made a ruling on the defense motion, and I thought you should hear it immediately so that you can be guided in your preparations for court on Monday."

He pauses, but neither Dylan nor I say a word, so he continues. "I have carefully reviewed the FBI material, and I have determined that it provides no new or relevant information to this case. Lieutenant Dorsey is mentioned only peripherally, and Mr. Cahill, or Stynes, is not mentioned at all. There is also no indication of another police lieutenant that may have been in a conspiracy with Mr. Dorsey.

"Therefore, my ruling is that the probative value of these documents as it relates to our trial is effectively zero and certainly not worth interfering with an FBI investigation. Any questions?"

Dylan, the victor, responds first. "Not from my end, Your Honor. I think you made the right decision."

"That's comforting," Hatchet responds dryly. "Mr. Carpenter?"

"Have a nice weekend, Your Honor."

The loss of this motion does not come as a great surprise. We have no choice but to shrug it off, and Kevin and I work until almost eleven o'clock on our defense strategy. Our plan is to work all day tomorrow and then take Sunday off, resting up before the battle begins.

Laurie is already asleep when I get into bed, and I lean over and kiss her lightly on her forehead. My concern for her is almost overpowering. We're heading into the homestretch, and she doesn't have a hell of a lot of horse under her.

I'm just dozing off when the phone rings, and I jolt upright, immediately alert. The last time I got a call at this hour, it started the chain of events that led to Barry Leiter's death. I have an initial desire to just let the phone ring, but I force myself to pick it up.

"Hello?"

The voice on the other end is immediately recognizable, as it should be, since I heard it a number of times earlier today. It is the computer-masked female voice that in the 911 call identified Oscar Garcia as Dorsey's murderer.

"Mr. Carpenter, you're not looking in the right place."

This of course is not exactly shocking news. "Where should I be looking?" I ask.

"Vietnam. That's where it began. That's where you'll find the connection."

"Connection between who? Dorsey and Cahill?"

There is no answer, and I'm desperately afraid she's going to hang up. "Come on, please," I say, "what about Vietnam? I need more to go on."

Again there is no answer; for all I know she may not even be on the phone any longer. Then she answers hesitantly, as if not sure whether to tell me more. "Talk to Terry Murdoch."

"Who is he? Where is he?"

Click.

I don't even put down the phone; I just dial Kevin's number.

"Hello?" he answers with not a trace of sleepiness in his voice.

"What time do lieutenant colonels go to sleep?" I ask.

• • • • •

KEVIN IS OVER BY SIX in the morning to jump-start our weekend. He informs me that, even though he planned to call his brother-in-law this morning, he couldn't resist and called him last night. It was a great thing to do, because it has already gotten the ball rolling.

Lieutenant Colonel Prentice has already contacted the Records Division at Fort Monmouth and instructed them to fully cooperate with our investigation. He's established a liaison there, Captain Gary Reid, to deal with us.

Laurie is just getting up as Kevin and I are ready to leave for Fort Monmouth. She's excited about the news and the possibilities it represents and amazed that so much has happened while she was asleep. I can tell it's killing her that she can't go with us today, but she's forced to leave it up to us.

Fort Monmouth is located on the Jersey Shore and is surrounded by beach communities. We've left early to try to beat the beach traffic, but the only way to really do so would be to leave in February.

It's a phenomenon that has always amazed me. People get in their cars in the height of the summer heat and crawl along for two or three hours, all for the right to spend an afternoon lying in grainy dirt, baking, sweating, and burning under a barrage of cancer-causing rays. Their only escape is to enter the water, which can best be described as a freezing, salty urinal. Then, unless they've endured the day covered with sticky grease, they can spend the two or three hours on the way home watching their skin blister.

As you may have noticed, I'm the type of guy who sees the ocean as half-empty.

We arrive at Fort Monmouth, though the only thing that tips us off to the fact that it's an army post is the "U.S. Army" sign at the main gate. It is basically an office complex of nondescript brick buildings, set in the middle of a residential area. For every soldier we see walking around, there are three or four civilian workers. Kevin, whose mind is filled with obscure knowledge like this, tells me that the fort is mainly involved with electronics and that its chaplain school has recently been moved to Maryland.

We head to the main building, and Captain Reid is there to meet us. He is the personification of the buttoned-down military man and looks as if he had his uniform pressed while he was in it. He openly tells us that the order from Lieutenant Colonel Prentice was quite clear: He is to do whatever is necessary to facilitate our investigation. Which is good, because there is no doubt that this is a guy who follows orders.

Captain Reid assigns four young enlisted men to do our bidding. It gives me a feeling of power; I'm tempted to send them into Guatemala Bay to rescue the otters. But first things first, and we request all military files related to Dorsey and Cahill, as well as a search for any records for a Terry Murdoch, the only stipulation being that he be someone who served during the Vietnam era.

Within moments we are looking at and comparing the military histories of Dorsey and Cahill. The files are quite detailed, listing on an almost daily basis every commendation, every assignment, every communication, even every illness that they had.

There are similarities to be sure. Both were Army Special

Forces, both had advanced infantry training and were considered outstanding soldiers, and both served a lengthy hitch in
Vietnam. Dorsey's time there started two months after Cahill's,
which means they overlapped for a long time.

Unfortunately, there is no obvious connection. The two
men came from different parts of the country, went to different schools, trained stateside at different posts, and were assigned to different divisions in Vietnam. There is no evidence,
at least none that we can see, that they knew each other. Certainly nothing that should have caused them both to die, their
deaths interrelated, all these years later.

Captain Reid comes in with the military records of two men
and one woman, all named Terry Murdoch. They all served in
Vietnam, but only one of the men was there at the same time
as Cahill and Dorsey. He was also Special Forces, advanced infantry, and much decorated, but again has no other obvious
connection to the others. Murdoch left the army in 1975, and
as with Cahill and Dorsey, that is when the army lost track of
him.

"Do you have any idea where we could find him now?" I
ask Reid.

"We don't keep those records," he says, "but we have some
resources we can call upon when it's absolutely necessary."

He says this cryptically and ominously, and I'm afraid to
ask him what he's talking about, since if he tells me, he might
have to kill me. Kevin's not the bravest guy either; right now
he wouldn't open his mouth if I offered him a raspberry
turnover.

"Lieutenant Colonel Prentice indicated everything was possible," I say.

Reid smiles. "Yes, he did."

Reid leaves, suggesting we go over to the mess hall, as
aptly named an establishment as has ever existed, for lunch. I
just have some coffee, then watch as even Kevin is challenged
to find something edible. Finally, he settles on a plate of what

looks like baked linoleum. He puts things in his stomach I wouldn't put in a Dumpster.

"It's not bad," he says, and goes up to see if he can negotiate another helping. The server agrees; I'm sure it's the first time he's ever been confronted with a request for seconds. Kevin is polishing off plate number two when a soldier comes in and summons us back to see Captain Reid.

"You guys get enough to eat?" Reid asks us when we return.

"I would say we both had as much as we wanted," I say.

"Good. Terry Murdoch has not exactly been a credit to the army since he went civilian."

"What do you mean?" I ask.

"He's currently serving time in Lansing."

Lansing is a federal prison in Pennsylvania, less than a hundred miles from here. "What is he in for?"

"Counterfeiting," he says. "Twenty-five to life, must serve the twenty-five minimum."

"Which means he can't get out until he's seventy-five years old. Can you get us in to talk to him?"

Reid hesitates. "Lieutenant Colonel Prentice didn't mention anything about interceding with federal prison authorities."

"I'm sure it just slipped his mind," I say, and then turn to Kevin. "He's your brother-in-law, why don't you call and ask him?"

Captain Reid shakes his head with authority. Actually, he does everything with authority. "Won't be necessary," he says. "When do you want to go?"

It's getting late in the day, and we haven't done any case preparation yet. I also want some time to figure out how to approach Murdoch, so I say, "How about tomorrow, late afternoon?"

Reid nods. "Done. He'll be expecting you. Whether he talks to you or not is up to him."

Reid tells me that I should not hesitate to contact him if I need anything else, so before we leave, I test that by asking if we can have copies of the files on all three men. Within moments I have them. This kind of power is so intoxicating that I've decided I want to be a lieutenant colonel when I grow up.

We get home, and after briefing Laurie on what we've learned, Kevin and I get started on preparing for our own witnesses. Edna is there, making sure we have pens, paper, coffee, or whatever else we might need. After all this is over I'm going to take some time to reflect on the concept of Edna working weekends.

The most difficult part of the preparation is our belief that a significant part of the defense will involve the Dorsey-Cahill-Murdoch connection, yet we don't know where that is going to take us. We may even have to try to string out our case, delaying and taking more time while we follow the dots. One of our problems is that Hatchet's never been real big on case stringing.

In order to maximize our time, and to pretend I'm a big shot, I agree to spend six thousand dollars to charter a private plane to fly to Lansing. Having somebody go to all this effort and expense just to see him will no doubt make Murdoch the envy of the entire cellblock.

I have Edna reserve the plane, and I'm so focused on the case that alarm bells don't go off in my head when she asks, almost offhandedly, "How much do you weigh?"

When I see the contraption she has chartered the next morning, the meaning behind Edna's questions becomes clear, and I immediately wish I had exercised more at Vince's gym. But Clyde, the pilot, seems like a nice enough guy, and he swears that we'll make it, no problem, so I get on.

I have a great time, the first relaxing moments I've had in a while. Clyde lets me take the controls, and I mentally shoot down about thirty Russian MIGs, anachronistically teaching those "dirty commies" what American skill and courage are all about.

As we land at a small private airport just outside Lansing, ground control tells the pilot that the prison has sent somebody out to meet me. Good old Captain Reid can really get things done.

A car pulls right up to the plane as we taxi in. I get out and am greeted by a thin, pasty-complexioned guy who gives me a limp handshake and actually introduces himself as "Larry from Lansing." My immediate mental connection is to a sports talk-radio show: "Hi, this is Larry from Lansing . . . I'm a first-time caller . . . uhhhh . . . how do you think the Mets are gonna do this year?"

I tell Larry I want to get right out to see Murdoch, but he says, "The warden sent me out to tell you there's a problem with that."

Uh-oh. "What kind of problem?"

"He killed himself last night. Slit his throat in his cell," says Larry from Lansing with the kind of passion normally reserved for readings of the telephone directory.

The news is simultaneously devastating, frustrating, and yet further confirmation that we are on the right track. I have Larry from Lansing take me to the prison, a collection of gray buildings surrounded by barbed wire in the middle of nowhere.

The warden is Craig Grissom, who looks and sounds just like Eddie Albert in *The Longest Yard*. When I meet him, it's immediately obvious that he isn't grieving too much over Murdoch's death; nor do I get the feeling he stayed up agonizing over the eulogy. The closest he comes to serious reflection is, "Things like this happen. You try to prevent them, but they happen."

I coax the particulars out of Grissom. The guard found Murdoch in his locked cell while making his midnight rounds last night. The doctor's estimate was that he had been dead at least an hour.

"How did he get the knife?" I ask.

He seems surprised. "Who?"

"Murdoch."

"You think he got the knife?"

"Larry said it was a suicide. That he slit his own throat," I say.

Grissom shakes his head sadly. "Larry's not exactly the sharpest tool in our shed. How many suicides slit their own throat from ear to ear, then still have the knife tucked in their hand after they bleed to death and fall to the floor?"

"So somebody got into his locked cell in the middle of the night and killed him? Warden, this is a maximum security prison."

He nods. "That's why they didn't hang him in the mess hall during dinner." He can see me getting more and more frustrated. "Look, this is not the Boy Scouts. We've got murderers in here, so we've got murders. We do our best, but it is what it is."

"Had he been told I was coming?"

Grissom nods. "I told him myself. He seemed to like the idea. Maybe somebody else didn't."

"Did he make any phone calls?"

"Hard to tell," he says. "We monitor the pay phones, but they can get access to cell phones."

"Cell phones in the prison?"

He shrugs. "They got money or things to trade, they can get whatever they want in here. Think of it as the old economy— a return to the barter system."

Grissom gets Murdoch's file at my request and tells me that he was serving a lengthy term for counterfeiting. It was only incredibly bad luck on his part that got him arrested. There was a fire in his house while he was out, and when the fire department broke in, among the things they saved were plates with American presidents on them. His lawyer had claimed that the evidence should be suppressed since the firemen had no warrant, but the judge correctly ruled that they had good reason to enter the burning building.

Referring to Murdoch's murder, I ask, "Are you going to investigate this?"

He laughs a short laugh, then nods. I've got a hunch the investigation is not going to be relentless, nor is it going to get anywhere. Just like I'm not going to get anywhere with Warden Grissom. I hope Burt Reynolds comes here, puts a football team together, and kicks his ass.

I have Larry from Lansing take me back to Clyde the pilot, so I can take my new frustrations out on those dirty commies.

I call ahead to Kevin, tell him what happened, and ask him to assign Marcus to find out everything he can about Terry Murdoch. The first thing I do when I get home is go through the military files again, looking for some connection, any connection, but there just isn't anything there.

Kevin and I finish our preparations for tomorrow's witnesses, and Laurie and I get to bed early. For the past couple of weeks, we've pretty much kept our conversations about the case out of the bedroom, more to help our insomnia than for any other reason.

But tonight Laurie breaks that unwritten covenant. "I want to testify," she says.

"I know you do. We're just not ready to make that decision yet."

"I'm ready, and I've made it. I'm not going to jail without having told my story. I'm telling you now so you can factor it in."

"Consider it factored," I say a little petulantly. I need to focus on tomorrow's witnesses, not a decision that is now, no matter what my client says, hypothetical and premature.

The problem is, now that it's in my head, I spend the next hour thinking about it. Like every other defense attorney practicing on this planet, I am generally loath to put my clients on the stand. There is just too much that can go wrong, and not enough potential upside to counterbalance that.

The main reason not to put Laurie on, besides the unseen pitfalls inherent in such a move, is that she doesn't have any evidence to present. It's not like she has an alibi for the night of the murder; all she can say are the things she didn't do. "I didn't kill him, I didn't frame Oscar, I didn't own the gas can."

Etc., etc., etc. These are self-serving statements which won't and shouldn't carry any weight with the jury. The truth is, anything positive that she might have to say about the facts of the case I can introduce through other witnesses, without exposing her to a withering cross-examination.

At this point the only reason I can come up with to put her on is to give the jury a taste of who she is. There has always been an incongruity between Laurie's demeanor, her persona, and the crime she is accused of committing. Dylan's task, even with the overwhelming evidence in his favor, has first been to get the jurors to consider Laurie capable of such an act. The more they get to know her, the harder it will be for them to believe it.

If Laurie does testify, she will be the last witness we call. Tomorrow morning will be considerably less dramatic, but it's important that we get off on the right foot. I have no doubt that if the jury were to be polled right now, they would vote to convict. Which means we have twelve formerly open minds to win back.

● ● ● ● ●

THOUGH THE PROSECUTION

builds their case brick by brick in logical order, my style of defense is to shoot random darts, jumping around so they won't know where the next attack is coming from.

Our first witness is Lieutenant Robert Francone, the officer who directed the Internal Affairs investigation of Dorsey. Since Celia Dorsey told me that her husband was in cahoots with an unidentified lieutenant, in my mind everyone with that rank is a suspect. However, Francone is widely considered above reproach, and Pete Stanton endorses that view.

I take Francone through the particulars of the investigation. He's not hostile, just reluctant, viewing the material as not meant to be public. Nevertheless, the information ultimately comes out, and the portrait painted of Dorsey is that of a corrupt cop, selling out to, and profiting from, the criminals he was sworn to combat. Those criminals will have to go unnamed during this trial, as per an edict Hatchet issued earlier in the case.

"So Ms. Collins was correct in her initial report about Dorsey?"

He nods. "She was, although she was just skimming the

surface. Most of it was brought out by our subsequent investigation."

"Did you think it was proper that he only received a reprimand?" I ask.

"That's not really my area. My job is just to report the facts."

"Then let me ask it a different way. Were you surprised when he received only a reprimand?"

"Yes."

"The people Dorsey was involved with, the criminal element you refer to, would you consider them capable of murder?"

He says yes quickly, before Dylan has time to object to my improper question. Since the jury has heard the answer anyway, I withdraw the question.

I get Francone to say that there were no complaints of any kind directed at Laurie in all her time on the force, and then turn him over to Dylan.

"Lieutenant Francone," Dylan begins, "regarding these alleged mob people you say Alex Dorsey was involved with, to your knowledge, did any of them ever cause him harm?"

"Not that I'm aware of."

"And they were in something of a partnership, is that right? Both sides benefited from the relationship?"

"Yes."

Dylan then asks him a few questions about the type of violence organized crime generally practices, and he says that decapitations and body burnings are very atypical.

Dylan lets the lieutenant off the stand, satisfied that he's done little damage to the prosecution. He's right: All we've managed to show is that Dorsey was not a choirboy and hung around with dangerous people. There is absolutely no evidence that those people had anything to do with Dorsey's death, but unfortunately plenty that Laurie did.

Next up is Celia Dorsey, a less important witness for us than she would have been if we were still contending that Dorsey is alive. Her testimony is a self-indictment of a wife looking the other way while her husband descended into a life of crime and violence.

With quiet dignity, she talks about their life together, about his increasing secrecy, the talks with the mysterious other lieutenant that she overheard, and his stealing their money before leaving.

"And he was gone for a week before the murder?" I ask.

"Yes."

"Were the police looking for him?"

She nods. "Yes. I told them that I didn't know where he was. But that if Alex didn't want to be found, they wouldn't find him."

"Why did you say that?"

"He was too smart. And he used to brag about being able to disappear, to blend in so well that he couldn't be seen. Said he learned it in Vietnam."

"But whoever killed him found him," I point out.

She shakes her head. "I don't think so. I think whoever killed him wasn't somebody he was hiding from. It had to have been somebody he trusted."

Dylan objects that this is speculation, and Hatchet sustains.

"What else did you hear him say about how he might disappear?"

"He said he would fake his death. That they might bury his coffin but that he wouldn't be in it."

I've debated with Kevin whether I should open the door to Celia's "fake death" story, and we decided it was something we needed to do, if for no other reason than to have the jury know we didn't create the idea out of thin air.

I turn her over to Dylan, who treats her fairly gently but makes the point that she has no actual knowledge of what happened to Dorsey, just theories.

Hatchet sends the jurors off on their lunch break, after which we catch a break of our own. One of the jurors has taken ill, either a bad stomach virus or food poisoning. Hatchet sends everyone home for the day, giving us some much-needed additional time in the process. A key strategy in our defense will now be hoping that whatever the juror has, it's contagious.

But I have to assume that the worst will happen, that the other jurors will stay healthy. Therefore, I must prepare for tomorrow's witnesses tonight, which will make for an excruciatingly boring evening.

The two witnesses we are likely to get to tomorrow are a blood spatter expert and a retired medical examiner. Their testimony, which I hope will be significant, will also be dry as dust, and Kevin has to force me to concentrate on the nuances of it. He knows this stuff better than I do, and I offer to let him handle at least one of the witnesses, but he thinks I have developed a good rapport with the jury, and to change lawyers, even for one witness, would be messing with that chemistry.

It's not until almost eleven o'clock that he feels secure enough with my grasp of the subjects to head home. I'm not tired, so as I do almost every night, I take paperwork that I have gone through countless times and go through it again.

It is a curiously relaxing part of my routine. I take a glass of wine and the documents into the den, and Tara grudgingly joins me on the couch. I hope to find something significant but don't expect to, since I've been over these things so many times before. So if I uncover a gem, wonderful. If not, my expectations are low enough that I'm not disappointed.

Tonight's no-pressure reading includes the respective military records of the recently murdered partners in the Green Beret firm of Dorsey, Cahill, and Murdoch. There simply has to be a connection between these men; the computer-masked, anonymous tipster was certainly right about that.

I wonder if she knows that by simply giving me Murdoch's name, she caused his death.

I am simultaneously all-powerful and all-oblivious.

The detail in the files is extraordinary. My admittedly uninformed mental picture of the military experience in Vietnam includes jungles, napalm, land mines, snipers, and daring chopper missions. Yet based on the size of these reports, half the people we had there must have been typists. Every hangnail, every training proficiency score, every reported enemy sighting, every move they must have made . . . it's all been dutifully chronicled.

I start out by taking Dorsey's file and randomly picking out items from his time in Vietnam. I then compare them to the two others, in the hope that there might be some overlap. For instance, if Dorsey went to the hospital for a vaccination, I look to see if by chance Cahill and Murdoch were there the same day. Their meeting could have been brief and appear inconsequential in these reports, but it could have somehow triggered the devastating events that have led us to where we are today.

I'm on my fourth glass of wine, and Tara has long ago fallen asleep with a chewy half hanging out of her mouth, when I notice something startling. Though the chronology of Dorsey's Vietnam stay covers eleven single-spaced pages, on page nine there is an entry dated August 11, 1972, and then the next entry bears the date February 4, 1973. The two notes seem to be completely ordinary events, and there is no indication of any reason for the six-month gap.

I can feel my pulse start to race as I grab Cahill's file and look for his records during that same six-month period. Sure enough, he is unaccounted for in that time as well, and Murdoch's file, as I expect, is identical in that respect. I'm so excited that if Tara's paws weren't under her chin as she sleeps, I would high-five her.

I can't keep this to myself, so I wake Laurie and tell her what I've discovered. Her reaction is identical to mine: She understands that this could be the break we've been searching for, yet she's all too aware that we have no idea what it means.

I place a call to Captain Reid's office at Fort Monmouth, knowing he isn't there but leaving a message for him to call me back as soon as he can tomorrow morning. I hang up and go upstairs to the bedroom, barely reaching the top of the stairs before the phone rings.

"Hello?"

"Captain Reid here. How can I help you?" he says in his crisp, professional tone.

I'm amazed he has called me back so quickly, and I apologize for disturbing him this late at night. He doesn't react either way, so I quickly get down to why I called, describing the six-month gap in the records of all three men.

There is a noticeable delay in his answer, and when he does speak, it is the first time I have heard him sound tentative and unsure of himself. "There are a number of possible explanations. Record keeping in wartime is not the most accurate, and—"

My bullshit meter is clanging so loud I'm afraid it will wake the neighbors. "Captain Reid," I interrupt, "it is vitally important I get to the truth, and really quickly. I believe that what I've discovered can be very significant, and I need your help in explaining it to me. Please."

Another pause, and then his voice is softer and even more serious. "I was not in Vietnam, so what I'm about to tell you is not something I know from personal experience. As it relates to your case, you should simply consider it informed speculation."

"Fine."

"It may not be true, and even if it is, it may not be true in this particular case. Do you understand?"

"Yes."

"I must have your word that you will never reveal where you heard this."

"You have my word." I hope this preamble is over before the jury reaches a verdict.

"I am told there was a practice of bringing together the most elite members of the Special Forces, often from different divisions, and sending them out in small groups to operate behind enemy lines. Actually, the way the battlefield was drawn in Vietnam, it would be more correct to say 'among the enemy' than behind their lines."

"Operate in what way?" I ask.

"In any way they saw fit," he says. "There were no rules, there were no restrictions. Their mission was to create havoc and destruction, by any means they deemed appropriate."

"Was there any accountability?" I ask.

"I'm not sure you understand what I'm saying. During the times these men were operating, they did not exist. Existence is a prerequisite for accountability, don't you think?"

I'm afraid I know the answer to my next question. "Is there any way I can obtain proof, written proof, that these men were together in one of these squads?"

He hesitates again. "I doubt that even Lieutenant Colonel Prentice could access that information."

I thank Reid, and warn that I may be calling upon him again. Then I spend the next hour processing what I've learned and trying to figure out how I can learn more.

I have no concrete proof that these three men were together in Vietnam, yet I'm certain they were. But even if I do prove it, so what? How does it make Laurie any less guilty, in the eyes of the jurors, of the murder of Alex Dorsey?

Unfortunately, not only are the jurors' eyes clear, but their stomachs are healthy, and the trial resumes at nine in the morning.

Every subject you can name, every single one, comes with a coterie of experts. And the places these experts hang out are the courtrooms of America.

Our first witness today is Dr. Brian Herbeck, widely considered the nation's foremost authority on the spattering of blood. We are paying him ten thousand dollars to impart that expertise to the jury, who will hear how much he is making and will no doubt hate him for it.

Once I establish Dr. Herbeck's considerable credentials as an expert, I have him examine the bloodstained clothes of Laurie's that were behind Hinchcliffe Stadium. He has of course previously examined them, and we've rehearsed exactly what he is prepared to say.

Dr. Herbeck points out in excruciating detail the pattern of blood spatter on both the front and the back of the blouse. His position is that they are essentially matching, which means that, while the blouse may belong to Laurie, neither she nor anyone else was wearing it when it became bloodied. The blood was applied to the front, and it caused a contact stain by going through to the back. If there had been a person in the blouse, he contends, the blood would never have reached the back.

It is a logical, albeit boring presentation, and as Dylan rises to cross-examine, his expression is sort of bemused, as if he and the jury have to deal with eccentrics like this and they might as well do it with a smile.

Dylan has obviously been well schooled in this area, and his cross-examination is impressive. He takes the good doctor back over the clothing, stain by stain, pointing out those areas that don't match quite so perfectly. Dr. Herbeck has answers for each of Dylan's points, but by the time it's all over, there's no way the jury could find any part of the testimony particularly compelling.

All in all, it's a depressing morning. My hopes are beginning to rest almost entirely on the outside investigation we are trying to conduct into the experiences of the three men in Vietnam. An investigation that has every possibility of going nowhere.

Kevin, Marcus, and I have lunch together in the court cafeteria, and they bring me up to date on our progress, or lack of it. Kevin has talked to the lieutenant colonel, who checked and confirmed Captain Reid's view that the information is not accessible. Marcus has learned about the crimes Murdoch committed to get himself put in jail, but this doesn't seem to shed much light on our case.

Having finished his lunch, Kevin cleans up the leftovers on Marcus's tray and my own. He seems about to ask the people at nearby tables if they're going to finish theirs, when Pete Stanton comes over. He had been in an upstairs courtroom testifying on another case and is just checking in to see how we're doing and to lend moral support.

"There have been happier days in defenseland," I say.

He nods and throws a light verbal jab. "Maybe you should let Kevin take over."

"That would help," I counter. "But what we really need is a bozo like you to cross-examine."

We both realize that this banter is halfhearted at best, and he inquires as to how Laurie is doing. He's been a great friend and supporter to her, which she and I will both appreciate pretty much forever. I tell him that she's doing okay and is stronger than I am. Both statements are basically true.

Across the room, having just finished his lunch, is Nick Sabonis. Nick and I haven't talked since he was on the stand, though our paths have crossed on a couple of occasions. My sense is that Nick has not forgiven me for implying that he could possibly be the mysterious lieutenant that Celia Dorsey spoke about.

"I'll be right back," Pete says, standing. "I've got to talk to Nick."

I'm not sure why it hits me this time, but it does, right between the eyes.

"What did you say?" I ask, though I know exactly what he said.

"I said I've got to talk to Nick."

"Call him over here," I say. "Please."

I'm sure that Pete, Kevin, and Marcus can all hear the strange tone in my voice, but I'm not concerned; my focus is totally on Pete and Nick.

"Hey, Nick," Pete calls out, waving. "Come here a second, will ya?"

Nick looks over, a little tentatively, obviously not wanting to be drawn into an uncomfortable situation with the enemy, meaning us.

But my mind is already elsewhere, and I turn to Kevin, just

about dragging him out of his chair. "Come on, we need to talk."

On the way to the phones, I tell Kevin what I've just come to understand. We call Captain Reid, who characteristically comes to the phone immediately.

I get right to the point. "Captain Reid, we need a list of every Special Forces lieutenant who was in Vietnam at the same time as Dorsey, Stynes, and Murdoch."

He doesn't burst out laughing, which I take as a good sign. After a few moments he says, "It'll take the better part of an hour."

I thought he was going to say week, so I'm thrilled. "Can you fax it to me at the courthouse?"

"Give me the number."

I do, and the list arrives an hour and five minutes later. It's five pages, and on page two is the name that is going to blow this wide open.

• • • • •

I'VE NEVER CONDUCTED a stake-out before, and I'm not sure this would qualify as one. I've got the obligatory donuts and coffee, but I don't have a radio to say "ten-four" into. I just sit in my car outside the FBI regional office, downing donuts and listening to an Eagles CD, while remaining ready to hunch down to avoid being seen.

I'm listening to "Life in the Fast Lane" for the fourth time when Agent Cindy Spodek comes out at about six-forty-five. She walks to her parking space and drives away. I let her move out a little, then I smoothly start following her without being detected. You would think I've done this all my life. Ten-four.

She leads me across the George Washington Bridge, up the Palisades Interstate Parkway, and into Rockland County. Rockland is on the New Jersey side of the Hudson River but is a part of New York State. It's not much farther from Manhattan than northern New Jersey or Westchester County, but almost as nice and much less expensive.

My fervent hope is that Agent Spodek is heading home, and not out to dinner or a book club or a rifle range or whatever it is that FBI agents do at night. This stakeout thing is tiring, and I'm very anxious to talk to her.

She gets off the highway and drives into a small town

called Pomona. It's a residential area, and since she may be nearing home, I start following her a little more closely. It would be beyond annoying to lose her now.

After a few more minutes she pulls into the driveway of a one-story redwood home. Kids play on the street, but none pay attention to her arrival. I realize I have no idea if she has kids or whether she's married or single. For my own limited purposes, I'd rather she lives alone, since I don't want her to have to consider other people when she hears my request.

I park on the street directly in front of her house, and she's looking in my direction when I get out of the car. I think I see a flash of panic in her eyes, or maybe it's anger, or maybe it's an eyelash. I'm not that good an eye reader.

She strides directly toward me. "What the hell are you doing here? I don't want you near my house."

She thinks that will intimidate me; she's unaware that women have been saying stuff like that to me my whole life. "I was hoping we could continue our conversation," I say.

"What conversation is that?" she challenges.

"The one about Terry Murdoch."

This time I'm pretty sure the eye flash is panic, but she doesn't back down. "I don't have any idea what you're talking about. Now, please, I—"

I interrupt. "Did you know that Terry Murdoch is dead? Someone killed him to stop him from talking to me."

She sags slightly and closes her eyes. "Oh, God . . ."

"Can I come in?" I ask.

She doesn't answer, just nods in resignation, turns, and walks toward the front door. I follow her inside. Chalk up another successful stakeout for the good guys.

We're no sooner in the house than she asks me, "How did you figure it out?"

I don't want to tell her the truth—that I wasn't even absolutely positive I was right until I saw her reaction to the news about Murdoch's death. So I simply say, "Dorsey's wife said he called someone 'Lieutenant.' I assumed it was someone within the police department, until I realized Dorsey was a lieutenant himself, and people of the same rank don't talk that way."

I pause for a moment, preparing to drop the bomb. "It had to have been Dorsey's commanding officer in the army, the special unit he was in with Murdoch and Cahill. It turns out that your boss Hobbs was a lieutenant in Vietnam at the same time as Dorsey, which makes him the logical choice. Also, the 911 call referred to Garcia as the 'perpetrator.' It's a word you might use."

She doesn't react with any surprise at all; she's been living with this truth for a long time. "You can't prove it. Nobody can."

"I don't have to prove it," I say. "I just have to shine a light on it."

"I can't help you," she says.

"You're the only one that *can* help me. And you've already tried to. But now it has to be out in the open. No more phone calls, no more masking your voice."

She smiles at my naïveté. "Do you have any idea what it would be like to come out publicly against a man like Darrin Hobbs? Do you know what they would do to me?"

I nod. "Laurie Collins faced the same decision with Dorsey two years ago. She knew it would be bad, and it's been worse than she could have imagined. It may well ruin her life. But she'd do it again ten times over."

She speaks quietly, as if she's really talking to herself. I have a feeling this is a conversation she's had with herself quite a few times. "I've wanted to be an FBI agent my entire life."

I shake my head. "I don't know you, but I'd bet you didn't want it like this. I don't think you can live with it like this, knowing what you know . . ."

"I'm telling you, I have no proof that your client is innocent. I have no information about her at all."

"I know that." I sense that she is weakening, and I am going to stay here and beg and plead and persuade until she caves. It is realistically the only chance Laurie has to stay out of prison. "I just want the information you have about Hobbs."

She nods. "I've got plenty of that."

I'm definitely making progress, and I want to be extra careful what I say so I don't blow it. "Would you tell me about it?"

She sighs her defeat. "Are you hungry? This is going to be a long night."

"The longer the better," I say. "Besides, I had four stakeout donuts in the car."

"What is a stakeout donut?"

This woman is an FBI agent? J. Edgar would snap his garters if he could hear this. "It's a technical term," I say. "You wouldn't understand."

The next three hours are the most exciting I've ever spent with a woman with my clothes on. Cindy has made a study of Hobbs from her vantage point as his subordinate/punching bag, and she has the goods on him.

From his high-level perch in the FBI, he has essentially been providing protection for his elite army squad, which has come together for some domestic work. There were at least four men under Hobbs, probably more, though it will take investigatory work to find any others.

All were involved in different types of criminal activity, still under Hobbs's command. But his blanket of protection was not total. Dorsey, for instance, drew too much attention to himself, and Hobbs couldn't keep him out of trouble without exposing himself. Murdoch had the bad luck of having his counterfeit plates found by the fire department, and it became public so quickly that Hobbs was powerless to intervene.

For all intents and purposes, Cindy can prove what Hobbs has been up to, but with some glaring gaps, the main one being the Dorsey murder. She believes that Hobbs either murdered Dorsey himself or more likely sent Cahill to do it, but the evidence simply does not exist to get Laurie off the hook.

By the time I leave her house at eleven o'clock, I've got a plan formulated. I call Kevin and bring him up to date, then I give him a list of subpoenas to start serving. I also tell him to call Captain Reid and ask for some special help. For us to have any chance to pull this off, we've got to start now.

Laurie is waiting up when I get home; she would have stayed up if I didn't come home until November. She devours what I have to say and wants me to tell her exactly what we're going to do from here on in. I describe it as best I can, but a lot of it is going to be reactive, and she's just going to have to trust me.

We get to sleep at two and we're up at six-thirty. I've got to be ready to play a different role today. I've spent most of my adult life in courtrooms, but today, for the first time, I'm going to be a witness.

Kevin and I meet at the coffee shop to do a crash preparation for my testimony, since we didn't have a chance to go over it last night. What I learned from Cindy Spodek has changed our goal for my testimony. Rather than provide the crucial basis for our defense, I am in effect a setup man, helping the jury understand what they will later be presented with.

Dylan again objects to my testifying, and Hatchet shoots him down. Kevin takes me through the basics of my relationship with Laurie, from our first meeting until today. I openly admit our romantic attachment; the jury knows about it anyway, and it's better that we acknowledge it voluntarily than let Dylan appear to be exposing it.

Within fifteen minutes we're at the meat of what I'm here to say. I talk about the day that Stynes came into my office, describing my attorney-client privilege dilemma, my subsequent decision to defend Oscar, and my sending Laurie out to the stadium to retrieve what I thought were Stynes's clothes.

"Did you ever see Stynes again?" Kevin asks.

I nod, and for the first time I'm in danger of losing my focus and becoming emotional. "I asked a young man to help me find Alex Dorsey. His name was Barry Leiter, and when it was discovered that he was helping me, Stynes shot him to death in his home. The police killed Stynes on the scene, but it was too late to help Barry."

After a few more questions Kevin and I make eye contact, and I can tell that we both feel we've covered the facts that we wanted the jury to hear. He sits down and lets Dylan have a shot at me.

"Mr. Carpenter," he begins, "did anyone else hear Stynes's confession to you?"

"No."

"Had you ever met him before?"

"No, I had not."

"Was he referred to you by someone?"

"No."

"So out of the blue he came into your office and told you a story, which you are now telling the jury. A story which just happens to argue against your client's guilt. Your lover's guilt. Is that what you're telling us?"

"Yes. That's what I'm telling you."

"This is a woman you want to spend the rest of your life with?"

Kevin objects as to relevancy, but Hatchet lets me answer.

"I certainly do."

"And that would be difficult if she were in prison?" he asks.

"It would. Which makes me glad the truth is on her side."

Dylan objects, and he and Kevin fight it out for a while in a bench conference. When it concludes, Dylan veers off from this area and focuses on my involvement with Oscar Garcia. His contention is that I was less than zealous in my representation of Oscar, questioning me about my inability to uncover the bank tapes in the supermarket. The clear implication is I was throwing Oscar to the wolves to make sure Laurie stayed in the clear.

Dylan asks, "If Mr. Garcia had been convicted, then Ms. Collins would likely not have been charged. Isn't that true?"

"I can't answer that. You're the one who charges people

without regard to the facts, so you might want to testify after I do."

The jury laughs, which pleases me but infuriates Dylan. We spar for a little while longer, but he seems even happier to finally let me off the stand than I am to get off.

The testimony went very well. We got out the story about Stynes without having to reveal what we know about his military connection to Dorsey, even without revealing that his real name is Cahill. The less of this that comes out before Hobbs takes the stand, the better. That's if we can get Hobbs to take the stand.

Tomorrow will be the key to the entire trial, and Kevin and I go over our approach until past midnight. Marcus calls to report that the subpoenas have been served and that Hobbs was furious to receive one. Marcus served that one personally. He thought the level of Hobbs's anger was pretty funny; the fact that Hobbs might well be a Green Beret killing machine did not intimidate him. If I ever meet someone who intimidates Marcus, I am going to be very afraid of that person.

Simply put, we have to make Hobbs look bad on the stand. So bad that suspicion gets cast on him and away from Laurie. We cannot prove that he murdered anyone, but we can prove some other facts, and the trick will be to get him to perjure himself by denying those facts. It's risky; if he detects our strategy, he can just admit to the facts and explain them away with minimal embarrassment. That would be it for our defense.

Which means that would be it for Laurie.

• • • • •

DYLAN HAS SMOKE coming out of his ears when I arrive in court. He has been confronted by a roomful of potential witnesses that we have subpoenaed, none of whom were on our witness list. Which means he has not prepared for any of them.

Those witnesses consist of four members of the Paterson Police Department, including Pete Stanton, as well as three FBI agents. Two of those agents are Darrin Hobbs, who is angry at the imposition, and Cindy Spodek, who is secretly privy to our scheme and nervous about her crucial role in it.

Before the jury is called in, Dylan objects to the witnesses' appearance, based on our not having put them on our list, and also based on relevance. Hatchet agrees to hear argument on the matter, and I suggest that we might as well let the witnesses be in the courtroom to hear the argument themselves, as well as each other's subsequent testimony, should it be admitted. Dylan agrees, as I hoped and expected he would.

If we don't get these witnesses in, we are dead in the water. "Your Honor," I say, "these people were not included on our witness list because they are rebuttal witnesses, called to rebut the specific testimony of Captain Franks."

Hatchet is properly suspicious of my motivation here, since

this is clearly overkill to rebut a relatively innocuous witness like Franks. "I didn't realize Captain Franks was that powerful a witness, nor that significant a part of this case," he observes dryly.

"Respectfully, Your Honor, I disagree. He portrayed Lieutenant Dorsey as cut down in the prime of life just before reaching sainthood. I believe these witnesses will paint a truer picture, and it is important for the jury to hear that truth."

"This is a delaying tactic, Your Honor," Dylan argues. "As well as an attempt to muddy the water and blame the victim. I urge you not to allow it."

I jump in before Hatchet can say anything negative to our side; this is not an issue I can be passive about. "Your Honor, it is entirely possible that all of these witnesses will not be necessary. And if you determine that I am not eliciting significant and relevant facts, you can stop me in my tracks with a ruling."

Hatchet stares another hole through my forehead. "Are you saying you will abide by my future rulings? Is that your idea of a concession?"

He's caught me; I can't help smiling. "No, Your Honor. I am saying that you will find I would never waste the court's time."

Hatchet lets the witnesses testify, putting me on a short leash by announcing he will not let this drag out if he feels it's repetitive. He also takes pains to confirm that I am not using Hobbs's presence as a backdoor attempt to get in the FBI report that he has already ruled out. I feign horror at even the prospect of it.

I do have another request of Hatchet. "Your Honor, if we call Special Agent Hobbs, I would like to qualify him as an adverse witness. He has been antagonistic towards the defense throughout these proceedings."

Qualifying a witness as adverse, or hostile, allows me to question him as if it were a cross-examination, giving me the leeway to ask leading questions. At this point the request does not seem to be a big deal to Hatchet or Dylan, and it is granted without objection. Satisfied that I've gotten what I need, I call FBI agent Albert Connolly.

Connolly had been mentioned in the FBI report as one of the agents involved in the surveillance of Petrone's people and therefore of Dorsey. There is really nothing I want to get from Connolly; I am merely questioning him so that Hobbs will not realize that he is being targeted. When Hobbs is asked the same questions that he has heard asked of Connolly, he will be less likely to realize that we are laying a trap.

So, with Hobbs and Cindy Spodek watching from the gallery, I have Connolly identify himself and describe his role in the Petrone investigation.

With a glance at Hatchet, I tell Connolly, "I am not interested in the details of your investigation. I am simply trying to get your knowledge and impressions of Lieutenant Dorsey. Do you understand?"

"Yes, sir," he says.

"Good. Had you known or had any contact with Lieutenant Dorsey before you encountered him on this investigation?"

"No, I had not."

"Did you have occasion to have any direct conversations with him during the investigation?"

"No."

I take him through his observations of Dorsey during this investigation. My questions are brief and designed to elicit quick responses, since there is a very real danger that Hatchet will intervene.

Connolly says that he really hadn't had much occasion to watch Dorsey, nor had he had much knowledge of his activities. Clearly, Dorsey was involved with members of organized crime, in ways that his police bosses would not have approved.

"Are you familiar with a man named Roger Cahill, who also goes by the name Geoffrey Stynes?"

"I am not."

I let Connolly off the stand, and Dylan does not cross-examine. Instead, he calls for a bench conference, during which he again asks Hatchet to stop "this unproductive waste of the court's time." Since it is out of earshot of Hobbs, I promise that I will not call four of the seven witnesses I brought in today and will end the parade after only two more, Agents Hobbs and Spodek. Hatchet accepts the compromise, and I call Darrin Hobbs to the stand.

I can count on zero fingers the number of times I've seen witnesses knowingly make self-incriminating statements. I would love trials to be like the one in *A Few Good Men*. I could get Jack Nicholson on the stand so he can scream, "You can't handle the truth!" at me and then, in a rage, admit his own guilt. But I never get that lucky, and I'm not going to get that lucky with Hobbs. He will incriminate himself only if he doesn't believe he is doing so; he will expose himself to danger only if he is unaware that the danger exists.

"Good morning, Agent Hobbs."

"Good morning."

"As I told Agent Connolly, I am not interested in the details of your investigation. I am simply trying to get your knowledge and impressions of Lieutenant Dorsey. Do you understand?"

"I do."

"You were in charge of the investigation which included Lieutenant Dorsey. Is that correct?"

"He was a peripheral figure."

"I understand. Had you known or had any contact with Lieutenant Dorsey before you encountered him on this investigation?"

Hobbs doesn't even flinch; the son of a bitch lies through his teeth. "No, I had not."

"Did you have occasion to have any direct conversations with him during the investigation?"

"No."

"How about since then?"

"No."

As with Connolly, I ask Hobbs a few quick questions about Dorsey's activities during the investigation. My final question is,

"Are you familiar with a man named Roger Cahill, who also goes by the name Geoffrey Stynes?"

"No, I am not. Other than what you've told me and I've read in the paper."

"Thank you," I say. "No further questions." I want to add, "I've got you, you son of a bitch," but I control the impulse.

Dylan again declines to cross-examine, and I surprise him and Hobbs by asking Hatchet to keep Hobbs present and available for recall this morning. I can see a flash of worry across Hobbs's face, but he still has no real idea of the hole he has just dug for himself.

"Call Cindy Spodek."

Cindy rises and walks to the witness stand, passing Hobbs on the way and staring him right in the eyes. If he didn't know he was in trouble before, he should now.

"Agent Spodek," I begin, "who is your immediate superior at the FBI?"

"Special Agent Darrin Hobbs."

"The man who preceded you to the stand?"

"Yes."

"Were you present in the courtroom during his testimony?"

"Yes, I was."

Out of the corner of my eye, I can see Hobbs alert, listening intently. "Did you listen to Special Agent Hobbs's testimony in its entirety?"

"I did."

"To your knowledge, was he being truthful?"

"He was not."

Dylan and Hobbs simultaneously jump to their feet. When Dylan gets there, he screams an objection. When Hobbs gets there, he has no idea what to do, so he looks around, a puzzled expression on his face, and sits back down.

Hatchet calls us over for a bench conference to discuss Dylan's objection. Dylan is steaming, and once the jury cannot hear us, he lets loose. "Your Honor, Carpenter is making a mockery of this courtroom."

Starting a conversation with Hatchet by telling him that his courtroom is a mockery is not a shrewd strategy. He didn't get the name Hatchet by treating lawyers with kid gloves, and it's possible we could have another beheading on our hands. I just stand there, well behaved and totally innocent.

Dylan realizes in an instant what he's said, and he backtracks. "I apologize, Your Honor, but these tactics are truly reprehensible."

"Which tactics do you mean, Dylan?" I ask with a voice as sweet as sugar.

Dylan is not about to be drawn into a conversation with me; he speaks only to Hatchet. "Your Honor, the defense called Agent Hobbs under false pretenses."

"Which pretenses do you mean, Dylan?" I purr.

Hatchet now turns his glare on me. "I would say it's time you announced where this is going, before I stop you from going there."

I nod. "Your Honor, I said I would question these witnesses, including Hobbs, about their knowledge of Dorsey. I did that. I admit I suspected Hobbs would lie, but I couldn't know that for sure until he did. Those lies, as I will demonstrate, bear directly and crucially on this case."

"He's impeaching his own witness," Dylan complains.

"My own *adverse* witness."

I know for a fact that Hatchet is annoyed with me. He feels I manipulated the court for my own ends, and in fact I did. But I didn't lie, and there's no legal reason for him to prohibit me from going forward.

"Mr. Carpenter, I'm going to allow you to proceed, but be very careful. If I sense you are being dishonest with this court, you will find yourself in very unhappy circumstances."

"Yes, Your Honor, I understand."

I prepare to resume questioning Cindy, who has sat stoically on the witness stand, no doubt watching her career flashing before her. Hobbs has been staring at her, trying to intimidate her. Not a chance.

"Agent Spodek, you said that Special Agent Hobbs was being untruthful in his testimony."

"He was lying, yes."

"Which part was a lie?"

"Almost everything after he gave his name."

The jury laughs, but Spodek doesn't crack a smile. This is one tough lady.

"I'm paraphrasing, but Special Agent Hobbs claimed never to have had contact with Lieutenant Dorsey. Was that a true statement?"

"No. I witnessed their meeting at least half a dozen times."

"How did that come about?"

"Usually, we were out in the car, working on a case, and we would stop at an apparently prearranged location. Lieutenant Dorsey would be there, and they would talk."

"Did you hear any of the conversations?"

She nods. "Parts of two of them."

"What were they about?"

"They were discussions of Lieutenant Dorsey's activities with certain criminal figures. About protecting Lieutenant Dorsey from prosecution by the local authorities."

"Lieutenant Dorsey was worried about that?" I ask.

"Very worried."

I steal a glance at Hobbs, who looks like a newcomer to acting class who has just been instructed by the teacher to "show outrage." The funny thing is, he thinks this is the worst part. Just wait.

"Agent Hobbs also said he did not know Roger Cahill. Was that a lie as well?"

"Absolutely." She goes on to describe two meetings that he had with Cahill, though she hadn't known his name until she saw his picture in the paper after Barry's murder. It was a major reason she called me about Murdoch, another man whom she knew Hobbs was meeting with before he was sent to prison.

I take her through some more discussion about Hobbs's

perjured testimony, then ask her if she knows anything about the original 911 call that implicated Garcia in the murder.

"Yes," she says. "I made that call."

"Why?"

"Agent Hobbs instructed me to. He said that he had information that Garcia was guilty but that he didn't want to involve the Bureau."

"Do you know why he didn't make the call himself?"

"No, I don't."

"Could it be that he wanted the call to come from a woman so that the prosecution would accuse the defendant of making it?"

Dylan objects, and Hatchet sustains. I tell Hatchet I want to recall Hobbs, and Dylan reserves his cross-examination of Cindy until after Hobbs is finished. Dylan is smart enough to know he is walking into a minefield, and he's hoping Hobbs will at least provide him with a map.

Hobbs takes the stand again, a considerably less confident and self-assured man than he was last time he was there.

"Agent Hobbs," I begin, "I take it you listened carefully to the testimony of Agent Spodek?"

"Yes."

"Do you wish to change your previous testimony as a result of it?"

"I do not."

"So would it be fair to say that your position is that Agent Spodek was herself being untruthful?"

"She was lying through her teeth."

"Do you have any idea why she would do that?"

"Agent Spodek is a bitter woman of very low competence. I have been considering recommending her termination from the Bureau. I suspect she is aware of that and has taken what amounts to a preemptive strike against me."

"So she is lying and you're not?"

He nods. "She is lying and I'm not."

"You did not know either Alex Dorsey or Roger Cahill?"

"I did not."

At that moment, by prearrangement, Captain Reid, dressed in military uniform, enters the courtroom. He goes to Kevin, whispers something, and hands him a piece of paper. Kevin looks at it, smiles, and indicates for Captain Reid to sit with the other witnesses. Then Kevin walks over to me and pretends to whisper in my ear. Hobbs watches all of this take place with barely concealed horror.

"Special Agent Hobbs, were you in Army Special Forces in Vietnam?"

Hobbs doesn't answer. I can see his brain reacting to figure out what to do as surely as if I were watching it through a CAT scan.

"Did you not hear my question?"

This brings him back to face his current dilemma. He is positive that Reid must have brought absolute evidence of his military connection to Cahill and Dorsey. To deny it is to commit perjury even more blatant than previously.

"Were you in Army Special Forces in Vietnam?"

"Yes."

"Was your rank first lieutenant?"

"Yes."

"Did you command a small secret unit which operated behind enemy lines?"

"That is classified."

"I think that war is over, Agent Hobbs. Were Roger Cahill and Alex Dorsey under your command?"

His answer is soft, as if he's hoping no one will hear it. "Yes." The resulting buzz from the gallery and jury says they heard it loud and clear.

"So you knew them? Had contact with them?"

"Yes."

"So Agent Spodek was right? You were lying before when you denied contact with them?"

"I didn't realize you were talking about in the army. I thought you meant more recently, during the investigation."

"That's another lie, isn't it, Agent Hobbs?"

"No, it isn't."

"So let me see if I understand," I say. "You knew them in the army but haven't had any contact since?"

He nods. "Yes. That's correct."

"You say this fully aware of the perjury laws in the state?"

"Yes."

I introduce as evidence a tape recording supplied by Cindy. It is Bureau practice that all calls from agents' offices are taped, in order to protect the agents and help in investigations. Thinking she might need it to protect herself, Cindy had confiscated a tape of one of Hobbs's conversations with Dorsey, and I play it for the court.

It is a devastating record of a conspiracy between Dorsey and Hobbs, and though Hobbs doesn't directly implicate himself in any criminal acts on the tape, there is no doubt in anyone's mind he has committed multiple perjuries in his testimony today.

I ask Hobbs if Murdoch was in his squad and if he knows that Murdoch was recently murdered. He acknowledges the army connection but denies knowing about the murder. Not a person in the room believes him.

I'm finished, and Dylan doesn't even cross-examine the shell that was Special Agent Hobbs. His defeat is total; the man is ruined.

Heh, heh, heh.

• • • • •

WE ARE A SUBDUED GROUP

during our nightly meeting. We're nearing the end; the only issue to resolve before closing arguments is whether or not Laurie will take the stand.

Laurie still wants to, but in light of today's positive developments, is willing to listen to arguments. Kevin and I tell her the basics: that there really is nothing for her to add and that the dangers are potentially enormous.

I feel compelled to point out that, while we did really well today, we are still in very precarious shape. The jury could easily find that our entire defense, centering on Hobbs, Dorsey, and Cahill, is interesting but off point. The only tangible evidence in the Dorsey murder still points to Laurie, and the jury may follow that evidence—in fact is more likely to than not.

It's a lively discussion which finally ends with Laurie trusting our judgment and agreeing not to take the stand. This allows us to focus on the closing arguments, which in this case are going to be even more important than usual. It will be up to us to make the jury understand that what we have been saying matters, and creates at least a reasonable doubt as to Laurie's guilt.

The media are filled with the trial news, and there is open

speculation that Hobbs will be indicted and tried for perjury. The FBI director himself has issued a statement saying that Hobbs is being put on temporary leave, and both federal and state investigations are under way. It's gratifying, but it's small consolation if it doesn't result in Laurie's vindication.

Our first action in court is to announce that the defense is resting, and Dylan tells Hatchet that he is ready to give his closing argument.

"Ladies and gentlemen of the jury," he begins, "I stood here at the opening of this trial and told you that the evidence would show that Laurie Collins murdered Alex Dorsey. I told you the defense would utilize tricks and mirrors to make you think otherwise, but that what you needed to do was focus on the facts.

"My message today has not changed. The evidence has been presented, the facts are clear. The defense has been even more illusory than I expected, presenting a wild tale of Green Berets, frame-ups, and conspiracies.

"In the process, an FBI agent has been shown to have lied. I won't dispute that; we all saw it before our eyes. But what does that mean to this case? No evidence was presented implicating him in the murder you are here to judge. In fact, as a federal officer, he had nothing to do with this case whatsoever; it was handled by the Paterson police. Nor did anyone come up here and say he had a grudge against this defendant. Why would he have framed her? It doesn't make any sense.

"Yes, Agent Hobbs lied, perhaps to hide his embarrassment at his relationship with criminals and a cop gone bad. It's interesting, it's troublesome, and it will be investigated, but it has nothing—I repeat nothing whatsoever—to do with the murder of Alex Dorsey.

"The state has proved its case, proved it well beyond a reasonable doubt, and I ask you to return a verdict of guilty against Laurie Collins for the murder of Lieutenant Alex Dorsey."

I get up to give our closing argument aware that we have a big hill to climb. In a perfect world, a lawyer wants to be able to recap and summarize the compelling evidence he has presented during the course of the trial. This case being tried in a less-than-perfect world, I have the task of explaining what the hell our evidence has to do with it.

"Ladies and gentlemen, there is absolutely nothing in Laurie Collins's background, not a shred, which would indicate she could possibly be capable of a brutal act such as the murder of Alex Dorsey. On the contrary, her entire life has been devoted to furthering the public good and the cause of justice.

"The prosecutor says she did it, and points to certain items of evidence. I say she was framed, and that the same evidence was planted to further that end.

"But Mr. Campbell completely rejects the idea of a frame-up moments after he tells you that the reason he first charged Oscar Garcia with the crime is because he was framed! Mr. Garcia could be framed, but Ms. Collins could not? Why doesn't he explain that?

"And let's look at what he does say about it. He says that Ms. Collins framed Garcia to avenge one of these grudges that he thinks she carries around. Yet an FBI agent, Cindy Spodek, testified that she made the call accusing Garcia. Ms. Collins had nothing to do with it. Mr. Campbell was wrong about that, as he has been wrong about so much in this case.

"Which brings me to Special Agent Hobbs. Even Mr. Campbell admits Hobbs perjured himself. Now, I don't know exactly what Mr. Hobbs did, or why he did it, but I'm going to give you a theory. It may be right, or it may be wrong, or the truth may be somewhere in the middle.

"I think the evidence shows that Hobbs led a squad, much of the same squad he led in the military. I think they got into positions where they could abuse the system and commit crimes, and Hobbs was in a position to protect them and to take a healthy cut of their profits.

"And he did protect Dorsey, but it got to a point where he couldn't protect him anymore. Dorsey didn't want to go to prison, and he threatened Hobbs with exposure. Dorsey may well have intended to fake his own death, but that wasn't good enough for Hobbs, and he either killed him or had Cahill kill him. And when Murdoch was going to talk to me, Hobbs had him killed as well.

"Before killing Dorsey, he either tricked him or forced him to tape a message to Ms. Collins, which he played in a phone call to her, making us think Dorsey was alive. Because as the actual murderer trying to deflect attention from himself, Hobbs had a very strong interest in Ms. Collins getting convicted.

"Now, as I've said, this is just a theory, though I believe it is plausible given the facts before you. Don't you have to admit it's possible? I believe that you do. Can you say beyond a reasonable doubt that I'm wrong? I don't think so.

"One of the many unusual aspects of this case is the fact that the lawyer for the defendant was a key witness in the defense. I sat up there and told you that Roger Cahill confessed the murder to me and told me about the bloody clothing behind the stadium, clothing he said was his own. I also told you that I sent Ms. Collins out there to retrieve the clothing.

"If I was telling the truth, Ms. Collins is innocent. It's as simple as that. You may or may not believe me, but can you say beyond a reasonable doubt I was lying? I don't think so. And if you can't, then you must vote to acquit.

"I know Laurie Collins very well, probably better than I know anyone in the world. She could no more commit a murder like this than she could get up and fly out the window.

"A murder of anyone, no matter what their actions in life, is a tragedy. Please don't compound that tragedy by turning Ms. Collins into another victim. She is innocent, and she has been put through hell. I ask you to do what is right and give Laurie Collins her life back."

As I turn and walk back toward Laurie at the defense table, I experience a totally selfish moment. I realize that the life I have been fighting for as much as Laurie's is my own.

I simply cannot envision living my life while Laurie wastes away in prison. It would be an incomprehensibly horrible existence, and the knowledge that twelve strangers can turn it into a reality bores a panic-filled hole in my stomach.

Kevin and Laurie shake my hand and whisper that I was wonderful, but the jury sits impassive, not looking at me, or Laurie, or anyone else. I want to go over and shake them until they understand who the good guys are. And I want to memorize their faces so that if they convict the woman I love for murder, I can hunt each one of them down, cut off their ugly heads, and set their stinking bodies on fire.

Hatchet reads them his version of the law, which when boiled down from its one-hour length, basically says, "If you think she's guilty beyond a reasonable doubt, vote guilty." He sends them off to deliberate, though they inform him that since it's late, they're going to get started in the morning.

Kevin comes over again tonight, basically out of force of habit, since there's nothing else we can do. I'm going to be hard-pressed to stick to my usual style of waiting for a verdict, which is to be totally alone (except for Tara), totally obnoxious to anyone who interrupts that solitude, and totally superstitious.

I can't be alone, at least not in my house, since Laurie is confined there for the duration. I don't want to be obnoxious, since she is no doubt going through a greater agony than I am. The only thing I can be is superstitious, so I'm sure I will do that with a vengeance.

I know we shouldn't, but we are physically unable to avoid watching news coverage of the verdict watch. Some commentators give us a decent chance, but most feel that if the jurors follow a strict interpretation of the law, we'll probably lose. All agree that if not for the Hobbs revelations, we'd be dead in the water.

The area of most agreement is that the longer it takes to reach a verdict, the better off we are. If the jury rejects our theories about Hobbs as irrelevant, they'll vote quickly to convict. If they're willing to accept them, or at least examine them, it will take considerably longer. Of course, this "longer the better" theory does not take into account the likelihood that we will soon all have strokes and die from stress waiting for the jury to come back.

We're eating breakfast at nine A.M. when Laurie and I make eye contact and realize that at that very moment, the jury is meeting to begin the process of deciding her fate. It's enough to make me choke on my pancakes.

The doorbell rings and we get a FedEx delivery. It's from the opposing law firm in the Willie Miller suit, and inside is a cashier's check for more than eleven million dollars. Since two hundred thousand dollars of it is Edna's, she is more than happy to take it to the bank and deposit it.

I call Willie and Kevin and tell them the news. Willie tells me that he's decided what he's going to do with some of the money. I assume he's going to buy a yacht on which he can tool around the inner city, but he tells me otherwise.

"It's an investment," he says. "But it ain't gonna make any money."

"Most investments are like that," I say. "But you don't usually know it going in."

"I want you to come in for half," he says.

I'm really not in the mood to deal with this insanity now, so I say, "After the trial, we'll talk to cousin Fred."

Kevin comes over at noon, and along with Laurie and Edna, we sit around waiting for the call that we hope doesn't come for quite a while. At one point I get up and open a window; it's not hot, it's more to let the pressure out.

At three-thirty, Edna answers the phone and nervously tells me that it's Rita Golden, the court clerk. It takes what seems like an hour and a half for me to walk the eight feet to the phone. There are a lot of things that this could be other than a verdict. The jury could want testimony read back, one of them could be ill, they're ending deliberations for the day, etc., etc. Any of the above would be fine with me.

"Hello?" is my clever opening line.

"Andy," Rita says, "there's a verdict. Hatchet wants everyone here at five o'clock."

"Okay," I say, and she gives me a few more instructions. I hang up, turn, and break the news to Laurie, Kevin, and Edna. They've all been a part of our discussions hoping for a long deliberation, but no one voices the pessimism we all now feel.

"What time are we leaving?" Laurie asks.

"In about an hour," I say before dropping a bomb that Rita dropped on me. "Laurie, you're supposed to pack some things. Just in case . . ." I don't finish the sentence, since it would have sounded something like "Just in case last night was the last one you will ever spend out of prison."

Laurie nods and goes to the bedroom to pack a suitcase. Kevin hasn't said a word; he's feeling exactly what I'm feeling. It's a sense of powerlessness and fear. The powerlessness comes from the awareness that our ability to influence events is over, and the fear is from knowing that those events have already been decided.

The truly chilling part is that we both feel we have lost.

The scene outside the courthouse is chaotic, but they get us through and into the courtroom just before the appointed time. Ever since we got the phone call, I've felt as if I'm watching things in slow motion, yet at the same time realizing that they're moving at high speed.

Laurie hasn't said a word since we left the house; I don't know how she's bearing up under this pressure. Kevin has been spouting optimistic one-liners, none of which he truly believes. The bottom line is that how any of us are acting and feeling does not matter; the result has been determined, and within moments we are going to have to deal with it, one way or the other.

Hatchet comes in, issues a stern, cautionary warning against outbursts after the verdict is read, and calls in the jury. Their faces are somber, expressionless; their eyes are averted from both the defense and the prosecution.

Laurie leans over and whispers in my ear. "Andy, thank you. No matter what happens, you've done an amazing job. And I love you more than you can imagine." I don't know how to respond to a comment as caring and generous as that, so I don't.

Hatchet instructs the foreman to give the verdict slip to the bailiff, who carries it over to the clerk.

Hatchet says, "Will the defendant please rise?"

Laurie stands quickly, almost defiantly. Kevin and I are on our feet a split second later, and I take Laurie's hand. I'm not sure which one the shaking is coming from.

"The clerk will read the verdict."

The clerk looks at the form for the first time and seems to read it silently for a few moments, as if she wants to be the only person besides the jury who knows how this ends. There is not another sound in the room, and her words come through so clearly that it is as if I am hearing them through a stethoscope. I know I'm standing on my legs, but I can't feel them.

"We, the jury, in the case of the *State of New Jersey versus Laurie Collins,* find the defendant, Laurie Collins . . . not guilty of the crime of murder in the first degree."

I'm sure the gallery must be in an uproar, I'm sure Dylan must be upset, I'm sure Hatchet must be banging his gavel, but I'm not aware of any of it. All I'm conscious of is a three-way hug between Laurie, Kevin, and myself, a hug so tight that I think they'll have to carry us from the room in this position and pry us apart at the hospital.

Laurie tells us both that she loves us, and Kevin, his eyes filled with tears, keeps saying, "It doesn't get any better than this." He's wrong; it would be better than this if Barry Leiter were alive to see it.

But this is pretty damn good.

Hatchet thanks the jury, releases Laurie from custody, and adjourns the proceedings. Dylan comes over to offer his surprisingly gracious congratulations, and they take Laurie away for some quick processing and paperwork.

When she comes back, she has a smile on her face and no bracelet on her ankle.

She looks great.

• • • • •

LAURIE DECLINES MY OFFER of

a get-away-from-it-all vacation to some island paradise. At this point, her idea of paradise is to live her life unshackled, to run errands with impunity, and to sleep in her own house every Tuesday, Thursday, Saturday, and Sunday.

I've given Edna a couple of weeks off, and in fact haven't even moved the files and things back to my office. If it took me six months to get back in emotional work-mode after the Willie Miller case, I'm figuring six decades this time.

The press conference was intense after the trial, again bestowing hero status on me. Surprisingly, it hasn't died down, though the focus has switched to Darrin Hobbs. New revelations seem to be leaking from the investigation daily, and it seems that there may have been as many as eight ex-army buddies who have been committing crimes under his protection. It appears almost inevitable that he is going to be arrested and charged.

I've heard from Cindy Spodek, who is getting the hero treatment from the press and the cold shoulder from most of her colleagues. She tells me that the dominant emotion she feels is relief, and I know exactly what she means.

The ever-unpredictable Willie Miller has reacted with apparent nonchalance to his sudden wealth, behaving responsibly and prudently. Fred has invested most of the money, leaving some aside for Willie to have some fun. It turns out that Willie's idea of fun is to buy a Volvo, because he's read in *Consumer Reports* that it's a really safe car.

Willie, is that you? Willie?

I'm going to get a firsthand look at the new Willie in a few minutes, as he's coming by the house to pick me up and drive me to what he says is going to be our investment together. He's keeping it a surprise, but I assume it's not going to be anything too formal, since he suggests I bring along Tara.

Willie pulls up and I get in the beige Volvo. Tara jumps into the backseat with Cash, and I get in the front. After instructing me to put my seat belt on, Willie drives off.

About fifteen minutes later we pull up at an abandoned, dilapidated building, with an old sign identifying it as once having been called the Haledon Kennels.

"Come on," Willie says, and gets out of the car before I have the chance to tell him that this would not be a good investment, and I wouldn't want to run a kennel even if it were.

Willie lets Tara and Cash out of the car, and they walk toward the door with us. It's locked, which is not a problem for Willie because he takes out a key and opens it.

"You have a key?" is my perceptive question.

"I should. I own the damn place. *We* own the damn place." This shows signs of being a disaster.

We enter and I'm not surprised to discover that inside the dilapidated kennel is a dilapidated kennel.

"What do you think?" Willie asks, positively beaming.

I decide to be direct. "I think you're out of your mind."

He's surprised and wounded. "Why? I thought you love dogs."

"I do. But I don't want to take money from people to stuff their dogs in cages while they go on vacation."

He laughs. "Is that what you think this is?" He points at Tara and Cash. "Look at them, man. Tara was gonna be killed in the animal shelter, and Cash would have been history if they caught him."

I'm not understanding. "So?"

"So *we're* the shelter," he says. "Come on, man. We rescue dogs from the other shelter, from the street, whatever, and we take care of 'em until we can find them homes. It'll be one of those nonprofit things, like a foundation or something."

He's finally getting through to me. "Damn," I say in wonderment and admiration.

"And I'm gonna run the place," he says. "That's gonna be my job."

I put out my hand and shake his. "And I'm gonna be your partner."

Willie and I spend the next couple of hours talking about our upcoming partnership. We discuss things like what we're going to do to the place, how we'll take care of the dogs, the need to get veterinary care, etc.

I've spent the better part of a year looking for a charity to call my own, and Willie comes up with one a week after getting his money. I'm not about to abandon the needy otters, but I'm genuinely excited to have this project. I'm even more excited that Willie has agreed that we can call it the Tara Foundation. Cash doesn't seem to mind.

I get home and call Laurie to tell her about the venture, but she's not home and I leave a message on her machine for her to call me. Tonight being Thursday, I won't be seeing her. I have no idea where she is. I'm not jealous or insecure, but I wonder how she'd feel about wearing an ankle bracelet so I can monitor her activities.

I call Danny Rollins for the first time in months and place a bet on the Mets against the Braves. I order a pizza, grab a beer, sit with Tara on the couch, and start watching the game. Life is back to normal, and the last thing I remember before falling asleep is a Mike Piazza home run in the fourth inning.

When I wake up, the television is off, but so are all the lights. My first reaction is to assume it's a summer power failure, due to overuse of air-conditioning in the hot weather. However, I can see a streetlight on outside, so the outage must be within the house.

I'm annoyed as I stand, ready to grope around for my flashlight. I hear Tara barking near the back of the house. It is unusual for Tara to bark, and there is always a reason. The last time it was a head being buried on my property. In an instant I go from annoyed to scared, because I know that there is no way Tara would consider a blown circuit breaker a reason to bark.

On a gut instinct level, I know what is going on.

Darrin Hobbs.

I make my way to the phone, but I'm not surprised to discover it has been shut off along with the power. My cell phone is in my car, and I don't think my chances of getting to it are very good.

I hear Tara come into the room, moving toward the other side of the house. I can use her in this fashion as a sentry, but I know that Hobbs would not hesitate to shoot her.

"Here, girl. Come here," I whisper.

She comes to me, and I grab her collar and half coax, half drag her to the closet. I open the closet door and push her inside, closing the door as quietly as I can behind her. She starts barking again, but it's muffled, and she's relatively out of harm's way.

Now it's just Hobbs and me. A Special Forces killing machine head-to-head with an out-of-shape, chickenshit attorney. I'm not thinking about winning; I'm thinking about escaping . . . about surviving.

I inch out of the room, trying to make it to the back door of the house. It's very difficult in the darkness, and with the need to be perfectly quiet.

"It's show time, asshole."

It's Hobbs's voice in the darkness, but suddenly it's not completely dark anymore. There is the beam of a flashlight, moving back and forth slowly across the inside of the house. I duck down behind a couch as the beam approaches, but I'm very aware that eventually I will be found. And if I am found, I will be killed.

I am more physically afraid than I have ever been in my life, but for some reason it is not a debilitating fear. My mind is totally alert, my senses exquisitely tuned, as I try to come up with a strategy for staying alive.

And then I realize that silence is not my ally . . . it's his. I need noise, disruption, anything that will attract attention and cause him to move faster and with less caution. If he is free to take his time and methodically hunt me down, he will.

I peer out and follow the beam of the flashlight. It helps me see where the window is, and I pick up a vase and throw it toward the window. I'm right on the mark, and it crashes through.

Hobbs turns toward the noise, and I pick up a paperweight and throw it against a lamp, knocking it over and shattering it. All of this is making a racket, but not enough. I start screaming, "Help! Call the police!" at the top of my lungs, all the time moving from hiding place to hiding place.

The beam of light glances on me once, while I'm on the move, and Hobbs fires his weapon, though the sound is muffled by what must be a silencer. The bullet misses me, but breaks another window. Good.

I'm near the entrance to the hallway when an opportunity presents itself. I throw a plate down the hall, and Hobbs moves toward the entrance, not knowing that I'm there. Ironically, the flashlight allows me to see him, even though he can't see me. As he nears me, I leap for the light, crashing into it and Hobbs as hard as I can.

I land on top of him and can hear him swear. The flashlight falls to the ground, casting a reflected aura on us as we fight.

Fight is probably not the right word for it. I turn into a maniac, desperately trying to hang on to him, trying to rain blows on him, while all he wants to do is separate himself from me so he can take me apart. Or shoot me, if he is still holding the gun.

We knock over a table, but he manages to back off for a moment and deliver a stinging blow to my forehead. I rush forward again, winding up and blindly throwing as hard a punch as I can. It connects, sending shooting pains through my hand as I land on him and we tumble into a cabinet filled with china and glass-ware, sending it crashing to the ground with a noise that may be louder than any I have ever heard.

I feel like I hit him hard. My hand is aching and wet from what feels like blood, either his or my own. I summon the strength to try to do it again, while readying myself for his return barrage. But he's not retaliating, not attacking, not moving, and I realize that I've knocked him unconscious.

Suddenly, the flashlight moves, rises on its own power, be-wildering me, since Hobbs is lying at my feet.

"Andy, are you okay?" is what Laurie says, as beautifully crafted a sentence as any I've ever heard.

"I think so. It's Hobbs. I knocked him out."

I can almost see her grin in the darkness. "So I shouldn't have shot him?"

She points the light on Hobbs's face, and there is a neat little hole in his forehead, which I don't think was made by my fist.

"No, you did fine . . . but it wasn't necessary. I used my right cross. It's the punch against which there is no known defense."

I go to her and we hug, though I can feel that she is still hold-ing the gun in her hand, just in case. "How did you know to come here?" I ask.

"Pete called to tell me that they went to arrest Hobbs, but he had taken off. Pete tried to call you, but your phone wasn't work-ing. I was worried, so here I am."

"And you didn't think I could handle it?" I say with mock of-fense.

Suddenly, the house is washed in light, streaming in from po-lice cars outside. "Apparently, Pete had some doubts as well," she says.

I let Tara out of the closet while Laurie goes outside to bring Pete and the other officers in. That gives me about sixty seconds to figure out a way to spin this so I seem heroic.

It's not enough time.

• • • • •

IT'S HARD TO BELIEVE how much

progress Willie and I have made in just seven weeks. The renovation of the building is almost complete, we've hired two permanent staff members, and we've arranged for veterinarian care. Willie has been amazingly focused and driven, and I thought he was going to cry when I told him I wanted him to be president of the Tara Foundation.

Laurie is doing great. Her saving my life sort of evened the emotional score, enabling her to stop gushing her gratitude for my keeping her out of prison. I've decided not to belabor the point: that her intervention was not necessary and that neither Hobbs nor anyone else could have survived that right cross.

Cousin Fred is in the office more than I am, counseling Edna and Kevin on their investments. Laurie is no longer thrilled to have to use her share of the Willie Miller settlement to pay for my legal work, and she's been quibbling over the bills.

I've told her that the bills are justified, and I thought she had backed off, but she's just presented me with bills of her own. At first glance they seem unfair. Twenty thousand for a pancake seems high, but I could live with it if she weren't charging me for Kevin's.

And you don't want to know her price for basil.